A Steele Family Saga

Living with Elizabeth

BETTY LOU RAY-SUNDQVIST

TATE PUBLISHING
AND ENTERPRISES, LLC

Published by Tate Publishing & Enterprises, LLC
127 E. Trade Center Terrace | Mustang, Oklahoma 73064 USA
1.888.361.9473 | www.tatepublishing.com

Tate Publishing is committed to excellence in the publishing industry. The company reflects the philosophy established by the founders, based on Psalm 68:11,
"The Lord gave the word and great was the company of those who published it."

Book design copyright © 2013 by Tate Publishing, LLC. All rights reserved.
Cover design by Rhezette Fiel
Interior design by Jomar Ouano

Published in the United States of America

ISBN: 978-1-62854-093-2
1. Fiction / Historical
2. Fiction / Romance / Historical / General
13.10.21

In Loving Memory of

Husband – John E Sundqvist b. 1922–d. 2009 – Cancer
Son – Charles Todd Stetler b.1968–d. 2005 – Diabetes
Son-in-law – Michael Correll b. 1953 – d. 2009 – LAS

Dedication

I'd like to dedicate this book to each of my children:

Dana Lynn, Julie Ann, Lisa Faye, and Eric Reed. Each of my children were tremendously helpful to me in getting my manuscript completed and ready to send in to the publishers. I am proud of each of them and would like to say, "Thank you, kids."

Chapter  1

The place where Harrison Steele and his wife, Ellen, built their home and lived with their four children was located in a lovely valley where the bluegrass waved softly in the gentle breeze of early spring just outside of Corbin, Kentucky. Corbin was the best possible place to raise a family, according to Harrison's way of thinking. He built the farm which they struggled so hard to hold on to through the Civil War years, when so many others were not so lucky.

Those were hard times for everyone though, and many who did live through those times were unable to keep their property, so they would move away. There were other folks who would find the resources to buy the land, so it meant new neighbors like the Boggs family, as well as the Jones family. Luckily for the Steeles, they were able to keep their land intact. The new neighbors were hardworking, God-fearing people with children of their own to make friends with the Steele family and keep life on the farm lively for them all.

Now it was the spring of 1878, and that year was already looking good. Harrison took the tobacco crop to London,

Kentucky, after the first of year, hoping to get the best price, and was pleasantly surprised to get the best price ever. This was a good sign for better times to come for him, his wife, and children. So he planned to increase his tobacco crop that season; but even in the hard times, they were able to continue to keep the farm growing, improving it by their hard work and conservative way of life.

To date, Harrison had managed to increase his herd of black and white Holstein breed milk cows to number six; they were good for milking twice a day. He also had increased the number of beef cattle. He himself was fond of raising an English breed, which was a hardy red stock with white faces. He always kept an eye out for horses with a good bloodline too.

Now as Harrison stood, he was thinking his twenty-two-year-old son, Joel, had been a great help in making the place what it was at present. Joel was a handsome young man with dark-brown hair, always-tanned skin, and light-grey eyes with a dark circle around the irises, very distinctive, that also helped lend him an air of seriousness. Joel seemed to be favored by the young ladies as well, but because of his serious nature, he usually had other things to think of than women. As a young boy, he was eager to learn how to do the work that would help his mother with the outside chores so she was able to consecrate her work inside the home.

Now Harrison's thoughts turned to his daughter, Elizabeth, who was now eighteen and pretty as a speckled pup. She had pale-blond hair, a lovely fair complexion just like her mother's, and she had the most brilliantly blue eyes. She was also a natural beauty that needed nothing more than soap and water and a face cream that her mother made from herbs they collected with other ingredients, which Ellen kept a secret. Harrison had to smile— his Ellen had her ways—and Elizabeth took after her mother somewhat, not so much in looks, but she did have her sweet nature. No father could be more proud of his children.

Elizabeth loved her family and was totally satisfied with her life as it was. She said she doesn't want anything to change anytime soon, but Harrison was positive it would change if she met the right person. Letting go of one's children was a cross he and Ellen hadn't had to bear yet, but with the good Lord's grace, they would be prepared. One thing he knew for certain, unless whoever came to call for his children had faith and believed in the Lord, there would be no matches made.

Elizabeth and her brother Joel were great friends as well as brother and sister from the time of her birth. Joel was four at the time, but he adored his little sister. As she grew, he thought her the cutest little thing he had ever seen. With her blond curls and the big blue eyes, he always thought her special, so she became his pal. Then when David came along, as the three of them grew up, they had lots of fun together because the boys didn't treat Elizabeth as just a girl. They became even closer because of shared responsibilities while they were younger, actually too young, but from necessity they needed to help out. Harrison thought back to those days, and he was amazed at how much he and Ellen had depended on their children's help. Elizabeth, together with Joel, took care of their brother, David, and their younger sister, Lily, while Ellen needed to help in the fields with the crops. David wasn't a problem growing up, and he even helped with Lily, who wasn't easy to care for.

Harrison and Ellen both admitted that Lily had always been difficult. She always had a temper, plus she seemed to find a way to get out of helping with chores, while the rest were expected to do chores in the house and outside as well.

I suppose Ellen and I were just too busy and didn't realize how out of hand Lily had become, Harrison was thinking. And she wasn't anything like her brothers or Elizabeth in nature. In fact, it had become obvious that Lily was resentful of the others, so it was never a problem when he and Ellen asked the others to help and they just let Lily be, which was more than likely a mistake, but at the time they didn't have the time or energy to deal with her.

David had a sunny nature and loved to tease. Poor Joel never knew what to expect from his brother, but when David would play his pranks, he seemed to take it all in stride and even got his own back now and then. David was almost too handsome though. At the age of sixteen, he was now as tall as most men. His hair was a darker blond with an impish wave to it, and his eyes were a lighter blue than his sister's but just as bright. His smile was beautiful. Elizabeth liked to say it was just like sunshine after a rain with a rainbow thrown in! David wasn't afraid of work either. He was always eager to learn from his father and brother. Now that they had survived the hardships of the war years and the recovery, he could look back and smile. "Honor the Lord with thy substance, and with the first fruits of all thine increase." (Proverbs 3:9, KJV) Harrison really did have a lot to be thankful for, and talking to the Lord was one of his favorite pastimes.

It was a warm day and it helped that their everyday work clothes were made from a lightweight fabric—a white shirt and dark pants. Since David loved to play practical jokes, when he and Joel were in the barn, he had been known to grab a handful of straw, stuff it down the back of Joel's shirt; and if your shirt was wet with sweat, that would really have to be uncomfortable, so naturally, Joel would retaliate with taking a handful of straw and rubbing it in David's hair, since David was so proud of his golden locks.

Winter was their favorite time of year with its snow to play with. Elizabeth can throw her fair share of snowballs in a fight too. The boys never expected it, but she was very good at getting her own back as well. David was most often the main target since he would usually be the one to throw the first snowball.

Sometimes Joel and Elizabeth would together gang up on him and get him from different directions, but it was always done in fun and with laughter.

Well, enough daydreaming for him, I have things to do now, Harrison thought, but he can't help but be thankful because God had blessed them.

Later that same day, Joel and David were cleaning out the stalls in the stables when they heard barking. Joel called out, "Hey, David, is that what I think it is?"

"Sure sounds like barking to me," David replied.

So the two of them put their pitchforks aside and started looking around. When they came to the stall of Joel's horse, King, they realized the barking was coming from inside. When they looked over the half door, they could see this little ball of fur lying in there with King. The guys were shocked since the horse had never been friendly to anyone or anything before! King didn't seem to mind having the little pup in his space though. It was the cutest little black-and-white puppy and must have made its way under the door to get in the stall. Where the dog came from is anyone's guess, and King was such a spirited horse that no one could just go into his stall. They had cut a section off the bottom of the door so that food and water could just be slid under it, and cleaning out King's stall was a monumental task.

Joel said, "We need to go check with mom and ask if she has something to feed this little guy."

When David explained to their mother that they had found this pup, he exclaimed, "Mom it's no bigger than a minute and so cute. What do you have that we can feed him?"

"Well, let's see what we can find." So Ellen went to the table and took a biscuit from a plate, left over from breakfast, which she broke into pieces in a pan. She then put gravy over the bread. "Tell them this should do for now," she said, "and just keep the pan out in the barn for the pup." When the food was set inside the stall, the little guy wasted no time in eating it.

The next day, when Joel turned King out in the paddock for the day so he could clean his stall, he lay an extra hay in the corner for the pup. Though the dog was new to the farm, he made friends quickly and easily with all of them.

When Harrison got his first look at the little mutt, he said with a chuckle, "I would say since one can hardly tell what breed it is, his daddy must have been a traveling man, don't you think? But I can see he knows which side of his bread is buttered, the way he has made up to all of you guys."

He still stays with King when he's in his stall, and this big horse will put his nose down to nudge the little thing now and then. It was amazing how well they got on together.

Now Lily, at fourteen, was the youngest of their children, but she hardly ever acted her age. She still played with her dolls, and Lily was disruptive whenever it pleased her—which was most of the time—and seldom ever smiled. She had no interest in the pup and didn't see why everyone else had either. Elizabeth helped her mother in the house and mused that it would be nice if Lily would help occasionally too. Somehow Lily seemed to never be around though when there was work to be done. Come to think of it, Lily didn't join the family even when they were just relaxing. And when they were younger and played together in the house, if the weather was bad, Lily was never with them then either.

Elizabeth was thinking of how their father had taken a board, cut it in a square for them, then showed them how to draw the blocks to play a game called fox and geese, with shelled corn and dried beans for game pieces. They would get the game out from a drawer in their father's desk. Their mother had made a small drawstring bag from leftover dress fabric to keep the game pieces in. They would lie on the huge round braided rug in the front room. She remembered how very small she felt those times being surrounded by all the furnishings—a large desk and chair where her father sat to work in his account books, a grandfather clock, the couch and chair frames her father had made so her mother could make the loose feather-filled cushions for both the couch and chair then change them as often as she liked; the fireplace mantel seemed so tall too. But now, she was thinking how odd it was as one grew; the size of things seemed to even out.

They would play for hours though. Of course, Joel would win most often, but she and David didn't like it when he would let them win either, which he would do occasionally. Then the three of them would put the game away and also played hide the thimble until they would grow tired enough to take a nap lying on the braided rug.

But she also remembered how hard her parents had worked in those days to keep their farm going. Her parents were such hardworking people, but they were never really neglectful of their children. Ellen and Harrison Steele, to her way of thinking, were the best of people. They all worked hard, but it was her father's job to keep everything on the farm in good working order and looking presentable, with the help of his family, of course.

Her mother was the same with their home. She kept her appearance neat as well. At the age of ten, Elizabeth began to help her mother make their clothes, but then most people they knew did make their own clothes, and she loved to help. Ellen Steele had a natural talent for style and colors as well as what looked good on different people. They would buy some of their clothes for Sunday church, of course, especially the men. They would buy their Sunday suits and dress hats for the men and women in Corbin, or even in London, Kentucky, when the chance came.

One day, Elizabeth felt pretty and twirled around in the sunshine. She was wearing an everyday dress made from lightweight fabric in a light shade of blue, a simple style that she made herself, with short sleeves and lower neckline than usual because of the heat; also great to wear while doing chores. She had her hair tied back away from her face with a blue ribbon; it was cooler that way. It was a beautiful day in early spring—the trees were leafing out, the flowering trees were getting buds, the grass was greening up, which was good for the cows, especially since she was taking them out to pasture. Her father and brothers were busy that morning starting their work in the tobacco patch, so she was asked to take the milk cows to pasture after the morning milking. Joel's horse, King, was out in pasture behind the barn and so the new little dog chose to come along with her and the cows that morning. Her brothers haven't named the dog yet, but she called him Little Jo. The pup seemed to answer to it. It was such a beautiful morning; the birds were singing and sounded like they had their own little choir. Elizabeth remembered an old saying of her mother's, "Beauty is best when plainly drest," and this was certainly a beautiful day even though she had the chore of taking the cows to pasture. She still planned to be back in plenty of time to help her mother prepare the milk for the spring house.

It's so good to be outdoors, she was thinking again. The air smells heavenly, well away from the barn that is; and to her way of thinking, early spring was her favorite time of year. There were more birds singing now with the bees buzzing and butterflies flying around all the new budding flowers, and Elizabeth was lost in the music and in thought, so she was startled when she noticed a man watering a horse in the creek that runs by the lane leading to the pasture.

It was unusual to see a stranger this close to the house. She decided it best just to ignore him, tried to get the cows past him, and hoped he didn't notice her either; but no such luck because Little Jo started barking up a storm. The man looked up just then. He stared at her while standing there in the middle of the creek. He then began walking toward her while leading his horse.

She quickly turned away, gasping, "Oh no." She had been taught at an early age not to talk to strangers, so she just wanted to get away fast.

The man called to her and asked, "Hey there. Can you tell me, miss, who's property I happen to be riding through? I noticed the creek here and decided to let my horse have a drink, but I'm afraid I lost my way back to the main road."

When she continued to keep her eyes straight ahead and didn't answer, the man asked, "Can't you at least look at me, Missy?"

Elizabeth turned, and with a glint in her eyes, she said, "You, sir, should leave. My father doesn't like for strangers to be on his property, and not this close to our house especially."

She was focused on the man who was still staring at her when there was a splash, and she turned to see the cows had all gotten in the creek. "Oh great, now look what you've caused." Elizabeth started running after the cows, and Little Jo was running, too, and barking, which only made the cows scatter more. She was trying to pull her shoes off as she was hopping around after the cows.

With a deep sigh, the man called to her. "Just stay where you are, Missy, and I'll get them rounded up." Elizabeth bristled at his tone. How dare he treat her as if it were her fault! The man climbed back on his horse then said to her, "I'll get the cows out of the creek, but stop that dog from barking." She reached down and picked the dog up started humming to calm it down. The man walked his horse back in the water, and used him to herd the cows back out in the lane again.

He called out in a not so friendly tone, "Where do these cows belong anyway, girl?" Elizabeth stood there amazed and thought how easily he had managed to work with his horse to get the cows out of the creek and back out in the lane again. But then she didn't want to be impressed, as she remembered the way this stranger had talked to her, and just then he called out to her again. Elizabeth turned to look at him finally; she was hopping mad now. The stranger dismounted and was now standing by his horse, waiting for her to answer him. Elizabeth grimaced and then she pointed toward the pasture gate.

"Well then Missy, do you think you could at least open the gate so these cows can go in there?" Elizabeth didn't like his attitude one little bit, but she didn't say so. She just set the pup down, opened the gate for the cows, then she tried to close the gate; but he was there and reached out over her shoulder to take hold of the gate as he said, "I'll do that." He was standing much too close for her comfort.

Elizabeth had had enough. She bent her head and said a quick prayer, asking the Lord for this man to just leave and head back to the main road. Stiffly, she turned to say, "If you will just leave now, sir, I can handle this myself."

The stranger went right ahead, closed the gate anyway, then he turned to stand closer to Elizabeth. She heard his breath catch as he looked at her. In a deep husky voice, he asked, "What did you say your name is, Missy?"

"I didn't say, sir," she answered. "Now will you please leave?"

"Tell me your name first. I also wish to offer an apology for my bad manners. I have been riding all night and feeling the saddle, then I lost my way. I know that is no excuse, but will you please accept my apology?" He smiled at her apologetically or He shyly smiled at Elizabeth. "Here we are now. Say, has anyone ever told you how pretty you are, miss? You still haven't told me your name, you know."

Elizabeth didn't realize she had been staring at his mouth until she heard him ask for her name; then as she raised her eyes to his, she thought, *Oh my, he has the most beautiful green eyes.*

She was mesmerized and just couldn't look away, but then she heard him say, "If you keep looking at me that way, Missy, I won't be responsible for what happens."

Hearing what he said brought her back to herself. "Well, that's something you will never know, so you can just go now, sir." That statement was like waving a red flag in front of a bull. Before she could react, he pulled her to him, gave her a hard kiss. Then once their lips met, the electricity zapped both of them and he softened the kiss to the sweetest thing he had ever known. Shocked and surprised himself, he let her go too quickly because he felt as if he had been burned. That was a mistake as she began to lose her balance, so he reached his hand out to steady her, but Elizabeth jerked her arm away and said, "Don't touch me again! Now please, just leave!"

"I know I should apologize again, but I won't. I'm not sorry I kissed you. Will you at least tell me who you are, please?" he asked softly.

"If I tell you my name, sir, will you then please leave? I need to get back to help my mother." This man was still looking at her in a way she didn't understand, so she blurted out, "My father is Harrison Steele, and my name is Elizabeth. So, you can leave now."

"Elizabeth, that is a very pretty name, almost as pretty as you." He extended his hand to her. "By the way, my name is Noah Bennett. Do you think I could come back to see you again?"

"No!" *Elizabeth's answer came out sharper than she had meant.* "I shouldn't even be talking to you now, sir, much less agree to see you again. I don't think so. Now, for the last time, goodbye."

She turned to walk away, but as she did, she heard him mutter under his breath, "Oh, I'll see you again, Elizabeth."

Noah mounted his horse and rubbed his chin. He thought to himself, *I have to see her again. I have to understand what it was about that kiss. I felt something I've never felt before.* He was watching her with the little ball of fur following her.

Noah sat there watching as she walked away till she was out of sight. Then he rode back across the creek to find his way to the main road. She was in such an all-fire hurry for him to leave but she could have at least given him directions. After that kiss, he had forgotten about it himself, he thought with a smile, so he really couldn't blame her.

Later, when Elizabeth reached the house, Little Jo trotted back to the stable, which was his habit, as she continued on into the kitchen. Her mother looked up from her preparations to get the milk ready for the spring house. "Your face seems flushed, dear. You didn't need to rush back, you know, but the milk's all ready for you."

"Thanks mom," Elizabeth said and blushed even brighter but hoped her mother wouldn't guess something was different about her. With six cows to milk twice a day, it made for a large amount of milk each day, and it meant plenty to keep them busy.

Ellen used some of it to make butter. She had two large churns, which almost always one churn will be ready to make butter in the mornings while the other one will be ready by the next day. Ellen will sour the milk in a large pan on the reservoir used for heating water. The reservoir was attached to the side of the wood cookstove; it will sit there overnight, then after it was ready to be churned, she will use her own recipe to make butter. The family liked the buttermilk too.

Ellen will sell some of the milk, cream, and butter they made. There were also eggs to sell because there were plenty of chickens. Some of the neighbors will either pay money or trade stuff such as garden or flower seeds. So for the present, she was using the wooden wagon their father had made for the boys when they were young. Elizabeth remembered how Joel would pull her and David around in it and how they would laugh. Now, it was perfect to load the cans of milk in and pull to the spring house. As she was putting the cans of milk in the cool water, she was thinking how nice it would be to linger a while to cool off, but of course, there was still more work to do.

As she was walking back to the house though, she looked around at her home. She thought about all the hard work her father had put into building the house, her mother's flowers all around. She has always loved her home and was so thankful for the way of life she has had. The house may not be as fancy as some of their neighbors', but that didn't matter to her. The homestead was begun when Harrison knew he was going to ask for Ellen's hand. He built a sturdy home for them as newlyweds then added rooms as the children came along, and then he kept adding— whatever it took to please Ellen—such as the large front room. Then what had been their front room was now the dinning room.

There were two bedrooms downstairs and a large kitchen along the back of the house, four bedrooms upstairs with a large attic room, with an extra bed and room for storage. There were two windows overlooking. the front yard and two windows facing the back; a porch across the front of the house that the family used all the time; they especially enjoyed sitting out there when the weather permits. Her father had built it all to suit his family, although the kitchen was built to suit her mother. It had a cabinet built by her father, the top part of which had shelves for dishes; it had glass in the doors; also a flour bin underneath and butcher block top space, with a large mixing bowl that always sat there for when her mother made biscuits. There were also shelves underneath to store bowls. There was a work table also, with space to store pots and pans under it. Her father made a large kitchen table with eight chairs; in fact, he made most of their furnishings. Other things, of course, he bought. So all in all, their home was special to her. *Well, enough daydreaming—* she thought—*best hurry back to the house now.* When she did return, she found her mother in the pantry, which is something else she had asked to be added to the kitchen.

Ellen was going through her herb basket. Elizabeth had to smile to herself, for her mother enjoyed searching for herbs and finding new ways of using them. She was already able to treat so many different ailments using the herbs. People often came from far and wide to ask her for advice and purchase the tonics she made too.

Ellen looked up to see Elizabeth standing there. "Oh, there you are, dear. I was thinking maybe you would like to go with me today to gather more of my herbs. I'm running short of some."

"I would love to go with you, mom, and maybe learn more about the different kinds of herbs you use." Elizabeth thought it was a great idea, so she asked, "When were you thinking of leaving?"

"Well, I thought we could go now. I just put a pot of pinto beans with ham on to cook while we're gone. The fire's banked with enough wood to keep it cooking until we return. Then we can prepare the wild greens I plan to find to finish up dinner."

Ellen already had her basket on her arm, and she walked over to take her bonnet off a hook near the door. While she was tying it on her head, Elizabeth was thinking it was such a shame for her mother to cover her beautiful hair. It was a dark auburn red, and she kept it pulled back in a neat bun. Ellen Steele is still a very pretty woman even being the mother of four grown children; and after years of hard work helping her husband in the fields, she still appeared to be young. This is mostly because Ellen had such a youthful attitude and she was pure of heart. She took care of her skin, made her clothes to fit her still-slim figure, and always looked lovely on Sunday mornings when she dressed up for the Lord and church services.

Elizabeth was reminded of a saying her mother used a lot: "She looketh well to the ways of her household, and eateth not the bread of idleness." That really did sum up her mother to a tee.

That day, she was wearing a dress she made in a pretty shade of blue gingham with a small pink flower print, simple style, with a round neckline and elbow-length sleeves. Her dress was ankle length as was the style then; it suited her too. She said that style was preferable to the old one of the hooped skirts, with all the petticoats which was the style when she was a young girl. "Let me tell you, dear, the dresses were terrible in the heat of summer. In those days," she continued, "the young women wore wide-brimmed hats usually decorated with flowers and berries."

Ellen and her daughters saved their best clothes and hats for Sunday church services. Now as they walked in the woods overlooking the creek where Elizabeth had met that awful man that morning, she couldn't help but think about how he had kissed her. She put fingers to her mouth to touch her lips and remembered how that kiss felt but then gave herself a shake because she didn't want to think about it. Besides, her mother had been speaking to her. Ellen had been telling her they would need to go farther into the woods now to find the sassafras roots she wanted for making tea.

"We can get dandelion root too. It makes a pretty good tea as well, you know. Some people have been known to make wine with it, too, but of course I have no interest in doing that," she said with a chuckle. "But the tops can be used, maybe, which is—what I wish to do is to find other wild greens to go with them for our dinner. I know your father will surely appreciate them." Sure enough, they did find the sassafras root. Ellen Steele seemed to have an uncanny way of knowing where to find what she was looking for.

Elizabeth said, "You know, Mom, you never fail to amaze me at how you just seemed to know where to look for the herbs you need."

"You must remember, dear, that I have been roaming the woods and gathering herbs since I was a young girl."

After gathering up quite a bit of sassafras, Ellen noticed some white willows growing along the creek.

"You know dear," she said. "I'll come back another time to get some of the bark from those trees. It's good for treating inflammation or joint pain."

They also found dandelion roots and the tops they cut to go with the wild lettuce and other wild greens they had found.

As they were walking back, Elizabeth asked, "Mom, I've been wondering. How did you and Dad meet? You never talk about it, and you don't really talk about your childhood or any other family either."

"Well, I hope you realize, dear, I never intended to keep anything from you children," Ellen replied. "Its just that your father and I both were orphans. We lost our families in a typhoid fever epidemic sometime around 1840 while we were still children in a small community called Bee Rock. It is near the Laurel River, where the water became contaminated after a flash flood. Anyway, that's what people believed at the time. My parents died, and I assume so did your father's parents, with others who as well were unaware the water was unsafe to use. Luckily, some of the people knew to boil the water before drinking it. So, both Harrison and I survived along with other people."

"Although your father and I didn't know each other at the time, I don't remember anything about my parents, but Harrison has some memories of his family, since he was older, but he still doesn't have a lot to say about them. The church women took turns taking care of me, and they were good enough, but it still isn't the same, you know, as having your own family."

"But like I said, your father was a little older, and he was in an orphanage till he was age twelve. That's when he decided to go out on his own to find work. He did go to work with a man making furniture, cabinets, and just about anything that could be made with a log of wood, which you know is something your father is good at."

"He really learned a love of woodworking as a useful skill. Of course, the home he built for us is proof of the love and care your father puts into his work, don't you think?"

"Yes, I know," Elizabeth answered.

"Well, you see, I met your father at a church gathering," Ellen continued. "We knew from our first sight of each other that we wanted to know one another better, and we were married within days of our first meeting," she said with a smile. "The teachers at the orphanage used to tell your father daily that what you are is God's gift to you; what you make of yourself is your gift to God. Well, I can tell you that I thank the Lord above that your father took those words to heart. We made a promise to each other that since we never really had family growing up, we would have as many children as the Lord would allow us. We were blessed with you four children; we're so proud of you too. Now I do understand that Lily can be difficult at times, but do you realize that because of all the work trying to keep the farm going, when Lily was very small, she was left to herself so much of the time. Don't get me wrong, I'm not saying that is an excuse; just that Lily has had a different time growing up. Now dear, we do need to return to the house and finish up dinner before the men get there and find there's nothing for them to eat."

The noon meal, which was called dinner, was ready to put on the table just as Harrison and his two sons came into the kitchen. "I'm sure hungry, Mom," David was saying, "but mostly we all need water to drink. Just can't seem to get enough because of this heat; it's terrible."

David reached for the water bucket and left the dipper on the stand, and continued to the back porch to bring it back full of cool water straight from the pump. He put the dipper back in the bucket, took glasses from the cabinet, then dipped each of them a cool drink.

As he handed his father a glass, Harrison said, "Thanks, Son, that sure tastes good, and I agree with you about the heat."

Joel spoke up to say, "I second that. And thanks for the water, brother."

Harrison added, "It's as warm today as I can remember for early spring weather." Then he sat down at the head of the table just as Ellen and Elizabeth set out the meal.

Ellen asked, "How's the work coming along? Are you going to have enough tobacco plants to finish up with?" but wasn't surprised to hear him say, "We do, and plenty left over, in case some of the neighbors run short."

Harrison raised his own plants. It was quite a process, too, to prepare the ground. He will have his sons burn the ground "to help prevent weeds and bugs," he would tell them. Sometimes, even Elizabeth would help gather brush from the woods. Harrison will wait for a day or two until the ground has cooled down to clear away the ashes and stuff, then start working the ground to the consistency of cornmeal. He would plant the seeds then cover them with cheesecloth. And he always had the best plants around, more than he needed, too, which he felt was better than not having enough. He repeated an old favorite saying, "Wisdom is knowing what to do next, skill is knowing how to do it, and virtue is doing it."

Ellen was lost in thought when she felt Harrison's eyes on her, and he said, "Anyway, for now, wife"—he held up his plate—"I'm more interested in getting you to break off some of your good cornbread, lay it on here, and cover it with some of those ham and soup beans. They smell wonderful and look even better. I don't know about the boys, but I'm hungry. Some wild greens on the side, please. "Joel, will you pass the boiled potatoes?" he said with a twinkle in his eye. "Elizabeth, are those green onions some of the first from our garden? Just lay a couple of those on there, too, thank you."

"Yes," Ellen told him. "The onions are the very first"—she returned his smile—"but I do need to get more onion sets out, you know, and more bean seeds planted, too, with Elizabeth's help, that is. Maybe we can do that after the kitchen is squared away."

"Sure, Mom, I'll be glad to help. It's such a beautiful day; I'd like that."

"Beautiful and *hot*," came David's teasing remark.

"That's true, dear," Ellen told her. "You really should wear one of my bonnets or a straw hat when you're out to keep the sun off your face. You could get freckles, you know." Her mother said with another smile, "In my day, that would have been a no-no."

Joel reached for the onions and said, "Now, Mom, there's nothing wrong with Elizabeth's skin. Other girls her age should be so lucky to have complexion such as hers. Anyway, William Jones seems to think it perfect." Teasing his sister is one of Joel's favorite things to do—all in good fun, of course.

Elizabeth fired back with, "Oh, thanks, Joel. And just so you know, the next time we have the chance to go to a gathering, I believe I should let all the girls there know how well you like to dance."

Joel's smile froze on his face as he said, "I certainly hope you're teasing now, sis."

David started laughing out loud. "I think you put your foot in your mouth this time, brother. She's pretty good natured to us most of the time, but this time she's stinging you like a bee."

Elizabeth passed the wilted greens to her father as she said, "Well then, David, maybe since you seem to like having girls around, I should let it be known you're looking for a steady girl," Elizabeth said with another sweet smile.

David looked stricken, and Joel was still sitting there stunned with disbelief when they both said, "What in the world has gotten into you today, sis?" That got them all laughing, and Harrison looked over at his wife to smile. Ellen was watching their children tease and have fun with each other. They always enjoyed being together and teasing one another.

But now, Lily was coming into the kitchen from the front room and balefully looked at them all and wanted to know why no one had let her know dinner was on the table.

Harrison asked, "Where have you been, girl? If you had been in here helping your mother, then you would know when a meal is on the table. Now sit down and join us."

Lily sat down with a sulky look but didn't say anything more. Her father said in a more gentle tone, "Eat, child. Your mother worked hard to cook this meal."

So Lily took out a little of the beans and some cornbread, but she just started pushing it around on her plate. Elizabeth was watching her sister and thought how Lily would be pretty if she would just smile more. Lily caught her watching. She made a face. Elizabeth gave a sigh and turned and looked Joel's way. He just shrugged his shoulder to let her know there was no use worrying about it.

After the meal, their father had a habit of resting for a while on the front porch "to let his dinner settle," he will say. Their mother is also in the habit of letting the dishes wait, so they would all go out to the porch to sit for a while. Elizabeth would go because she enjoyed being with her family, but Lily never bothered. She had a place beside the porch where she would play with her dolls. She was out of sight but liked to hear what was being said. Lily wouldn't come back in the house as long as there was work to do.

Chapter  2

After the men had left for the field again and the dishes were done, the kitchen was clean again. Ellen asked if Elizabeth was ready now for the garden work.

"Of course," she agreed. "I'll get a hoe from the shed, Mom, and meet you out there." After getting the hoe, she chopped weeds while her mother planted her bean seeds and put the onion sets in the ground. When they were finished, Elizabeth put the hoe back in the shed. When she returned to the kitchen, her mother was busy getting out ingredients for baking.

"What are we making, Mom? Need help?"

"Well, yes, I thought we could make some gingerbread to take out to the men in the field and also take them a jug of cool water from the spring house, since the weather's so warm. Like David said, they can't get enough water to drink. So if you'll help, we can have this done in no time."

A few minutes later, Lily came running into the kitchen to tell them that William Jones was coming up the lane.

Ellen said, "Elizabeth, you go out to greet him. I would imagine you're the one he is here to see anyway."

Lily stomped her foot. "How do you know he's here to see her?" She pointed to Elizabeth.

"Hush now, Lily," Ellen told her, and then turned to Elizabeth to say, "You go on out to meet William."

Elizabeth was walking out on the porch. As William opened the gate, he walked up to where she was standing. He had been away for a while, so he stood there just admiring her and thinking how she was more beautiful than he remembered. He told her so as he reached for her hand.

"How have you been, Elizabeth?"

"I've been fine, thank you, William. And you?"

"I'm fine too," he said laughingly. "You would think from our greetings here, we just met."

Elizabeth laughed too. He felt his heart skip a beat. He squeezed her hand, looked her in the eyes, and told her, "I can't get over how lovely you are, my dear." She couldn't help but blush. He squeezed her hand again as he said, "You're even more so when you blush, sweetheart." Elizabeth blinked at him in surprise this time. "Does it bother you for me to call you *sweetheart?*"

"I suppose not. I was just surprised, is all," Elizabeth replied.

"Then you don't mind?" he asked with a grin.

Elizabeth laughed again. "No, I don't mind, William. Would you like to come inside the house? It may be a little cooler, but I can't promise."

"That would be good," he said. "Actually, I came to invite your family over to a party my parents are having Saturday evening. It will be a sort of kick off to start the racing season. So, would you be my date, Elizabeth?" She stood there surprised again and told him so.

"Why are you surprised, honey?"

"William, you must know that you could ask any girl in the county, and they would gladly accept."

"But I want you for my date, Elizabeth. So are you going to turn me down then?"

"No, not if you're sure you really want me for your date."

"I do," he said. "Now let's go see your mother."

Together they walked in to talk with Ellen. Elizabeth led the way into the front room. When she called to her mother, of course, Lily came out of the kitchen first. She walked right up to William, held out her hand for him to take as she said, "I'm Lily, you're William, right?"

William said, "Yes, Lily, that's who I am." He shook her hand and let it go. He walked over to Ellen to say, "Mrs. Steele, how are you and the rest of the family? Well, I hope?"

"We're all fine, William." Ellen answered. "It's good to see you, and I hope your family is well too"

"Yes, ma'am. My parents are fine. One of the reasons I'm here is to invite your family to a party Saturday night. I do hope all of you can make it."

"How nice," Ellen said. "I hope we can too, William. And thanks for the invitation. Now come, Lily, we have work to do in the kitchen."

When Lily said, "I wanted to stay," Ellen took her hand. She said, "Come on now, I need your help." So the girl had no choice but to go back to the kitchen with her mother, although she made it quite plain she was not happy about it.

After they left the room, William turned to Elizabeth. She smiled shyly, as they both knew her mother was giving them time alone. He said, "I really need to go, you know. I have more errands to run for my father, but would you walk out with me, sweetheart?" Elizabeth agreed to walk outside with him. Before he was ready to mount his horse, he took her hand to say, "I'm expecting to have you by my side at the party, okay." Then he gave her a quick kiss, turned to climb in the saddle, and he rode away without looking back.

Elizabeth couldn't help comparing William's quick kiss with the one she received earlier from the stranger. She thought it odd, but as she was always lighthearted, she put the thought out of her head and walked back in the kitchen. Her mother had the gingerbread already made, sliced up, and put in a basket.

"Now we'll take this jug"—Ellen handed it to Elizabeth with tin cups—"and get cool water from the spring house so we can go now. Lily, are you coming with us, dear?"

"No!" came a shout from the young girl. "I'm staying here. Besides, you don't care if I'm with you or not anyway." She ran out the door.

Ellen has this mystified look on her face as her daughter ran out.

Elizabeth quickly said, "Mom, don't worry. Lily's only doing this for attention, you know. Let her be for now. We'll take your bread to the men, and they will certainly love the break."

So they did. David was the first to see them, and he called out to his father and brother for them to come take a break. When he reached them, he took the basket from his mother. He said, "Here mom, let me help you sit on this log."

As Joel made his way to them, he took the jug of water and cups from Elizabeth. "Sit there by Mom, sis. By the way, thanks for the water."

"What do we have here?" Harrison asked as he walked over to the women. He gave Ellen a peck on the cheek then sat down on the other side of her.

David pulled the cloth off the basket and gave a whoop. He said with a wink, "Man, oh, man. Dad, would you looky here at what your beautiful wife has brought us." He passed it around for the others to have some. Then he took a piece himself when the basket came back to him. While Joel was pouring water, Ellen and Elizabeth told them to drink it all.

"We can get more for ourselves when we get back to the house," his mother said. Then Ellen mentioned casually while looking down at her hands, "William Jones came by just a while ago with an invitation to a party this Saturday evening at their place."

"Ah, and is this treat to soften us up for the invitation?" Harrison teased his wife.

"Now Dad," Elizabeth spoke up. "That isn't fair. Mom was already making the bread before William came by."

"There's no need to defend your mother to me, daughter, I am well aware of her kindness," he said softly, not taking his eyes off his wife. "I know she wouldn't do such a thing. Would you like to go to the party, dear?"

Ellen looked up at her husband, and with a twinkle in her eye, she said, "Yes. As a matter of fact, I think it would be good for everyone to have a break, away from the work for a short time. Not that I believe any of us minds the work. It's just for one night. Do you think it would be okay, Harrison?"

"Yes dear, I also think it would be good to take a break. And may I ask you to save me the first dance? I seem to remember that you used to love to dance," he said with a grin. She smiled back warmly.

Joel spoke up. "I wanted to know what it was like when the two of you were younger. Were you able to go to many parties?"

Harrison laughed out loud, "Hey now, son, you make your mother and me sound old. I will have you know your mother was—and still is, mind you—a beautiful woman. I just about needed a stick to fight the young men away. We met at a church gathering and danced till dark, if I remember right. Times were very tough but there were always plenty of church socials and dancing."

Ellen stood up and looked at her children to say, "Well, let me tell you three. Harrison Steele was one of the best-looking men in the county, a real charmer and, of course, he still is. And if I was a jealous woman"—Ellen smiled at her husband as she told them—"I'd have been mad all the time." Their children laughed at that. She continued, "Just take notice at the Jones's party and see if he doesn't get more then his share of second glances," she said with a cute grin as Harrison helped her to sit back down again.

Their three children were very pleased to share in what their parents were telling them and how both exchanged smiles and glances as they spoke. It was so fun to think of them as young and full of love and life. It was as if God was smiling on them all, and they realized how blessed they were.

After a bit, Harrison told his sons, "Come, we need to get back to our work now." He stood and reached out his hand to help his wife to her feet. "That was a very good break, dear. Thank you both for thinking of us. We'll see you later."

As they were walking back to the field, Elizabeth stood watching her father and brothers return to their work. All three were handsome men—strong, tall, well muscled from all the work they do. The three of them all had different hair color, but their builds were all alike; and if you couldn't see them, it would be hard to tell their voices apart. They all wore lightweight white cotton shirts, sleeves rolled up past the elbow, and dark-colored pants and work boots. As for hats, her dad preferred the same as he had worn for years, with a short brim. He also preferred suspenders to a belt. He says they are more comfortable now that he's older. Joel and David preferred the wide-brimmed hat as most of their friends do.

Ellen brought Elizabeth back to the present when she asked, "Are you ready to head back to the house now, dear?" They took the basket, the jug, and tin cups and began to walk back to the house and the rest of their chores.

Early the next morning, after Harrison had finished reading his Bible, as he was in the habit of doing, he gently laid it back on the sideboard, as always, while breakfast was set on the table. Then after they are finished with their meal, he announced heartily, "We should be done with the tobacco planting this afternoon. Since the party is tonight, we'll be back in plenty of time to get the chores done and be ready for the party, so there's no need for you to worry. I'll save my strength to be able to dance the night away, dear," he told his wife. "Well, maybe just a dance or two, and we will watch our boys and girls dance the night away."

"You know me too well, dear, but I will be looking forward to that dance tonight, good sir."

"That will make two of us, my dear." He turned to look at his sons. "Are you two ready to get this tobacco chore over with?" But as they were leaving, he gave his wife a kiss full on the lips as he said, "See you later. dear."

"Wow!" David said as his father was ready to walk out the backdoor. "It really is a special day," Joel spoke to say seriously. "I sure hope I find someone to marry that's as loving and devoted to me when I am Mom and Dad's age." Harrison, while standing in the backdoorway, turned to Ellen and smiled at this statement, then he told his sons that his old pastor had taught him: "Daughters will probably be like their mothers; therefore, the mother is a good guide for a young man when selecting a wife. To me, that was good and wise advice. He also knew both your mother and I were orphans, but then old pastors can't help themselves from handing out advice."

Ellen surprised him by voicing her opinion. "You children should learn age has nothing to do with it either; it's the love."

Joel looked at his mother and asked, "What do you mean, Mom?"

"Your father and I have loved each other since the day we first met twenty-five years ago. That has not changed; it's still the same today. Love is the answer. Marriage, for any reason, is risky; but for love, it's right."

Joel said, "That's good to know. It helps me to set a goal for myself." He gave his mother a peck on the cheek then said, "Hey, David, dad has already left. We best be on our way, too, before he comes back looking for us." Then as an afterthought, he asked, "Sis, do you need any help getting the cows out of the barn and headed toward pasture this morning?"

"No," Elizabeth said too quickly and blushed. "I should be able to do it myself, but thanks anyway. Actually, I best be on my way too. I'll be back shortly to help you, Mom." Then she walked out with her brothers who went on to join their father.

Elizabeth walked into the barn to start letting the cows out of their stalls, concerned at the thought of the stranger showing up again that day. The man had told her his name, but she couldn't seem to think of him as anything but a stranger—a stranger with an electric smile. She shouldn't even be thinking of him. As she began to get the cows moving down the lane, Little Jo showed up with a yip, and soon she had them headed to pasture. The cows were being much more cooperative that day, and she was singing to herself as she was headed down the lane, with Jo running alongside. It was another bright sunny spring morning, and Elizabeth was so caught up enjoying it all that she didn't notice at first that the stranger was back.

"Oh no," she groaned.

She had hoped this wouldn't happen again. He was standing just where the lane made the jog to the right along the creek and the pasture. He stood beside his gleaming black horse. He was as tall as her brothers—even David, at age sixteen, was a good six feet—or better. The man was standing there leaning against his horse and dressed in a loose-fitting white shirt with the sleeves rolled up, black pants, Hessian boots that came to his knees, and a black, wide-brimmed hat. It was strange that she hadn't noticed any of this yesterday. She was too upset, she guessed.

He straightened and was standing as if he was ready for battle, but when she came closer, he spoke with a smile, "I told you that I would see you again."

Elizabeth gave him a cool look and replied, "But if you remember, sir, I told you not to come here again." She stepped past him as she was trying to get the cows to the pasture gate.

He moved forward to say, "Here, let me help you," and in no time, he had opened the gate, the cows walked through, then he closed it behind them. He turned back to face her.

Elizabeth said, "Thank you, sir. Now if you will excuse me, I need to go back to the house before my mother becomes concerned." She started to turn away just as he reached out to touch her arm, but Elizabeth pulled away. She said, "I told you not to touch me again."

She started to turn away again, but this time he took hold of her arm and pleaded, "Please wait. I wish to talk to you, Elizabeth."

This did stop her, and she gave him a stern look. "Now just a minute," she said. "You shouldn't use my given name. I do not know who you are, sir."

"But I told you my name is Noah Bennett! I have thought of your face and name since I last saw you. Are you telling me that you didn't remember mine?" he asked sharply with a hurt look.

"I don't have the time, sir, to think about such things," Elizabeth told him, which was partly true. "Now let go of me. I need to get back to help my mother with the milk." She tried to pull her arm away, but his grip only strengthened a little, and he wouldn't let go. Suddenly, Noah pulled her to him and captured her lips with his and thought, *It's as if she is a magnet to me and I can't let go.*

Elizabeth didn't realize she was holding her breath, but she couldn't even think to breathe when he kissed her. She went to gasp. Noah was about to take advantage of this opportunity to deepen the kiss, but he realized Elizabeth is trying to get away.

When he finally raised his head, he looked into her eyes and they both realized what had just happened. The shock of it hit them both for very different reasons. She had never even thought of being kissed like that before, and Noah couldn't believe how much this girl affected him. He let her go too quickly again, since Elizabeth's feet hadn't completely touched ground yet. After he let her go, he had to reach out his hand to keep her from losing her balance. This galvanized her into action, and she brought her hand around to slap him.

But Noah caught it before she made contact with his jaw and said softly, "Now come on, sweetheart, I'll let you go. But do not try to slap me again; I will not allow it." He slowly let go of her. Elizabeth stepped back to glare at him. Noah thought she was probably trying to look menacing, but to him he thought she looked adorable. He wasn't about to say so. However, he did say, "Listen, I'm sorry, okay? I know I shouldn't have kissed you."

"Why did you kiss me?" Elizabeth asked hesitantly.

"Well, to be honest, I couldn't help myself," he said. "I know, Elizabeth. I don't understand it either, but will you please forgive me?" he asked.

"Yes, if you will just go away and leave me alone," she told him.

"I can't seem to stay away from you," Noah responded. "And I will not leave until you say my name, I want to hear you say it, and I want to talk to your father. I'm going to ask his permission to court you."

"No! You can't do that. I don't want you to court me. I am just going to pretend I don't know you," Elizabeth told him. "I have a date tonight with a young man I have dreamed of all my life. He has finally asked me to be his date at a party tonight, so please stay away."

"What man? Who is he?" Noah hated himself for asking but didn't like the thought of Elizabeth with someone else. He didn't want to startle her, but he couldn't seem to help it.

Elizabeth answered, "Not that it's any of your business, but his name is William Jones. His family is having a party tonight, and he asked me to be his date."

"Why has it taken him so long to ask you for a date?" Noah asked.

"Well, he has been away and just returned. Now please, I must go. My mother will worry if I'm not back soon." Before Noah could respond, she turned and ran back toward the house then called for the little dog. Soon he was running hard on her heels.

Noah stood watching her go. He felt as if she was taking his heart with her. Never in his life had any woman have this effect on him before now. He didn't understand why this slip of a girl had gotten to him, and so quickly too! He had known other women, some more beautiful and striking than she is, but there's just something about Elizabeth—the shine of her golden hair, the brilliance of her blue eyes that took his mind to a peaceful place, the pout of her lips. He thought of the kiss they shared; it went straight to his heart. What a puzzlement. Maybe it was because she was unpretentious. Most women he knew worried too much about their looks and knew how to flirt and flounce about, but Elizabeth didn't seem concerned with any of that. She was mostly concerned with getting back to help her mother and not causing her to worry. Elizabeth had made it plain that she didn't seem to care for him or share his feelings, but he couldn't accept that as how she really feels. With one look, he knew this girl was the one whom he could build a life with, and talking to her only confirmed it. Fate couldn't be so cruel as to not let them end up together.

Noah sighed deeply, then turned to his horse to mount. He sat there watching after Elizabeth. She was almost out of sight now with the little dog when a younger girl joined her, and then they were both no longer visible.

Noah turned his horse, a huge black stallion that went by the name of Ebony. Ebony was as handsome as they come. He was one of the best horses he had ever owned, but he could be an ornery cuss when it suited him. Come to think of it, so were a lot of women he had known. He just hoped Elizabeth wasn't like that. Noah headed back across the creek at the spot he had found yesterday. He should be going back to the horse farm he owned with his brother, about ten miles east on the other side of Corbin, Kentucky. But he wasn't going back home just yet. He was going to find out about this Will or Bill that Elizabeth had mentioned. He needed to know what kind of man he is and just what his intentions are toward Elizabeth. Noah couldn't help but feel possessive of her already. He still didn't understand his feelings for her so quickly, but he couldn't and wouldn't see her come to any harm. Hard to believe it had only been twenty-four hours since he happened to meet this young woman; it seemed much longer.

Before Elizabeth could get out of sight of that man, Lily was waiting for her and wanting to know who that man was whom she had been talking to.

"I don't know. He was lost and asking for directions," Elizabeth answered.

Lily wouldn't give up though. "I'm going to tell Dad I saw you kissing him."

Elizabeth stopped and told her, "I will tell Dad that you don't know what you're talking about and just making up stories. Now, I need to go help mom, Lily, unless you would like to help her with the milk yourself?" Lily turned and began stomping across the yard. "I didn't think so," Elizabeth muttered to herself.

Little Jo had been sitting there watching the back-and-forth conversation between the two sisters as Elizabeth started walking on toward the house. He was still sitting there looking after Lily who was still stomping her feet. The little dog ran to the safety of

King's stall, and Elizabeth smiled to herself to think that a horse like King, as large as they come, was better company for the little dog than Lily.

Elizabeth came into the kitchen hoping her mother wouldn't notice how flushed her face is this time either. No such luck.

Ellen asked, "Why have you been rushing so? Your face is red as a beet."

Her daughter laughed and said, "Oh, you know, Mom, the cows have a mind of their own sometimes." It wasn't exactly a lie, but she had her fingers crossed behind her back, hoping her mother would let the subject go and the Lord will forgive her for the half-truths.

Ellen had the milk ready for the spring house, so Elizabeth pulled the wagon out of the pantry. Her mother asked if she needed help to get it loaded, but she said, "No, Mom, I'm okay." After she had it loaded, she slowly went out the backdoor. When Elizabeth returned to the house, she and her mother did some light housework. Elizabeth told her mother she would do the upstairs rooms. While she was working in Joel's room then onto David's room, she had to smile. There was hardly anything but a light dusting needed here. She thought, *If I ever marry, I hope the man will be as neat as my brothers are.* Then she wondered where that thought came from but went on with her work. She decided to leave Lily's room for her to do; she can at least clean her own room. Besides, she isn't nearly as neat as their brothers.

Later after they were finished with house work, Ellen asked Elizabeth if she had decided on a dress to wear for the party that night.

Elizabeth answered, "No, not really, Mom; I haven't thought about it."

"Well, dear, you really should," Ellen told her. "Why don't you go do that now? You know that blue is your best color."

Elizabeth headed back up the stairs to her room. She stood in front of the wardrobe her father had made. He put a full-length mirror on the door. He had also made one for Lily also, with a chest of drawers for all the bedrooms. So now, she is looking over her choices. She found a pretty blue dress with white trim at the round neckline and with short cape sleeves. More than likely, this dress was the one her mother was thinking of. She held it up to her chin to see how it looked in the mirror and smiled at the color and style of it. Her mother had helped her pick out the fabric and decide on the design. She lay it on her bed and looked for some ribbons to match, thinking maybe she would wash her hair now so it will have plenty of time to dry.

Elizabeth took a towel and a bar of the scented soap that her mother made for the women in the family to use. She liked the scent of lilacs, so she took a bar and went back downstairs, out on the back porch where there was a pump with a tub to catch the water. She knew the water in the tub will be warmed by the sun, so she took a pan to dip out some, set the pan on the washstand, then she wet her hair thoroughly and soaped it up. She inhaled the lilac scent deeply, as she worked it through her hair before she rinsed the soap out. Then she reached for a second pan of water to rinse it again because her hair was so long and thick—it is a real chore to wash and rinse out all the soap—so she kept at it till she is sure it is rinsed thoroughly. Picking up the towel, she wrapped her hair in it. She decided she would take some of the warm water to her room later to bathe before dressing. For now, she went to sit on the front porch to towel dry her hair.

She was busy combing it out and didn't notice or hear a horse and rider coming up the lane. When she did notice, they were at the front gate. At first she couldn't see the rider well enough to tell who he is, but then she recognized the horse—that beautiful black horse—and her face flushed. Her eyes brightened as he came closer—Noah Bennett. Elizabeth breathed and was amazed. She didn't want to look at him though. She didn't want to feel this way about him either. She had dreamed of William Jones since she was in pigtails. He was the man she wanted to spend time with tonight. She didn't want Noah showing up to spoil the evening for her now. *Please Lord*, she thought, *help me to see what you have in store for me.* William Jones was such a good man—strong, kind, hardworking and good to his folks. Elizabeth had known him most of her life and she had always hoped to gain his favor. Now, here comes Noah Bennett, and there's no way to just ignore him, not the way her heart was beating. She could feel the heat of the kiss they shared earlier all over again as she remembered his lips on hers. With her mind lost in her musings, she didn't notice he was just sitting there before her, on that beautiful horse, staring at her. She couldn't think of what to do, and she wasn't sure she could move if she tried. Noah continued to stare then he just lazily tipped his hat, turned his horse around, and rode back down the lane. Elizabeth felt a sense of loss that she didn't understand. She did not want to see him, or did she? She still wanted to be William's date tonight. It didn't make sense to her that Noah's presence could change her mind. She had been looking forward to the party since William had invited her, and she planned to enjoy it.

Once her hair was completely dry and combed to a high shine, Elizabeth went in to see if her mother needed any more help. There will be food at the party tonight, Ellen had told them at the noon meal. They wouldn't need to prepare the evening meal at home.

"Sounds reasonable to me," Harrison replied. "That gives you ladies more time to spend on getting yourself dressed for the party tonight."

"Well, you would think so," Ellen replied, "except it really means we can spend more time preparing for our Sunday meal."

With a small grin, Harrison said, "Sorry, dear. I should have known you would not just rest for an evening. Anyway, I'm looking forward to the party. Do you ladies plan to dress early tonight? The boys and I will help after doing the milking. We will take the milk to the spring house when it is ready so we can all rest a little before getting dressed for the party. Now let's get to it, boys, shall we?" With that, Harrison and the boys headed back to the field to finish with setting the tobacco.

Elizabeth pulled her hair back in a knot, then she helped her mother prepare the food for Sunday dinner and pulled the little wagon out for her brothers to use for hauling the milk and smiled at the thought of how loving and generous her family is. No matter what the chore is, they all pulled together to get the work done. Well, there is Lily who is usually off to herself; and when she was made to help, she made the work miserable for them all. No one was fooled by her actions; they knew she just wanted them to tell her to go away, but really, it was better for her to go off on her own.

After Elizabeth helped her mother prepare the milk after it was brought in the kitchen, David loaded the milk in the little wagon and he called over his shoulder, "Hey, sis, this wagon works pretty darn good for hauling the milk."

"I thought so," she answered, grinning at him as he is heading out the door.

After their short rest on the porch, Elizabeth took water with her as she went upstairs to bathe and dress, then after she has the blue dress on, she put her hair up but left a few curls hanging loose. Usually, she didn't like to spend a lot of time on herself; just as long as she looked presentable, she was happy. But tonight, she wanted to look her best for William, so she went on the hunt for shoes to wear. She only had her work shoes for doing chores, then one pair to wear with everyday dresses. There are two pairs of shoes to wear with her best dresses for Sunday Church. She chose the soft dove-grey shoes that she thought would look best with the dress and be sturdy for dancing. She twirled and spun then laughed. With the length of her dress, no one couldn't even see her shoes anyway.

Tonight she felt pretty and light as air, as she made her way downstairs. Her father and both brothers were already dressed and looking comfortable even though they would rather be dressed more casually. Joel looked so handsome that she knew the girls would swoon over him, but she also knew he wouldn't notice. Then there was David who was just as handsome in a different way, maybe even more handsome than Joel, if that were possible, with his light curly hair and startlingly blue eyes and teasing way. Their father was still a handsome man as well. He always stood tall and straight with a sense of confidence that only love of the Lord and family can provide. All three men were dressed in white shirts, black pants, and vests. Harrison was wearing a black vest which covered his suspenders. Joel's vest was grey and matched his eyes perfectly. David was wearing a forest-green vest that looked really good with his wavy blond hair and makes his blue eyes sparkle. Her brothers were laughing and joking around with each other, when Joel noticed Elizabeth standing at the bottom of the stairs, watching them. He had been leaning against the fireplace mantel. He straightened up with a wide smile and said, "Hey guys, look at our Elizabeth here. Doesn't she look as pretty as a picture?"

"Yeah, Dad. We best take a big stick along with us to keep the men in line," David teased.

"Oh, I believe we'll have help from William on that score tonight," Joel joked.

"Well, you three men certainly look very handsome this evening," Elizabeth told them. "I am so proud to be allowed the pleasure of your company tonight, and I know Mom will be too."

Lily came into the room from the kitchen and is standing in the doorway as she piped up, "What about me, Daddy?"

Harrison turned to see his youngest daughter dressed in a pretty pink dress trimmed in white. It had a white collar with short sleeves.

He answered, "Of course, sweetie, you look pretty as a spring flower."

Lily twirled around the room and turned to Elizabeth, gave her a sly look, and asked her father, "Am I prettier than Elizabeth, Daddy?"

As she continued to twirl around the room, Harrison's smile froze and his voice stopped Lily's spinning when he said, "Why would you ask such a question?"

Lily realized she had overstepped her bounds and began to backpedal. "I'm sorry, Daddy."

He then said, "Both my girls are pretty and wonderful to me."

Lily had that sulky look again till their mother came into the room. Her face broke out into a big smile.

Thank goodness Mom didn't witness Lily's little scene earlier, Elizabeth was thinking.

All three men walked to Ellen and gave her a kiss on the cheek. David told her she would be the prettiest lady at the party and meant it.

"You do look pretty, Mom," Elizabeth told her. Ellen had on a pretty green dress which brought out the green flecks in her hazel eyes. "You and Dad make such a handsome couple."

"We will be a handsome family then," Ellen replied. "It's about time for us to leave, don't you think?"

Harrison took his wife's arm. He said, "Yes. Let's go, my dear." David and Joel had hitched the horse to the buggy and saddled their horses earlier, so now they were ready to help the women up to be seated. They mounted their horses and headed out for the short ride to the Jones's farms.

When Harrison pulled the buggy up, Joel and David had already tied off their horses. They were waiting there to help the women step down. Harrison came around to give Ellen his arm as they took the lead into the barn where the party is.

Joel was telling them, "This building was used mostly for storage, but it makes a great place for a party, don't you think?"

"Yeah, and one can never have enough barn space, you know," Harrison replied.

"You're right about that, Dad," Joel was saying as they had reached the door. Elizabeth was thinking, *Everything about the Jones place was great—the house is huge, it is beautiful and looks rich, too, but I still like our house better. It may not be as fancy as this one, but it has a homey feel to it, lots of space, and it held such sentiment because it is where I, Joel and David, with Lily grew up and played hide and seek as children.*

They walked inside and saw William right away. He had been speaking with a group of people but standing so he could keep an eye on the door as well. When the Steeles arrived, he then excused himself to walk over and greet them. Elizabeth thought him very handsome. He is tall like her brothers, and his hair is a light brown with glints of sun streak from all his work outdoors. His eyes are hazel, the same color as her mother's. This night, his smile was for Elizabeth alone. Dressed in a dark-blue suit with a white shirt and a dark string tie, he looked ever so smart. When he reached them, Joel had to grin because William was playing the gentlemen he was by shaking hands with Harrison first, though his eyes were always aware of Elizabeth. Then he came to his friend who had to tease him a little by saying, "You very much look the part of a gentleman, Farmer William." They laughed.

"You do too, pal." He slapped Joel on the back. "Good to see you."

Then he shook hands with David, said a few words, and walked to take Ellen's hand in both of his and told her she was looking very pretty that night. "I realize now where your daughter gets her good looks," he said with a wide smile.

"Elizabeth! It's so good to have you here." As he reached for her hand, William thanked her for being his date and asked her, "Are you looking forward to dancing this evening? Do you promise me the first dance?" Now he was smiling into her eyes as he asked if she would like for him to show her around the place, but Lily came forward just then and reached out her hand to William.

He stopped and said, "Why, yes, Lily I can't forget about you. How pretty you look tonight, too. I do hope you enjoy the party." Then he turned back to Elizabeth and asked again if she would like for him to show her around. Elizabeth asked her parents' permission.

Harrison said, "You go ahead, enjoy yourself, honey. We will see you both later. And remember, your mother and I plan to do some dancing ourselves; we will see you out there." He looked at Ellen, "What would you say to a cup of punch first, dear?"

Ellen gave her husband a bright smile and said, "Yes, please."

William took Elizabeth's hand. He said, "Come with me, then. Would you like to see the horse we are setting our hopes on to win the derby this year?"

"I would love to see your race horse," she told him. "I think they are so beautiful." They walked through a side door of the barn and across to the stables. As soon as they entered the stables, this horse came up to stick his head out over the door, watching them as they walked his way. "Oh, William," Elizabeth cried excitedly, "He's beautiful. What's his name?"

William rubbed the horse's face and said, "Well, because of his coloring, he's what's known as a strawberry roan, and then with this white blaze down his face, his name is Strawberry Blaze."

"Well, it suits him, I should say." She reached out her hand, to touch the white blaze and rubbed his neck. "You're a beauty, and you know it too, don't you, boy?" she crooned. They laughed as the horse whinnied and shook its head.

William was watching her simple reaction to Blaze and he reached for both her hands. "You know, I never thought to be jealous of a horse before, but right this minute I am." He brought her hands to his lips and softly kissed each of them. He then moved them up to his neck as he bent his head to take her lips for a quick kiss. He then hugged her to him and whispered her name. They were standing there in an embrace, but Elizabeth was very disappointed. As much as she liked William, the kiss was nothing like what she felt when Noah Bennett had kissed her. What did this mean? Maybe if they tried again? William's head was descending again, and this time she really put her heart and mind into the kiss. William pulled her closer to him and deepened the kiss. His tongue shot into her mouth and she was startled by it. Sputtering, she backed away a little and realized this just wasn't going to work. Then William was saying, "Elizabeth, honey, you should know I want you this very minute. I thought maybe if I brought you out here and showed you how much I feel for you, you would respond the same." Elizabeth looked up at him incredulously. He knew from the look on her face, though, what he said had been a mistake, so he said, "Just listen to me, please. I realize now that you're more special to me than hidden kisses and lovemaking in a stall. I want an open and honest relationship between us."

"I would really hate to slap your face, William, at your family's party," Elizabeth told him with so much emotion it was hard for her to speak.

"Are you telling me you would actually slap me?" he asked and seemed to be offended that she would even think to do such a thing.

"Yes, I would!" Elizabeth answered. "And if you still don't think I should be upset, we have nothing more to say to each other, William."

"No! Please, Elizabeth. I thought you wanted me to kiss you. I thought we had that in common. But I'm sure that if Joel knew that I was making a pass at you, he would pound me into the ground, and rightly so. Putting that aside, please believe me when I say I'm sorry, really sorry. Can you ever forgive me, Elizabeth? Can we just go back to being friends for the evening?"

"Well, as long as we understand each other, William, then yes."

"I will be the perfect gentlemen for the rest of the evening, I promise," he said. "I want you to have a good time, okay?"

"Now, we really should get back to the party before we're missed," Elizabeth told him.

"I know," he said. "But are you still upset with me, Elizabeth?"

"No, not upset but I am disappointed in your behavior. I will take you at your word though, William, as I do want to get back to the party now."

William gave Elizabeth his arm as they made their way back inside. Luckily no one had seemed to miss them. He asked if she would like to meet some of the other people there.

"I would love to," Elizabeth replied. So that's what they did. After meeting several people and getting acquainted a bit, they came to a group of young ladies. There were four of them standing in a little circle. They were all so pretty and their dresses put hers to shame. Elizabeth noticed she had never seen dresses this pretty before, not even at church. William then introduced her to them; they glanced in her direction but barely acknowledged her. Then all four of them focused their attention back to him to ask, "Where have you been keeping yourself, William?"

"I've been introducing Elizabeth around," he said, but still none of the ladies paid her any attention. One young lady in particular was insistent on holding William's attention. As he was turning to make their excuses, she said, "Well, I have missed you. Why haven't you been to see me?"

William turned back, and with a bland look he finally said, "I have been away and just returned a few days ago, Eleanor. Now, if you ladies will excuse us." He nodded his head to them all and took Elizabeth's hand to turn away. They could hear one of the girls say, "Well I never," and another said, "I wonder who she is, some hick from around here." "Yes, I suppose," another one said.

William turned to Elizabeth to say, "I'm sorry you had to hear that. Best to just ignore them, don't you think?"

"Yes, I agree," Elizabeth answered. "But now I understand why you would feel that you could, as you said, have your way with me, or any girl. I would like to go over to where my parents are now," she told him smartly.

"But wait, Elizabeth, you're nothing like those girls, and that's what I like most about you," he told her. "You have to know that. They can't hold a candle to your beautiful face, but most of all you do not pretend to be something you're not. You don't get caught up in how you look and don't need to be complimented every five minutes to be content."

They walked in the direction of where she had seen her parents. They were both surprised to see each of their parents standing there talking together. William's mother, Sara, called. "Hello, you two. We are having such fun watching the children play and dance."

William said with a chuckle, "Well I hope you will enjoy this dance as well." He turned to Elizabeth to ask her to dance, but she was deep in conversation with her mother.

"Uh-hum." William cleared his throat and got Elizabeth's attention. "Shall we give the dance floor a whirl?"

"Actually, I'm not much for dancing right now," she said laughingly. "Maybe the next dance, if you're still in the mood."

"Maybe after a while," William said. "Yes, of course, whenever you'd like."

Sara spoke up to say, "Elizabeth, dear, your mother has been telling me about her herbs and how she uses them for healing, among other uses."

"I'm surprised," Harrison spoke. "Normally Ellen doesn't say much about her herbs because there are always going to be people who do not believe in the use of them for healing."

"Well," Sara replied, "I'm pleased to hear about the herbs and very interested in hearing more. Maybe you and I could meet up one afternoon, Ellen, and you could tell me more. How does that sound?"

"I would like that," Ellen told her.

Joel walked up then to say, "So this is where all of you have gotten to. I'm pleased you've finally become acquainted, since William and I have been friends for such a long time."

Harrison turned to say, "Yes, son, and Bob here tells me they are running short on tobacco plants, so I told him since we have plenty left, maybe he would like to come by our place to get the plants." Harrison added, "I will pull them for you."

"Dad is particular about his tobacco plants, I should warn you," Joel told Bob with a chuckle. "He grows them, you know, and pulls them carefully. He isn't stingy with them; he just likes to pull them himself since they can easily be bruised."

"That's good to know," Bob responded. "Harrison, maybe you can show me some time how you raise your plants."

Harrison said with a chuckle, "I'll be happy to any time, Bob. It will save you money too. Bring Sara when you come over. I will explain how I prepare the tobacco beds, and Ellen can visit with Sara about the herbs." They all liked the idea and had a good chuckle then.

The music was starting anew. William looked over and asked, "Is this our dance, Elizabeth?"

"Yes, William," she said, but not nearly as enthusiastic now. When he reached for her hand, she didn't hesitate, but as they were nearing the dance floor, he asked, "You don't feel the same toward me as before we shared that kiss in the stables, do you? Why was I stupid enough to try something like that with you? But you have to believe how sorry I am, Elizabeth. I have watched you grow from a young girl into a beautiful young woman, and I have been looking forward to this night, for a very long time. I know I spoiled it by letting my emotions get the best of me. Can you understand, dear, I would never do anything to hurt you?"

"I appreciate your being honorable enough to admit it, William; that says a lot about your character," Elizabeth told him. "I do believe that you regret it also. So let's just put it behind us and enjoy the dance." Elizabeth wanted to tell William not to be so intimate with her anymore like calling her *dear*, but she didn't seem to know how to say it. Now they were dancing and she wanted to enjoy it, so that's what they did. It was great fun, Elizabeth realized, and she's really enjoying herself. When the dance ended, William suggested they get something to eat. As they turned to walk over to the food table, she happened to notice no other than Noah Bennett standing not far away. She felt her face redden and a knot suddenly arrived in her stomach. He was dressed all in black, but he wasn't wearing the Hessian boots tonight. He wasn't wearing a hat either, and she could tell his hair is a dark blond. Her look of surprise did not go unnoticed by William. He asked, "Is something wrong, dear?" There he goes again, she thought, but she said, "No, I just thought I saw someone I met recently." She had been looking at William as she spoke but when she looked back to where Noah had been, he wasn't there. She scanned the building but Noah was nowhere that she could see.

William took a long look at her and asked, "Do you still want to get something to eat then?"

She answered, "Sure, we were heading in that direction anyway right?" On their way to get the food, they ran into her best friend Connie Boggs. She was with her brother Tom who was followed by Joel, so they stopped to talk with them.

Elizabeth greeted her friend warmly. "Oh, Connie, it's so good to see you. I hoped you would be here. We don't get a chance to see each other nearly enough, you know."

"We almost weren't able to be here tonight," Tom said, grinning. Connie got dad all worked up about quitting early in the tobacco field. She wouldn't let dad have a minute of peace, till he agreed. And let me tell you I was holding my breath he didn't get furious and make us stay till dark."

"Tom, you do go on," Connie said teasingly. "And you know very well dad wasn't mad."

"Well," Tom spoke back, "he did let us go early so we could get dressed in time for your party, William. We really do appreciate the invite for sure, old friend."

The music was starting up again and William asked, "Would you like to dance again, Elizabeth?"

Tom said, "Not fair, old friend. I just arrived, so I should get a chance to dance with the prettiest girl here." Tom stepped between her and William and reached out his hand to ask, "Will you dance with me, Elizabeth?" She looked surprised, and he said, "Didn't you realize I meant you. You're by far the prettiest girl here, so will you dance with me?" Elizabeth smiled and said, "How could I refuse such a request?" She looked at William and told him, "I'll see you later on."

Left standing there, William turned to ask Connie, "Would you like to dance with me, Miss Boggs?"

She said, "Sure. I may as well step on your toes, as anyone else."

He laughed at that and said, "Connie, you have always had such a good sense of humor. I like it."

"Well, I am glad you think so. Hey, William, has anyone ever called you by a nickname? Everyone always calls you by your given name and I was just curious."

"Yes, I have always been known as William," he said. "What about you? Is Connie short for something?"

"Constance," she told him. "But wouldn't you know it. Tom has always called me Connie, so it just stuck like glue."

"I think Constance is a very pretty name," William told her, "to match a very pretty girl."

"Well, thank you, kind sir," Connie said with a tiny curtsy and tongue sticking out. They both laughed at that, and when the dance was over they, thanked each other and headed back to look for their friends.

Elizabeth had known Tom most of her life also. He wasn't exactly handsome, but his manner and personality made up the difference. Looking for what is on the inside was something her parents had taught her how to do at a young age. It wasn't just a Christian issue, it was just the right thing to do, her Dad always said.

Elizabeth had enjoyed the dance they shared, and she told him so. "You made it fun, you know."

"Yep, that's me," Tom said, "a laugh a minute. I'm not sure that I want to be remembered by you in that way though."

"Oh, Tom, I didn't mean for it to sound that way. You should know you're one of Joel's best friends and I love you like a brother," she said as she touched his sleeve. He put his hand to his heart and looked stricken. "Oh no, not again." Then he grinned and told her, "I do understand, but you should know, Elizabeth, I've had a crush on you since we were children."

"Tom, are you pulling my braids again? Teasing me again as you used to tease me in school," she laughed and said, "I never know if you are teasing me any more than when Joel is."

"You wouldn't, dear girl, that's one of the reasons I care for you. Plus I have always known you were mooning over William."

"Yes, well, I did have a crush on him, but I may have been a little blind in my feelings for him. For now, I'm not ready to be attached to anyone," she said.

"That's a good idea," Tom said. "Don't rush into anything, honey." They joined the others now, and Tom smiled at Joel. "I brought her back safe and sound." And he nodded to William also.

Joel announced, "Now it's my dance. Come on, sis, let's show everyone how it's done."

But Elizabeth asked with a teasing smile, "What about all those girls who've been giving you the eye, brother dear?" Joel took her by both hands and pulled her toward him.

"Come on, dance with me, sis." Then he whispered only for her to hear, "I've something to ask you."

Elizabeth said, "Sure, now you have my attention, brother." Once they were out on the floor with the others ready to dance, she asked, "Okay now, what is it you wish to know?"

Joel gave her a serious look and asked, "I would like to know who that man was in here earlier. He never took his eyes off you. Do you know him?"

"Yes, I have met him. He was at the creek letting his horse take a drink when I took the cows to pasture yesterday morning and...again today. He said he would be back, then he told me his name was Noah Bennett. That is all I know about him," she told Joel.

"How do you feel about him?" he asked. "I noticed you seem somewhat cool toward William."

She said, "I don't know how I'm supposed to feel. William is not who I thought he was, and I know nothing about Noah," Elizabeth said.

"Well, if this Noah Bennett is there at the creek in the morning, then I'll be there to meet him too," Joel told her, but he didn't like the look on his sister's face. It looked to him like concern, so he asked, "Are you concerned for him?"

Elizabeth gave him an honest answer, "I don't know Joel, he really upset me this morning. He's so arrogant. He seems to have a huge ego as well, but there's also just something about him that gets to me. I can't explain it." She looked so confused and the scrunched look on her face pulled at his heartstrings.

The two of them had always been close, not just as siblings but as real friends, so he pulled her close and said, "It'll be okay, honey, you'll see. Together we will figure this out. Now that the music has stopped, lets go back to join the others. I'm sure William is waiting to dance with you again," Joel said with a small smile.

William did ask her to dance again, and of course, she said yes. William kept his promise and kept the conversation light, so they did enjoy themselves again. When the dance ended, he asked, "Elizabeth, would you allow me to speak with your father, so I may ask for permission to court you?"

"I don't know, William," she answered honestly. "That is something that would have made me happy before tonight. I don't think that is a good idea. It isn't only what happened tonight, but it has to do with other things I'm feeling right now too."

William looked at her, more or less pleading. "Elizabeth, give me a chance to show you that I am not the man you have seen this evening. I promise to be the man you deserve."

She said, "Well, I wouldn't say no if you still wish to court me."

William gave her a wide smile and said, "At least, you're not saying flat-out no,"

Smiling, she said, "Yes, I would like to meet the man I wanted to get to know."

William said, "Okay, thank you, Elizabeth. I hope that what happened tonight can be put in the past. I still can't believe I lost my head like that, but do you realize just how beautiful you are tonight? I'm not using that as an excuse, but when I saw you, all I could think of was to get you to myself. Do you believe me?"

Elizabeth told him, "I do not believe you would tell me a lie, William, but I don't understand why you thought you could treat me that way. I will wait to see if you can behave as a gentleman should." At that, she left William and went to look for her parents.

Harrison and Ellen were talking with their neighbors, the Boggs siblings, and Joel when Elizabeth walked up. Her father greeted her with a smile as he said, "I believe it's time we leave now."

Elizabeth answered, "Okay, just let me say good night to Connie first."

Her father nodded yes, so she walked over to say good night to her friends.

Connie smiled and hugged her. She said, "Yeah, Tom and I are leaving also. We'll have an early morning tomorrow." Together they all walked over to say good-bye to their hosts.

They all were leaving when Joel noticed David was no longer with them. He had to pull him away from a group of girls who didn't want him to leave.

Lily was happy to be leaving. "I didn't enjoy myself anyway," she said, but that was nothing new. They made it out to the buggy in the darkness and the evening had cooled off to give them all a shudder and a chill. Joel and David helped the women get seated. They covered up with the quilts they had brought along for just this purpose. David and Joel collected their horses. They were ready to leave. As they started down the road home, Elizabeth could see a horse and rider in the shadows, and she just knew it had to be Noah Bennett. She could feel his presence in the prickling of her skin on top of the goose bumps the chilly night had given her. *Why is he following us?* she wondered. But they were moving closer to home now, so if it really was him, she didn't think he would dare follow them there. Elizabeth pulled the quilt tighter around her and Lily and hoped no one else noticed him. She just wanted to get home, get warm, and put this messed-up day behind her.

Chapter  3

The next morning, the sun was playing hide and seek with some good-sized clouds. Elizabeth was on pins and needles and charged with energy wondering if Noah would come by this morning, and the meeting she was sure would take place between her brother Joel and Noah Bennett. That man was determined to meet her father and ask to court her. William let her know last evening he wanted to talk to her father as well. She had a hiccup laugh. If she wasn't so anxious about all her own feelings, her situation would be comical. She was lost in thought and didn't notice that Joel was grinning at her from across the breakfast table. When she did look at him, she ducked her head because she is sure he knows her thoughts, she just knew it! But she also knew that he was and always would be on her side, just as she would always be there for him. She had pushed her food around on her plate for long enough. Now it was time to get on with her morning chores. She was curious what Joel was going to say because she assumed David was unaware of her problem.

Elizabeth went about doing her morning chores and tried not to think about what if. She had taken the milk to the spring house, deposited it, and was on her way back to the house when she noticed Joel and David leaving with the cows. Joel said, "He had decided they would ride their horses today to herd the cows to pasture."

David said, grinning, "That's fine with me. Why walk if one can ride?"

Elizabeth watched them ride off and just shook her head. Joel told her he would help with her situation, but she hadn't thought of this. They walked their horses through the gate then headed out with the cows. When they came in sight of the creek, sure enough, there was the same man Joel had seen watching Elizabeth at the party last evening. As he and David came closer, they got a better look at him. He was standing beside a big, handsome black horse. As Joel and David drew closer, Joel noticed that the man stood a little straighter and stiffened up. Joel tipped his hat to the man as they stopped before him, since they were not looking for any kind of confrontation.

Joel spoke to say, "Hello, would you by chance be Noah Bennett?"

He answered, "Yes, that's me. And who would you be, sir?"

So he told him, "My name is Joel Steele. This is my brother, David, and Elizabeth is our sister. I noticed you watching her closely last evening at the dance, and since we don't know you, we became concerned. I asked her if she knew you, that's when she told me the two of you had met here at the creek, first by accident then on purpose. So we would like to know, sir, what are your intentions toward our sister?"

"Well now, I understand your concern, and I think Elizabeth is very lucky to have brothers such as the two of you. My intent is to talk with your father," he answered as he climbed up in the saddle. He tipped his hat, said "Gentlemen," and sitting in the saddle with ease, rode back across the creek.

David had taken the cows on to pasture while Joel was speaking to this stranger. Now he rode back to where Joel was still sitting watching this man ride off. "What was that all about, Joel?"

"I'm not totally sure, David, but I believe that man wishes to court Elizabeth. They met when she brought the cows to pasture three days ago, and I believe he feels something for her. He's been back every day since, and now he wants to talk to dad about her. So now...we wait to see what happens. Let's get back to finish chores, okay?"

When they returned, Elizabeth was waiting for them. Joel groaned. He didn't know what to say to her. But he could tell she wouldn't be put off, so he turned to David to say, "I'll be with you shortly." He dismounted, leading his horse as he walked to her.

Right away, Elizabeth asked, "Was Noah there?"

Joel answered, "Yes, and by the way, he wasn't happy to be talking to me instead of you, Elizabeth. I can see why you would think him arrogant."

She asked, "Did he get angry with you then?"

Joel told her, "No, but when I ask what he wanted, he said that he was only interested in talking to dad."

Elizabeth just said, "Oh, I see." Before she turned to go inside, she said with a small smile, "Thanks, Joel. I owe you one."

But since it was Sunday, the morning chores were done and breakfast is over. Everyone was dressed for church in their Sunday best. The three men in dark suits, white shirt, string tie—of course they look handsome, the women thought. The women are all wearing one of their best dresses: Ellen was wearing another pretty green dress with a white collar and long sleeves with white cuffs this time, and green is her best color, which highlights her hazel eyes and goes well with her red hair as well. Elizabeth is wearing another blue dress; it was simple in style but looked great on her. Although she spent little time on her appearance,

Elizabeth always looked great, but then she has a natural beauty that she inherited from their mother that other women envied. Now Lily, she could be pretty, too, if she would only smile more. It was time to leave now. Joel and David would be riding their horses of course. Harrison was taking the women in the buggy.

They arrived at the church, which is called Locust Grove Community Church. In the graveyard behind the church was where the people in the surrounding county buried their loved ones. Every year in the month of May on Memorial Day, all the families observed the day by bringing a picnic basket of food and spending the day clearing away weeds and leaves and then putting flowers on the graves, so it was referred to as Decoration Day. Everyone, as if by mutual agreement, would stop to eat. It was also a time to visit with neighbors and other people they may know. This is the way it had been since Elizabeth could remember. Elizabeth halfway expected to see Noah here today, but since he didn't show up, maybe he would forget about her. She should be pleased, but she felt sort of let down instead. Their church was like most any country church, she supposed, but it had always been a special place, not only for the service but to be with her friend Connie and enjoy visiting afterwards. Today, the Boggs family wouldn't be here, so she decided to just focus and enjoy the service.

Harrison thought the service was excellent! He told the minster so as he was walking out after the services.

"I enjoyed your sermon very much this morning, Pastor Seymour. I do believe the book of Job is an important one to take note of," Harrison told him.

This pleased the man greatly, and he said, "That's kind praise indeed, Harrison. I like to hear when my sermons are appreciated."

Harrison is saying, "You're a good man, and we would all do well to remember Job's patience, endurance, and never-wavering faith in God. And Pastor, I enjoyed when you were also saying that God is ready to lead us in the path of righteousness, but it is up to us to make the decision to follow him. I always enjoy hearing you preach, but today I believe you gave a most powerful sermon and I am glad to show my support of you, sir." Harrison would have continued, but he said, "For now, sir, I can see my ladies are ready to leave, so I best say good day and tend to them. You understand, I'm sure."

Pastor Seymour said, "Yes, of course," with a wide smile. I'll see you good people at the next services."

Chapter  4

When the family returned home from church, as usual, on Sundays after everyone has changed back into clean everyday clothes, Elizabeth would help her mother finish the noon meal, which wouldn't take long at all since most of the food had been prepared the day before they left for the party and was stored in the spring house. They had made such as fried chicken, potato salad, and deviled eggs. After they had eaten and the dishes were washed, they were all sitting on the front porch relaxing. Elizabeth has always loved times like this with her family. After a while though, Joel and David became restless and decided to go to the paddock and single out the horses that need to be broke to ride. Elizabeth had the bright idea to ask if they would mind if she tagged along. Both her brothers said it was alright with them, so while they were looking over the horses, Elizabeth was standing on the corral fence with her arms resting on the top rail watching her brothers. She thought how exciting it must be for them to be riding all these fine-looking horses. She was also amazed, too, at how unafraid they were and they really seemed to enjoy the challenge. How exciting it would be if she could ride one of the horses herself, she was thinking. Their father would only allow her to ride the work horses which were all Belgians. They are large, mild natured most often—no danger but not much fun either. When she had the chance, she would ask Joel if he would let her ride his horse, a horse Joel raised from a colt. Actually, Joel had helped bring him into the world and he believed "the General," as he named him, to be a very smart horse. He had trained him early and the horse was a quick study. The General's a big red horse with four white socks, and for Joel he's like an old friend.

When Elizabeth asked if he would let her ride him, Joel asked, "Are you serious, sis? You should know there's a world of difference in riding the General and the horses you have been on in the past."

"Exactly," Elizabeth answered. "That's the reason I'm asking you to ride him, Joel. I want to know what it's like to ride a fine horse like the General."

He gave her a guarded look, but after a few seconds, which seemed forever to Elizabeth, he told her, "Okay then, come with me." So he lead the way to the stables. Joel saddled his horse, turned to her to say, "I want you to do exactly what I tell you, is that understood?"

Elizabeth quickly said, "I understand, Joel." He then told her to follow him as he led the way back to the corral. He helped her up on the General, but she was sitting in the saddle with her dress all bunched up around her.

Joel sighed, "This isn't going to work, you know." He could see how disappointed she was, so he said, "If you really want to try, sis, we'll see how it goes. It's too bad you can't wear pants though."

She said, "Wait just a minute, Joel, I'll be right back." He helped her down and wondered why she is hurrying back in the house. She had an idea she knew the boys weren't going to like, but she was determined now so she went to David's room and found a pair of his old pants that were too small for him now. She also took one of his shirts then hurried back to her room. She tried to put the pants on over her petticoat; of course it wouldn't work. She took off the pants, then took off the petticoat, put the shirt on, then pulled the pants back on again, and they were a perfect fit. She then put on her work shoes, pulled her dress back on over it all, and hurried back to the stables. She ran to the tack room, pulled off the dress, since she thought no one would see her now, and she hung it on a peg then rushed outside where Joel was waiting with his horse.

David whistled when she came out. "Wow, is that really you, sis?" he teased.

But Joel reminded her, "Seriously sis, you better not let dad see you dressed that way," as he was trying not to laugh.

"I know," Elizabeth answered. "I have my dress in the tack room. I'm ready to ride the General now."

It was not hard to tell she's excited. Joel helped her up in the saddle again. This time, she felt comfortable. Now it felt wonderful, too, so Joel said, "Okay now, pay attention." He gave her the reins and said, "See what you can do, but don't forget what I already told you, and most importantly, don't make any sudden moves, okay? Just walk him around some till you feel secure with him, then you can go from there."

The boys watched, and before long, she had the horse trotting, then running. Joel and David both called after her. "You're doing great sis, you've a good seat, and you're a natural."

A few minutes later, Joel heard his father ask David, "Who's that riding the General?"

David was stunned and didn't know what to say. Neither one of them had heard their father walk up; they were both so intent on watching Elizabeth. David was about to try to come up with something when Harrison realized on his own it was his daughter. Just then she called out to say, "This is great, Joel, I love it."

Then she heard her father say, "Elizabeth! You get off that horse this second, girl." She jerked around but Joel called to her, "Easy, sis. Slow him down then just walk him over here to me." She did as he told her, and Joel helped her down.

She looked up at her father. His face was solid red. He said, "You go inside now. Change, and do not let your mother see you dressed in those clothes."

Elizabeth answered, "Yes, sir," almost in tears as she ran to get her dress. She pulled it on then ran for the house. She was determined that she wouldn't cry. She had best to go in the front way, as she was sure her mother would most likely be in the kitchen at this time. She managed to make it to her room to change without being seen. She put the clothes back in David's room then made her way to the kitchen to help her mother with supper.

Chapter  5

Ellen had put a whole chicken on to cook after their noon meal. She had chased it down and then killed it by wringing its neck. Elizabeth had often thought she would never understand how a woman of such a gentle nature as her mother could just wring a chicken's neck, but her mother had told her she learned when she needed to help in the fields and would be short on time to cook meals. Now it's just a habit she does without thinking about it. After taking the chicken off the bone, she then returns it to the pot. Now Ellen is making dumplings to put in the pot with the chicken. Ellen's dumplings are one of her family's favorites that she prepares. She had also put potatoes on to boil then to be mashed later, and a pot of green beans she had canned last summer were just coming up to boil. Elizabeth said, "Everything smells so good, mom. What can I help with?"

Ellen turned to say, "If you wouldn't mind going to the garden to pull green onions and lettuce, that would go great together for a wilted salad. That will round things out pretty well, don't you think?"

Elizabeth answered, "Sounds good, mom." So she took a basket from the pantry that they used for the garden and walked outside. She went down on her knees, made quick work of the onions, laid them aside, and began pulling the lettuce when suddenly she noticed a shadow, and she just assumed it to be one of her brothers'. She said teasingly, " I see you're just in time to help now that I'm almost finished."

"The loss is mine then, for I really did come to help you."When she heard the deep timber of the voice that she remembered so well, she was startled and was coming to her feet, but he laid his hand gently on her shoulder and said, "I promise, Elizabeth, to only help you finish up here." So she stayed where she was and he came down on his knees beside her. "Now, what are we doing here?" he asked with a killer smile.

She found herself focusing on that smile and not what he was saying, but finally she said, "I'm getting lettuce."

"Okay then, just tell me when we have enough." He went to work in helping her pull the lettuce.

Shortly, she said, "I believe we have enough now."

Noah stood then reached for her hand to help her stand. He picked up the basket, handed it over to her, then reached down for the onions. After placing them in the basket, too, he said softly, "I'll carry these, honey." Then walking side by side, they headed for the backdoor and went inside.

Joel had been watching this all play out and kept close but out of sight in case he was needed. He didn't want to intrude because he could tell there was something special going on between Noah Bennett and Elizabeth, so he followed behind them inside. When they all came into the kitchen, Harrison was sitting at the table reading his Bible, which was his habit usually while Ellen was preparing their meal. He set the Bible aside, lay his hands on the table, and waited for this man to be introduced to him.

When Elizabeth didn't seem to know what to say, Joel stepped forward and said, "Dad, this is Noah Bennett. I met him down at the creek this morning when David and I were taking the cows to pasture. I do believe he met Elizabeth the same way just the other day."

Harrison said, "Is that so, sir?"

Noah stepped forward to shake hands with Harrison who noticed the hard firm grip the man had. Noah said, "Yes, sir. I met your daughter Elizabeth, just as your son said, and she made quite an impression on me, sir. I can't seem to get past the notion that I want to get to know her better, so I'm asking your permission to court her."

Elizabeth let out a breath she didn't realize she'd been holding as Harrison replied, "Well, that's all very interesting, but I believe Elizabeth should have something to say about it." He turned to Elizabeth. "What do you say, daughter?"

Elizabeth turned to look at Noah, and his eyes seemed to be pleading with her to say yes. She felt her heart skip a beat and knew she couldn't say no. So she looked back to her father. "Yes, I agree, Dad. Everything Noah here and Joel has said is true." She felt relief come welling up from inside her and she knew this was the right decision. Noah's face split with a heart-stopping smile that showed off his beautiful white teeth. She could feel in her heart a lightness and joy of the days to come.

Noah whispered, "You won't regret it, Elizabeth, I promise." She beamed back at him, and he knew his heart belonged to her now; he just hoped she wanted it. The look between the two wasn't lost on Harrison or Joel.

Harrison asked, "Mr. Bennett, why don't you stay to share our meal with us?" He looked to Ellen and said, "If that's okay with you, dear?" Ellen, who had been watching all this happen from the kitchen sink, turned to say, "By all means. We always have plenty and I'm sure we would all like to know more about you ourselves."

Noah noticed that when Ellen smiled, she looked more like Elizabeth's older sister than her mother—the same beautiful smile and perfect white teeth as her daughter. He looked at Elizabeth, who gave him a nod of her head, so he said, "I would appreciate it, sir, *but*," he said with a wide smile, "only if you would call me Noah."

Harrison returned his smile. "I can do that, Noah. And by the way, I answer to Harrison. Now here, pull up a chair. Let's get out of the women's way while we wait for our supper."

Noah sat down at the table where he could watch Elizabeth as she helped her mother with the meal. He liked watching her. She has an unconscious grace about her that only added to her appeal for him. She wasn't concerned about her appearance either, which he saw there was no need to be. Her features were perfect. Just now she's wearing what he assumed was an everyday dress, and she still looks lovely.

Noah was so lost in his thoughts that he almost missed what Harrison had said to him. He thought he heard him ask, "Where do you live, Noah?"

Noah focused on Harrison and said, "My brother James and I have built a horse farm, east of here near Corbin. We're not far from here, actually. James is married to his lovely wife, Ann, and they have two young sons; Jimmy, six, and Bobby who is four now. We lost our parents when we were still young. We lost our father while we were still living in Ireland, where our parents lived and their family before them lived for generations."

Noah took a deep breath and let it out slowly then continued by saying, "Our father was killed working a horse, and after that our mother moved us all to America. She met a man on the trip over and remarried. James, who is older than me, and didn't get on with our stepfather. He never did trust him and just didn't care for the man and told him so. James was told to leave. When I stood up for James, I was told to leave with him. It was our stepfather's home; we had no choice in the matter. We kissed our mother good-bye and left. We went out together to find work.

The only thing we could find at the time was breaking horses to ride. We found out we were good at it and after a while we started riding in the races."

Noah tried to guess what Harrison was thinking about his life's tale when Harrison said, "Well, Noah, you have certainly had adventures and I would appreciate hearing more of your story later, but for now, looks like the women have our meal ready to set on the table."

David had come in at some time while Noah had been speaking to sit at the table, and Joel had been quietly listening while Noah told of some of his life to know. Both brothers came to their feet now to help with setting the food on the table, then Joel went to seat their mother while David was ready to seat their sister, but Noah was there ahead of him to seat Elizabeth beside him. They were ready to sit down again, when Lily came rushing in to ask, "What about me, sir, are you going to seat me too?" Before Noah could answer, Harrison said, "Lily, please sit down there beside David so I may ask the blessing." Lily sat quietly, but she was not at all pleased.

Harrison started by saying, "Lord, we pray you will bless this food set before us, prepared by loving hands, and may it nourish our body. We ask, Lord, that you would bless each of us present here. We have with us a new acquaintance to share our meal. We ask, Lord, that you bless him as well. We are thankful for this day, Lord, and all that you have given us. Lord, we will give you praise in all things. In Jesus' name, amen.

Now the food was being passed around, so Ellen said, "Mr. Bennett, did I hear you say you were born in Ireland?"

Noah answered, "Yes, that is correct, ma'am. I was nine and James was twelve when we lost our father and moved to America with our mother. We lost her also while we were still in our teens. Let me say, Mrs. Steele, this meal is really good. I was always of the opinion that no one could cook food as good as my mother, but you sure do." Noah took another mouthful and smiled. "These chicken and dumplings are the best I have ever eaten."

They all noticed that when Noah spoke about his mother, his Irish brogue was clearly there. Elizabeth was watching him as he was speaking and thought again, *He's so handsome.* Noah was dressed casually in a white shirt open at the neck and with the sleeves rolled up. He looked very comfortable and so at ease. He looked her way just then and caught her watching him. He winked at her which caused her to blush prettily.

Noah was about to tell her how he liked to see her blush when he heard Joel ask, "Noah, how large is the horse farm you and your brother have?"

Noah was feeling more relaxed now with this family, so he answered Joel by saying, "We just sold twenty head, so that leaves about a hundred."

The meal was finished, so Noah stood up. "This meal was one for the record books, Mrs. Steele. I really don't like to eat and run, but I must be going."

He turned to Joel and said, "Maybe we can talk more about horses at another time, but for now I really do need to get back to the farm. My brother will think I have run off."

With that, Noah laughed and thanked them all again for such a lovely meal. He turned to Elizabeth and asked, "Would you walk out with me to my horse?" Noah reached for Elizabeth's hand as they walked out the backdoor together. When they reached his horse standing where he had left him beside the garden gate, Noah turned to her, and with a wide grin, he said, "You have no idea, honey, what a relief it was for me, when you agreed to let me come see you. It has become all important to me, you know, that we should build a life together, and I was pleasantly surprised to catch you watching me while we were eating. So, did I pass the test?"

Elizabeth answered, "I don't know what you mean, sir," blushing prettily again.

Noah took her hand to say, "It's okay, honey. I realize now you don't understand. Please forget I asked the question. Would you mind if I kiss you good night?" Elizabeth looked up into Noah's deep-green eyes with such a look of wonder that he knew it was okay, so Noah put his arms around her, held her close tucked into his chest for a moment, then he lifted her face and touched his lips to hers but only kissed her lightly. This wasn't the way he wished to kiss her, but there will be time now for learning more about each other. Noah had known from the first time he looked into her beautiful eyes, then kissed her, that she is the woman for him.

He touched his hand to her cheek then said, "Good night. I will see you tomorrow, darlin.'" He climbed in the saddle, gave her one last smile, then he was riding back down the lane. Elizabeth stood watching him till he was out of sight, then with a deep sigh, she turned to go back inside and touched her fingers to her lips with a slow smile. How could she have ever thought for even a second that she didn't want Noah to court her. How blind she had been not to realize what a good man he was. *In fact, I have never met anyone to compare with him*, she thought—his green eyes and smile that just glowed; also, once he took off his hat, she could see he has hair coloring very similar to David's, and wavy too. Elizabeth had this warm feeling inside thinking about Noah, but with another sigh she noticed it was a little cool outside and she really should be getting back in the house.

* * * * *

Noah was glad to be heading home finally. He had just been hanging around till he could speak to Mr. Steele about Elizabeth. When he rode up to the garden gate that afternoon, he could hardly believe his good luck in finding Elizabeth in the garden. He had wasted no time in going to her only to find she thought him to be someone else. Noah smiled again thinking how young and innocent she looked sitting there looking up at him. She had been expecting one of her brothers to come out and help her. At first, she was uncertain about seeing him, but not unhappy, so that gave him hope. The sweet kiss they had shared before he rode away spoke volumes. Oh, how he missed her already, but to know he'd sleep in his own bed tonight was comforting, not to mention seeing his brother James.

It had been over two days now since he rode out, and James had to be wondering what had happened to him. Most of all, though, he was looking forward to his bed. Sleeping on the ground wasn't as easy for him now as it once was. When he and James had first set out on their own, they slept under the stars all the time because they had no choice, but that was a long time ago. Tonight, he would rest in his own bed and think about Elizabeth and the life they would share together.

❉ ❉ ❉ ❉ ❉

When Elizabeth walked in the kitchen, Joel and David were helping with clearing the table. Joel turned to Ellen, reached for the dishes she was holding, and said, "Mom, now that Elizabeth is back, you go out on the porch with Dad and relax. We have this covered, right, sis?"

"Yes, Mom, you go with Dad." The three of them watched, smiling as their parents walked out of the room holding hands.

"You know," Joel said, "the way I see it, guys, we're blessed to have parents that still love each other the way they do."

Lily spoke to say, "Well, I think it sick how they act." She complained with her face puckered as if she had bitten into a green persimmon.

"You would," Joel declared. "You're too selfish, Lily, to think of anyone but yourself. You should be ashamed, saying such things about your parents."

Lily ran out of the room calling over her shoulder, "Oh, Joel, you're so mean."

David stood there grinning as Lily was leaving the kitchen. He gave a mock sigh and said, "She always picks a fight with one of us. It must have been your turn. Oh well, she wasn't going to help us anyway, right?" Joel and Elizabeth had a good laugh, because it was sad but true. The three of them finished cleaning the kitchen then walked out on the porch to join their parents. They found them sitting close—Harrison with his arm along the back of the swing; Ellen was sitting close to him. It was so revealing of how they still feel about each other. They all visited for a while, then Elizabeth quietly stood and said good night. With that, she went up to her room. She really wasn't tired but just wanted to be alone with her thoughts. When she reached her, room she went about getting ready for bed. She changed into her nightgown, washed her face good, and then rubbed on some of the cream that her mother makes. With delft fingers, she combed out her hair then put it in a single long braid. Certain she wouldn't be able to sleep, she turned out the lamp and lay down. The night sky out her window glowed with a million twinkling lights.

It seemed as if Elizabeth had just closed her eyes when she opened them again to the sun shining brightly and the sounds of bustling downstairs. Thinking how rested and happy she feels, she went to the window and pulled up the pane. A soft gentle breeze billowed out the curtains. Elizabeth had such an overwhelming sense of joy this morning. She usually always had been of a pleasant nature, but this feeling was new to her. After washing her face, she took a quick sponge bath. She then rubbed cream on her face and more on her arms. She dressed in a simple light-blue everyday dress then pulled her hair back and tied it with a red ribbon. She made her way downstairs but as she walked into the kitchen, she was pleasantly surprised to see Noah sitting at the table, talking with her father and brothers.

Noah felt her presence as she entered the room. He turned to see her fresh and beautiful this morning, but no surprise there, he knew she would be. He was smiling at her, she noticed, and that smile meant so much to her. Harrison and Joel were watching the two of them just looking at each other. They seemed to be totally unaware of anyone else in the room. Ellen turned from the stove to look at the couple, then turned back to hide a smile. After a few seconds more, Harrison cleared his throat. Both Noah and Elizabeth were startled, and they jumped to see Harrison who just grinned then asked Ellen for more coffee. He asked Noah if he would like a cup as well.

Elizabeth said, "Oh, yes. Would you like a cup, Noah?"

"Sure," came the reply. She walked to the stove and reached for the huge coffeepot that Ellen insisted on using. When Noah realized what she was doing, he jumped up from the table and said, "Wait." He walked over to say, "Here, let me get that for you." She brought a cup to the table for him. He refilled the other cups then poured some for himself. He walked back to set the pot on the stove.

When he was sitting at the table again, he asked Harrison, "Do the women always lift that heavy coffeepot?"

"Now Noah, I have tried to get my Ellen to use a smaller pot, but she won't hear of it," Harrison said with a twinkle in his eyes.

Noah said, "Oh," then he asked Ellen, "Do you mind if I call you Ellen, ma'am?" Ellen turned toward him from the stove where she was frying eggs and told him, "No, I don't mind. In fact, I would rather you call me Ellen, but please drop the ma'am."

Noah laughed and said, "Good enough, Ellen. And I don't mean to be presumptuous, but I wanted to ask you a question. If I can find you a different coffeepot, a lighter-weight one that will suit you," then he pointed to the heavy pot, "will you retire that one? It's entirely too heavy for either of you women to lift."

Ellen studied Noah for a second then she smiled and said, "Maybe, but now, mind you, I won't promise anything."

Harrison laughed out aloud at that response. "That settles that." He was grinning at Noah. "That's what she says when she has heard what you say but intends to go on as she pleases anyway. You'll not get her to give up the pot now."

Noah smiled back and said, "We'll see." Breakfast was ready, and Noah was asked to stay and eat with them. "That's very kind of you and I am hungry from the mouth-watering smells."

Noah realized he would get to spend more time with Elizabeth. After eating a few bites, he just sat there amazed. The biscuits and gravy were so light and fluffy, and the eggs were done just the way he always liked them. "I have to tell you again, Miss Ellen, this is great food. Your biscuits and gravy happen to be the best I've ever eaten, and riding around the country, I have had a chance to eat in a lot of different places. There isn't any better food anywhere in the state"—he pointed to his plate with his fork—"than this."

Ellen thanked him with a pleased smile. Joel asked, "What do you do to be riding around the country?" He asked more from curiosity than courtesy.

Noah answered him, "Riding in the races."

"Are you kidding me?" David asked with excitement lighting up his young face.

"No, its true," Noah said. He couldn't help but be pleased by David's enthusiasm. "Because of our age at the time, that was the only work James and I could get. As we grew older, we decided we liked it and continued doing it. I haven't raced as much in the last two years, what with trying to build up the farm and breeding thoroughbred horses as well takes up most of my time now."

"Wow!" David said. "You sure have done so many different things, Noah."

"Yeah, I suppose so. It may seem that way, but it was all out of necessity then became something I enjoyed doing." He turned to Elizabeth to say, "I have done quite a bit of racing, honey. I don't mean to brag but I'm good at riding in the races. When James and I started, we needed the money. But now I'm phasing into the owner-breeder side of the business with my brother, James."

Elizabeth said, "I want to hear more about everything you've done and experienced."

He said, "It will be my pleasure to tell you anything you want to know, Elizabeth." He wasn't at all surprised when she blushed prettily. He smiled to himself again at how blessed he was to have met this girl and how much he was going to enjoy getting to know Elizabeth Steele.

"Well, as interesting as all this talk has been," Harrison said as he stood ready to leave the table, "there are the morning chores to be done, you know." Joel and David both were on their feet, too, ready to follow their father. Noah stood as well. "I'll come with you. Maybe I can help too." He turned to Elizabeth and asked, "Will you be able to get away later, honey?"

Elizabeth turned to her mother. "Would that be okay, Mom?"

Ellen was smiling at her daughter and said, "Yes, dear, I see no reason why not, after the kitchen is cleaned. You are always so good to help." It was agreed then that she would meet him out at the stables later. Elizabeth helped with getting the milk ready then took it to the spring house. She helped clean the kitchen and helped set things up for the noon meal, then walked out to meet up with Noah and found him at the corral watching Joel with one of the horses he and David have been wanting to break to ride.

Chapter  6

When Elizabeth walked up to Noah, he turned to put his arm around her and pulled her close. He looked down with a tender smile and said, "Hi darlin', I've missed you."

Elizabeth looked surprised. "Noah, it hasn't been that long since you left the house."

Noah said with a grin, "Doesn't matter. Anytime you're not with me is too long. Now, let's watch your brother here; he's quite good at this, you know." So they stood watching Joel ride the bucking and twisting horse till he wasn't resisting any longer. Joel walked the horse around the corral several times before turning it out in the pasture. David came out to take his turn. Joel was holding the reins for him as David climbed into the saddle.

"That horse isn't happy," Noah mentioned. "I really don't like the way he's behaving; your brother could get hurt." Sure enough, David was bucked off, but his foot had gotten caught in the stirrup. Noah was over the fence like a shot and had hold of the horse to calm it which gave Joel time to help David get his foot free. Thankfully, Joel was able to help get David's foot loose, and the two of them were able to get to safety. When they turned around, Noah had jumped on the horse and it was magic to watch him handle the gyrating horse until he was too tired to resist any longer. Noah trotted the horse a few laps then stopped and made the horse back up and spin in circles before he brought it to a stop before Joel and David, who were standing there in awe of what they had just seen. He dismounted and took the saddle and bridle off to let the horse out in the pasture.

Joel walked over to Noah who was wiping his hand across his forehead. He said, "Oh man, that was incredible riding. David sure gave me a scare and I don't ever want to go through anything like that again."

Noah told Joel, "Then just learn to watch for signs from the horse. I was worried about that horse just as David was getting in the saddle."

"But seriously," David was saying, "none of these horses want to have a rider on them, do they?"

Noah laughed and said, "That's true enough, but you can develop the feel for what is in their minds, David, and you will, I believe. Joel already has it; he just needs to improve on it a little. You're still young, David. You do a really good job now, but you still have some things to learn. Just don't try to rush it, okay?" David nodded his head and thanked Noah for the advice.

Joel said, "Seriously, Noah, you were able to calm that horse out there so smoothly, and that allowed me time to help David get his foot free. You must have something going on with horses that none of us here know about."

Noah told them, "Yes, I do seem to be able to calm a horse and have, since a young age actually, just by talking to them. Don't ask me what I say to them," he replied with a chuckle, "'cause I can't tell you. It's just something between the horse and me. Some people call it horse whispering."

Joel asked, "Noah, would you mind coming with me? I have someone I would like for you to meet."

Noah laughed and said, "If it's a horse, then I'll be happy to follow."

Joel led the way to a stall in the stable. Even before they reached the door though, they could hear a horse snorting and stomping. When he stuck his head out over the door with a look of the devil in his eyes, he let them know he was certainly not happy.

Noah said laughingly, "Well, I'll say one thing for sure, that horse demands attention." Joel laughed and said, "Yeah he's not happy most of the time. I call him King, 'cause he rules the stables and won't let anyone of us near him. Dad has been wanting to sell him, but you know, for some reason, I just can't let him go."

Noah was saying, "From the look of him, he's a horse that doesn't give his affections easily. You're right, Joel, there's just something about him. I can surely understand your reluctance to let him go. He has to be one of the finest-looking horses I've seen and just as black as my own horse Ebony. I didn't always like the color black for a horse for many years, but then I discovered the color of a fine horse doesn't matter. It's what's in their hearts and minds that is of real importance." Noah asked Joel, "Do you mind if I try to calm him?"

Joel said, "I wish you would, Noah. That's the best news I've heard today."

Noah said, "Okay, I'll give it a try." He opened the door to the stall and slipped inside. King started snorting again, getting more unruly. He began pawing with his right front hoof, then he reared up and began pawing with his hooves again. Noah stood his ground and softly started whispering to him. King came down on all fours and kept snorting and shaking his head, but his eyes were watching Noah as he slowly kept walking toward him. Elizabeth was so concerned for Noah but didn't express it. She instinctively knew he wouldn't hear her anyway. She didn't want to risk alarming King. The three people watching were mesmerized at what Noah was doing with King. He had gotten close enough to reach out his hand for the horse to smell. King was still reluctant but soon stuck his head out to sniff Noah's palm. Noah stepped in then to gently rub the horse's neck, and he didn't shy away. Instead, King seemed to be content to have Noah rubbing his neck. Noah softly asked Joel for a bridle, then he reached back with his left hand to take it and all the while he continued to rub his other hand down King's neck and kept talking softly to him. Soon, Noah had the bridle on him, and he told the others to stand back as he opened the stall door. Just then, to his surprise, this little dog came trotting along to follow King out.

"Hello," he laughed and asked, "Where did the dog come from?" He led King out of the stable. Of course, Little Jo was trotting along behind them boldly. "Oh, well, David and I found him one day, here in King's stall, no less. He just showed up out of nowhere and we couldn't believe our eyes that King would allow the little thing to be in his stall."

Noah asked, "Elizabeth, honey, is that the same dog that was with you when we first met?" She agreed that it was.

Once they were all outside, with reins in hand, Noah reached up to put both hands in King's mane, then pulled himself up on the horse's back. Suddenly, they were off in a flash with the little dog running behind. Of course there was no way the little thing can keep up, so finally Jo decided to just wait for King to return and plopped down.

Joel turned to the others and laughingly said, "Hey guys, can you believe what we just witnessed here? I'm gonna go find Dad to let him know, but he isn't going to believe it unless he can see for himself." Joel left to find Harrison while Elizabeth and David still stood there, too stunned to speak. Noah was gone for about twenty minutes. When he brought King back, they were all there, including Harrison and Ellen, watching. King came to a stop kicking up dust in front of them. Harrison waved the dust away laughing as he called to Noah.

"That's amazing, Noah. How ever did you get on the good side of that horse at all, let alone long enough to ride him?"

Noah replied as he was rubbing his hand down King's neck, "Well, it's just that I know how to calm an unwilling horse. I have to say, Harrison, I would bet any amount of money on this horse to win the Kentucky Derby. He has incredible speed." He gave Elizabeth a wide smile with a flash of white teeth. If she didn't already know it, she knew now she was in love with this man.

Joel asked, "Are you serious?"

"Yes," Noah answered. "Joel, there is no doubt in my mind this horse can outrun any horse I've ever ridden or even seen run, for that matter. Yes, I'm very serious. If there's any way it can be arranged, King should run in the Kentucky Derby this year."

Harrison couldn't believe what he was hearing and said, "Could we discuss this more at the house while we eat?"

Noah replied, "That's a good idea, but first I need to cool King down. Something you guys need to remember is anytime a horse runs the way King just did, he needs a cooling-down bath." By now, the dog had made his way back to make himself heard by barking up a storm, then he just sat to watch what they were doing with King.

"Just tell the two of us what we need to do, Noah," Joel said. "Isn't that right, David? You want to be part of this too, don't you?"

David answered enthusiastically, "You bet I do. This is so great and I'm learning so much more then I ever hoped for."

They all followed Noah, even the pup, as he led King around the barn to a big barrel of rainwater. "We will need a bucket and brushes too," Noah said to them over his shoulder, "so we can get rid of the sweat and lather." David turned to run back in the stable to grab a bucket and some brushes, then all three men worked on King to cool him down. Joel was still having trouble believing how content the horse seemed, and, of course, Little Jo was watching them and taking it all in.

Elizabeth is also watching it all. Then Noah was walking King back to put him in his stall while Joel was putting out a bucket of oats for him to munch on. He put out some of the food Ellen had given them for the dog also. Noah was watching the dog eating and said, "As amazing as it seems that King, being such a powerful and unfriendly horse before, he would even let this little scrap of a dog near him, much less take to him, but he and King seem to have bonded," he said with a chuckle. "Beats all I've ever seen," Joel said. "We never really gave the pup a name though."

"Well, I call him Little Jo," Elizabeth told them. "He seems to answer to it." She reached down to pet the pup and rubbed his ears. He was sitting at her feet now but watching Noah, so he reached down and gave the pup a petting. He said, "I think Little Jo suits him."

Then Noah reached out his hand to Elizabeth. He smiled down at her and asked, "Well, what do you think about all that's happened here today with King, honey?"

Elizabeth smiled, "Noah, I thought you and King looked magnificent together. You really are a wonder with horses. When you did that thing with King, I realized there's a lot to learn about you, isn't there? I really don't know you at all." She was telling him with a quizzical look.

"I like how you say that thing," he said with a chuckle, "but we have plenty of time. We will get to know each other better. You'll see, that's why I'm here, so that you can get to know me better, Elizabeth. I want to know everything there is to know about you, too, okay?"

She said smiling, "Yes, I want to know all there is to know about you, and I realize that may take a while."

They all walked to the house together. When they were in the kitchen, Noah sat at the table with the men while Elizabeth pitched in to help her mother finish up the meal.

Chapter  7

The men were discussing the possibilities of taking King to run in the derby. Harrison made the statement, "I have been thinking about something, boys. If you are serious about doing this, we need to introduce King to a track and then get a time on his laps. We can take a harrow up on that strip of land above the barn. You know where I am talking about?" he asked his sons. Joel and David both answered.

"Yeah, Dad, I believe it just might work too," Joel was saying. "Noah, if you're interested, we can take you up there to let you see for yourself this place we are talking about."

Noah smiled. "Sounds good to me. Anything that is going to help us get things moving toward getting King to the derby. You may already know this, but the very first race of the Kentucky Derby was 1875, just three years ago. It was held at Churchill Downs in Louisville, Kentucky. It's a mile and a half race track. My brother, James, and I were there. It was a thrilling race to watch. The horse to win that first race was Aristides, with a time of 2:37. After riding him today, I believe that King can beat his time." Noah looked to see if the men are still interested in what he was telling them, and the rapt faces of everyone led him to continue. "The next race after the derby is held in Baltimore, Maryland. The Pimlico track was opened in 1870 and the Preakness race is run on a mile and a quarter racetrack. I'm told it was named in honor of a colt named Preakness that won the first race of three-year-olds. Were you aware that the first racetrack built in America was constructed on Long Island, New York, in 1665?"

"No, we didn't know any of that. How come you know all this history about horse racing?" David asked.

Elizabeth was pouring Noah a fresh cup of coffee, and with a gentle smile, he said, "Thanks, honey." He then continued to answer David. "I have always been interested in learning about horses, or any kind of project I go into. It's just who I am."

Dinner was ready to be set on the table, so they changed the conversation for a while because everyone was ready to eat. The day's events had worked them all up, and after they asked for the Lord's blessing, they all ate with relish, talking about a variety of subjects. When the meal was over, the men were in a hurry to go see if Harrison's idea would work. While Joel and David put a harness on one of the work horses and hitched it to the harrow, Harrison walked with Noah up to show him the piece of land he was talking about. Noah was standing up there where he could see how the ground lays.

"You know, Harrison, this is a great spot."

"I thought it might be," Harrison replied with amusement in his voice. "Now don't get me wrong, I'm not surprised that you came up with the idea of putting in a track here, Harrison," Noah said, "but before coming up here and seeing this place, I just didn't see how it was possible. Believe me when I say I'm pleased to see that it is possible, more so that you are really getting behind the possibility. It's great."

Joel and David came up with the horse and harrow ready to work. Noah could tell they knew what needed to be done. It was easy to see that Harrison had taught his sons well. When Noah could help, he did by using the rake David had brought along and pulling the loose grass out of the way. When they were all finished with harrow, Joel and David took the horse with the harrow back to put it in the shed. They put the horse back in his stall with a good ration of oats for doing such a tough job. They talked of making markers for the track.

Noah was on his way to get King. As he stepped inside the stable, Lily walked out from a stall in front of him. Noah was surprised to see her in the stables, so he asked, "What are you doing in here, girl?"

"Well, I thought you would be pleased to see me," Lily answered with a haughty shake of her head. "We haven't had a chance to be alone yet, 'cause she's always around."

"If you're referring to your sister, Elizabeth? I want her around as much as possible." Noah asked, "Why would I want to spend time with you, Lily? You're just a kid. Besides, I don't have the time for this conversation now. So go do whatever it is you do." Lily ran off upset and angry.

Noah walked on down to get King ready for his first experience with the track they had made. He had yet to put the saddle on him, but after he had the bridle on, he led King out and tied him up to the hitching post outside the stall. Of course, his little companion trotted out behind them. Noah had to smile. He said, "Well, if you two aren't the most unlikely pair ever." But he reminded himself he was in a hurry, so by calmly talking to King as he worked, the saddle was on cinched and Noah was walking him outside, with Little Jo trotting right behind them.

He could see two lovely ladies walking toward him. He's so pleased to know Elizabeth would be watching. He felt certain Harrison would be pleased to see Miss Ellen there too. As they came near, he called to them with a bright smile, "Hey, pretty ladies. The sight of you two has made my day." Noah pointed up to the new track and said, "I'm sure there's another man up there who will be mighty pleased to see you, Miss Ellen."

Then Noah asked, "Ladies, do you realize that the state of Kentucky is known for fast horses and pretty women? I would say the two of you lovely ladies, with King here, are good examples of that fact."

Elizabeth said with a bright smile, "Well, thank you, kind sir." Ellen also thanked him for his kind words. "I'm only speaking the truth, you know." Noah answered with a wide smile. "Now, let us make our way up to the track. I believe you ladies will be pleasantly surprised."

Chapter  8

A s Noah and the two ladies reached the makeshift track, the others were all there waiting. When Harrison spotted Ellen walking toward him, he gave her a wide smile. He said, "You, my dear, are a sight for sore eyes."

"I thought you would be pleased, Harrison," Noah said.

Harrison reached for Ellen's hand and said, "Yes, indeed, and you can come over here to stand by me, dear." They were all busy now getting things set up so King could run the length of the track, which they had deliberately made into a mile and a half oval shape, the same length of the derby track. Joel and David had made the markers to put along the way. Joel planned to ride the General to the other end of the track to clock King at the halfway mark using Noah's stopwatch. Harrison was going to use his own pocket watch to clock King's time from the start to finish.

"You men have certainly been busy, and this was all your idea, wasn't it?" Ellen asked as she looked at Harrison. "I'm impressed, dear."

Harrison smiled at his wife. "Well, this is high praise indeed," he told her. Harrison knew Ellen always meant what she said.

Elizabeth was watching Noah now, and with the sun shining on his wheat-colored hair, she was noticing all the golden highlights from the time he has spent in the sun and by the little wrinkles at the corners of his eyes from looking into the sun with a squint. These things took nothing away from his handsome face; in fact, they gave him more character, and she guessed most of the lines were more likely laugh lines. He was still the most handsome man she had ever seen. And to think of her first impression of him was to be a man so arrogant with a huge ego at their first meeting. Now, she knew that it couldn't be farther from the truth. It was safe to say he has a strong personality, and he didn't have a problem with speaking his mind. He has good character that's not hard to see when you look a little closer, and her father was a good judge of character. Dad took to him right away so that pleased her so much. Noah's about ready to give King a good run to the end of this makeshift track around and back where they started.

Everything was set up. Joel was at the halfway marker of the track, watch in hand, and Harrison stood at the ready to clock King's time at the finish line. Harrison was also to give the signal to start, which was to raise his hand then drop it—that was the signal. Joel waved to let them know he's ready. Noah was in the saddle and ready. Harrison raised his hand and gave the signal. King's off running like the devil himself was after him. At the halfway mark, Joel began whooping and nearly fell off his horse as Noah and King raced by him. He clocked them then started after them to the finish line to meet up. Little Jo was running just as fast as his little legs would go from the start of the race to try and keep up. King and Noah were barreling for the finish line; and when Harrison pushed the stop button as they crossed the line, he was stunned. Joel was there on the General. After crossing the finish line, Noah dismounted and was cooling King down as he walked him back to where the others are. Harrison was still standing there staring at his watch then shook his head to focus and told the group, "Oh my, I wouldn't have believed it if I wasn't looking at this watch. Two minutes thirty-seven seconds," he stated proudly.

David looking over his father's shoulder was beside himself, too, with excitement. When he came riding up, Joel called out, "Dad, what time did you clock King at?" Harrison walked over to show him his watch.

Joel said, "That's amazing! I have him at one-twenty-seven at the half, so he picked up speed on the second half." Joel could not hide the amazement in his voice. Noah wasn't surprised at all at the time King's clocked at. He'd known the second he'd looked at the big magnificent horse with the legs and the sleek lines. He just needed to know if King had a heart to match them. "That's fantastic," he said. "We can let him cool off a while and then run him again later when it's a little cooler out and see if he can beat that time."

Joel stopped walking midstride. "Do you really think King can run faster than he just did?"

Noah replied, "Yes I do." He rubbed King's neck. "This horse is remarkable, and you people need to start realizing that King is a champion. Now we need to get him to the stable and finish cooling him down." So while Harrison and the others went back to do some chores. He turned to Elizabeth, reached out for her hand to ask, "Walk back to the stable with me, honey."

"Alright." She gave him a little smile. He was starting to think of it as Elizabeth's smile; it made his heart skip a beat.

Elizabeth let him take her hand. She said, "Thanks for asking, Noah, I know how excited you are by what just happened."

"You should know by now, darlin', I want you with me every possible minute." When they stepped inside the stables, Noah turned to her and put his free arm around Elizabeth to pull her closer for a quick kiss. He knew he didn't have time for more, with cooling down King. He took her hand again and said, "Come stay with me while I wash King down. I'm going to bring water in here this time." So Noah went about, getting several buckets of water. Elizabeth wanted to know how she could help, but he said, "Actually, you're only here to keep me company, honey." While he was pouring water on King, he took his fingers, flipping a few drops of the water on Elizabeth.

She jumped back and said, "Hey, that's not fair, sir." He just laughed with a wink. Elizabeth walked around while Noah finished up with King. She climbed the ladder to the hay loft and sat there thinking about all the times she and her brothers used to play up there. They would make up stories and act them out.

She was brought back to the present when she heard Noah put King in his stall, so she reached for a handful of straw and waited. Just when he stepped out the door, she let the straw fall on him. Noah was so surprised he just stood there for a second or two, then with a wide grin, he dusted the straw out of his hair as he headed for the ladder that would lead him up to the loft. Just as he reached the top, from his blind side she threw more straw at him, catching him off guard once again. Noah made a grab for Elizabeth but she was able to quickly sidestep him. He was laughing out loud but managed to say, "Come here, little clever one. He made another grab for her, caught her arm, and pulled her to him.

"So you think throwing straw at my head is funny?" This time she was laughing so hard she couldn't answer him. When she could speak, she told him, "You started it by throwing water on me." Noah threw back his head and laughed as he said, "I only sprinkled a few drops of water on you, honey, and you did not melt. Now I'll have to punish you, my dear," he said with a flash of white teeth as he pulled her into his arms. He was planning only to kiss her lightly in the spirit of the crime committed but when he took her lips, she tasted so sweet with laughter bubbling up that he couldn't stop. After they were both dizzy from the sensations stirred up, he struggled to pull away. He was breathing so hard it took him a second before he was able to say in a husky voice, "Elizabeth, honey, I believe you're too innocent to realize how much I want to make love to you this very minute. But sweetheart, I want you for my wife more than ever now. I have to say this is not how I planned to ask you, but Elizabeth, darlin', will you marry me?"

Elizabeth was still reeling from their kiss trying to regain her focus, but she understood what had just happened quick enough. She threw her arms around Noah's neck and cried out, "Oh, yes, Noah. I love you so much."

He was smiling, "I was afraid to hope, but hearing you say it makes me the happiest man alive." Noah kissed her again but kept it light this time. He said, "Elizabeth honey, don't make me wait too long for us to marry, okay?"

"I agree, Noah. I want us to marry right away," Elizabeth told him.

"I'm so pleased to hear you say that, sweetheart. Maybe I can stay sane a little while longer." He kissed her again and held her close for a few minutes, then Noah held her at arm's length. "Sweetheart, will you go with me to meet my brother, James, and his wife, Ann? They have two sons, Bobby and Jimmy. I really want the people I love most in my life to meet each other." Noah was smiling down at Elizabeth with question in his eyes.

"Oh, Noah, I would love to meet them. They are your family, and if we marry, they will be my family too, right?"

Noah said, "That's right, darlin', but seriously, don't say the word 'if' when referring to our marriage. It's not 'if,' it's 'how soon.' Have I told you I love you yet, dear girl?"

Elizabeth said teasingly with tongue in cheek, "No, not that I recall."

Noah tweaked her nose lightly. "But you did know it, right?"

"Let's just say I was hoping that you loved me half as much as I love you," she said with that cute little grin. Noah couldn't help but grab her to kiss her senseless again, though it was difficult for him to not let it go too far.

"If there's still any doubt, sweetheart, that kiss was meant to reassure you that I do love you. Now, we best get down from this loft before someone comes in the stable and wonders what we're doing up here," Noah said, grinning. "I want us to marry, but I don't want us to be forced into it, if you know what I mean." Noah went down the ladder first, waited for her, and asked, "Now darlin', would you like to go for a walk? I believe I will be able to keep my hands off you if we are out in the open."

Elizabeth said, "Yes, let's do. We could walk out past the race track. Joel, David, and I use to go snow sledding up there."

So Noah walked up the hill with Elizabeth, holding hands. He was looking around at the property which he hadn't really had the chance to do before now. He could see an apple and peach orchard, one or two cherry trees too. The scent of apple blossoms had always been one of his favorites. Noah turned to Elizabeth to say, "Your father did a great job when he was building this farm, didn't he? There's pretty much everything one would need here to support a family. Also you can see the whole of the farm from up here. I realize it's taken long hours of hard work to make this idyllic place here, and I can appreciate that it all is to your father's credit. Both of your parents are amazing people."

I agree," Elizabeth told him. " I have always loved our life here. I don't recall ever being bored. We use to play hide and seek down there among the fruit trees in summer; and in winter, after the first snow fall, we would drag our sleds up here and go sledding down this hill, when we weren't in school, of course."

When they reached the place where the ground sloped down to the creek, she told Noah with another cute grin, "That's the same water that flows around to where we first met, sir. When we used to go sledding, the trick was always to stop short of the creek. After getting wet a time or two," she said laughing, "I learned to turn the sled before I fell in the water. I have such happy memories here," she said with a sigh.

Noah was watching her as she had been talking and thought again she is just too cute for him not to kiss her again. So he did and said, "I can just imagine what a cute little girl you were, honey, and can't wait till we have one of our own. Now we best go back to the house where we will be with other people around. That way, I will have to keep my hands off you." They walked back down the hill holding hands to the house and around to the front porch where they assumed the others would be.

They sat in the swing for a little while, talking, when a thought came to Elizabeth. She said, "You know, more than likely the men are doing chores early, since you will be running King again later on, so Mom will have supper ready early, too. That means I should go in to help her."

Noah said, "Alright, just let me kiss you again to hold us both over for a while." After the kiss, he said, "Bye for now, sweetheart," then let her go reluctantly. He watched as she opened the door to go inside.

With a deep sigh, Noah turned to leave just as Lily came up on the porch. She gave him a long stare and said, "Now I know why you want her. She does whatever you tell her to, and I'm going to tell dad I saw you kissing and doing other stuff too."

Noah asked, "Why would you do such a thing, Lily? Your sister and I love each other. We kissed each other because that's what people in love do. Lily, you're a spoiled brat. I've noticed that you get away with not helping. I haven't seen you do one thing to help your mother, or anyone else for that matter. There's an old saying, 'Be sure to taste your words, before you spit them out.' Do you realize what it means, Lily? It means you should be careful what words you say; you can't take them back, you know."

She just looked at him for a few seconds, then her mouth puckered up. As she ran away crying, she yelled back, "You're awful, and I'll tell Daddy."

Noah did not regret what he said to Lily, but he was curious what Harrison would think about it. For now, he was going to find the others and help with the chores.

Everyone sat down for the evening meal, and after Harrison said grace, they all began speaking at once. Excitement about running King again was high and the only thing on anyone's mind so Elizabeth kept quiet about her and Noah's plans. After supper, everyone, well except for Lily, was back at the makeshift track to watch King run again. Everyone took the same places and all was just as before, but this time, King was one second faster—two minutes thirty-six seconds. The men were so excited. King was cooled down again, this time with David and Joel's help. Noah took Elizabeth off to the side and told her, "As much as I hate to leave you, I do need to make the trip home. I will see you again in the morning, darlin'." Since they were surrounded by her family, he gave her a quick kiss and said good night to everyone. He walked over to his horse Ebony, mounted up, and rode off with a look back just for Elizabeth. With Noah gone, the whole group was deflated, not just Elizabeth, so it was an early night then for them all.

Chapter  9

Next morning, when Joel brought in the milk, he told his mother they would be a little late and asked if she could delay breakfast a bit.

"Bob and William Jones are here for the tobacco plants." Then Joel turned to Elizabeth to say with a grin, "Noah is here too, sis."

Elizabeth frowned at him. He knew what this meant. Joel laughingly asked if she wanted to introduce them, or if he could have the pleasure. She turned away from him and said, "Mom, I'll be back to help in a few minutes, okay?" She then walked out the backdoor, not sure what to expect.

Joel caught up with her. "Hey, wait up. Why are you upset with me, sis?"

She said without looking at him, "Because you think all this is funny, Joel, that's why." "No, I don't, Elizabeth." With an afterthought, he said, "Well, maybe I did at first, but now I can see your side of it. You don't want to hurt William, do you? And he will be hurt, right?"

When Elizabeth turned to look at her brother, he could tell she was miserable. Her face was scrunched with a frown. It made his heart ache. He regretted the way he had told her that both Noah and William were here. Joel put his arm around his sister and said, "It isn't your fault, you know. You had no way of knowing that Noah would show up here the other day and turn your life upside down, now did you? Actually, with King, he has turned all our lives inside out."

Elizabeth looked at Joel and she softened. He was being so sensible it was hard to stay mad at him. She said, "I know you're right, Joel, but it isn't going to make it any easier to tell William."

"Well I'm afraid the time is at hand now."

William was walking toward them. Then Noah was coming toward them too. Elizabeth had no idea what to expect so she just waited. William reached them first and said, "Hey, good morning, you two. I realize it's pretty early, but Dad wanted to come get the plants and then start setting them out before the heat gets up." He turned to Elizabeth to say, "I know it isn't the time to talk to your father now, honey, but I will come back soon to make the request." Noah walked up just then and put his arm around her. He reached out his hand to William and said, "I don't believe we have met yet. My Name is Noah Bennett." Even though he didn't like seeing him here with his arm around Elizabeth, from habit William took Noah's hand, but he said, "Good to meet you, sir. My name is William Jones."

Noah said, "Since you are a friend of Elizabeth's, you can be among the first to know, William, that Elizabeth agreed to be my wife yesterday and made me the happiest man alive."

William stiffened then, and he looked as if he had just been sucker punched in the stomach. He looked to Elizabeth, and the look on her face told him this was true. Though still numb from the shock, he reached out his hand to Noah. "Congratulations, sir."

Joel took this as his cue and he went to help the others. William turned to take Elizabeth's hand. He said, "I will always be your friend, so please, if you ever need me, I will be there for you." With a tip of his hat, he said good day to them and walked over to where his father, Harrison, David, and Joel were talking and getting the tobacco plants packed in boxes and carrying them to the wagon.

Elizabeth stood watching William walk away. Her heart ached to think she had hurt him, and Noah could tell. He took her by the arm and turned her to face him. "Honey, look at me," he said. "I hope you don't believe I did that to be mean. I could see how difficult this was for you, and it was better for William to make a clean break. He loves you, honey. That was easy to tell. Does that make a difference to you?" he asked. "Do you want to change your mind now? I would rather die first, but I will release you, if that's what you want." Elizabeth looked to Noah with surprise, then with a frown. "Are you trying to tell me, sir, that you want out of our agreement?" He reached out to pull her to him and said, "Oh God, no, Elizabeth. Please don't ever think such a thing. I love you more than I ever thought it possible to love another person. I want what's best for you, and if that's William, I need to know." He held her out to arm's length. "You do believe me, don't you?"

Elizabeth hugged him hard and said, "Yes, Noah, I believe you. I don't want you to think that I have any feelings for William other than just friendship. He's one of Joel's best friends is all, way before I met you, and from childhood, really. I thought that I wanted him to court me. She used her fingers to measure, "For a short time, I was upset with you because after I met you, my whole life changed, but he is still the same person, Noah. Do you understand what I'm saying?"

Noah said, "Of course, I do, honey. I could see how you feel. That's one of the reasons I took charge of the situation earlier. Then he said with a crooked grin, "The truth is I didn't want to give him an edge."

Elizabeth had to laugh. "You do like to be in charge; that's what it amounts to, right?"

Noah said with a chuckle, "I'm afraid you found me out, dear girl, but more importantly, I have realized today that you are my primary concern now, darlin'. Can you get away later to go with me to visit with James and Ann? I told them I would try to bring you today. I hope you don't mind, I also told them that you have agreed to marry me. I realize we haven't told your family yet, so maybe we should do that now, don't you think?"

Elizabeth said, "Yes, I agree. We could do it at breakfast. That reminds me, I need to get back to help mom finish up the meal, so see you later. I'll mention to mom about going with you to visit your brother." As she was moving toward the kitchen door, she gave him a wave, then she opened the backdoor to go inside.

Noah walked over to where Harrison was carefully pulling the tobacco plants and putting them in wooden boxes. Of course, William and his father are there, too, loading the plants in the wagon. Joel took time away from helping to introduce Noah to Bob Jones. He is also telling Bob about King, how Noah is training him to race, and believe it or not he's certain King can win the derby.

"If that's true," Bob replied, "why not bring him over to our farm. Let him compete against our Strawberry Roan, we have hopes of him winning the derby, so we can see which is the better horse."

Joel turned to Harrison and Noah to say, "You guys should see their place. They have a sweet setup with the track," then he asked, "What do you think, Noah?"

"Well, in my opinion, it's always good for a horse to have competition, so I say yes."

"Well," Harrison said then, "I say lets do it."

Bob responded, "Sounds like a plan. When would be a good time to have this competition?"

"You decide, Bob, since you still have the tobacco plants to set."

"Okay then. Thanks for the plants, and we should be done with setting them in two days." Bob told them to make it Friday evening then. Harrison agreed.

Chapter  10

After the Jones men had left, Harrison turned to the others to say, "I do believe we're late for breakfast, men, so we best go in and hope the women didn't get tired of waiting and feed our food to the chickens." He finished with a chuckle, and the others grinned at the thought. But of course, the food's being set on the table as they came in the backdoor.

Harrison said, "Ellen, my dear, you've a hungry bunch here to feed."

Ellen answered, "Well there's plenty of food, always is, you know," as she set a large plate of biscuits down in front of them.

Elizabeth brought a large bowl of gravy, then came back with bacon and eggs next. Of course, there's always jelly and apple butter set out as well. The men ate hardy and are well pleased with the food.

While having their coffee, Noah announced, "Elizabeth and I have news we wish to share. Honey, do you wish to tell them yourself."

"Yes," Elizabeth smiled as she said, "I would like to tell everyone that Noah asked me to marry him, and I said yes."

David spoke, "Well, I don't believe that's a surprise to anyone," as he's stuffing a bite of biscuit spread with apple butter in his mouth." Everyone's laughing now, not so much at what David said but the way he's talking around his bite of food. He turned nonchalantly to say, "Hey, what's so funny?" Since Elizabeth is standing near him, she reached out to ruffle up his hair. With David, touching his hair is a no-no, so he moved back out of her reach.

Well, anyway, she said smiling, "What I wish to say is Noah has asked me to go meet his brother, James, and his family today as well." She looked at her parents to ask, "Is it okay?"

Harrison looked at Ellen. She smiled then gave a nod, so her father said, "As David so ineloquently put it, it's no surprise to any of us to hear the two of you want to marry." They were all smiling as he said to Noah, "We all wish you both a lifetime of happiness."

Joel spoke up with, "You know, Noah, when we first met, I don't believe either of us cared much for the other. But now, after being around you, watching how you are with Elizabeth, and, of course, what you have done with King, I've gained respect for you. I have to tell you though," he said with a wide grin, "I was rooting for my friend William to court Elizabeth. Then I also realized Elizabeth loves you, so I do hope you love her too."

Noah told him, "I will tell you there is no reason to worry because as I told her, I love Elizabeth more than I thought possible to love another person. I also believe one reason we didn't hit it off at our first meeting, Joel, is you're the big brother." When Joel looked puzzled, he rushed on to say, "No, seriously, I thought at our first meeting that Elizabeth is lucky to have you and David both as her brothers. I also believe we're more then a little too much alike, don't you think?"

Joel answered with another wide grin, "Maybe."

Harrison smiled, too, as he said, "Now back to your question, Elizabeth. Your mother and I are okay with you going to meet Noah's family. We realize they will soon be your family as well." As Harrison finished speaking, Noah was laughing as he said, "Speaking of soon, is when I want the wedding."

Everyone else had a good laugh too. Joel told Elizabeth, "You go on get ready, sis, since you're going with Noah. David and I will help with clean-up chores." Elizabeth said, "Really, Joel, I do appreciate it."

He said, "Then go," with a smile. She gave him a hug with a peck on the cheek. She also gave David a hug, too, with a kiss.

He said, "We're happy to do it, sis." He touched his cheek. "Like Joel said, go now before we change our minds," but he's grinning.

Noah's pleased that Elizabeth didn't take long at all to dress. She had changed into the dress she wore to Sunday services. He told her, "Most women I know take far too long to dress, but you didn't, and you look very pretty, honey. If you're ready, we should go now." So they left in the buggy that Noah had brought that morning. He'd come prepared.

As they were riding along, Noah seemed preoccupied now. So finally, Elizabeth asked, "Noah is something wrong?"

He still didn't say anything for another minute before he pulled the buggy to the side of the road and tied the reins off. He turned to face her and took her hands to say, "Elizabeth, I haven't been totally honest with you, honey. Let me tell you a story. Back when James and I were asked to leave our mother and home, we had a friend. His name was Tom Miller, who had a similar situation at his home. So we all left together. It was hard for a long while. But since James was older, he was able to get a job at this stable, which kept us in food. Then he started riding in the races. Soon, Tom and I were able to do the same. We tried to see our mother as often as possible. But our stepfather didn't make it easy for us. He didn't try to reach us when our mother first became ill either. So she died before we could get home." Noah was silent for a few seconds, overcome with emotion, then he drew a long breath and continued.

"We were glad we had no more ties to that man!" After another sigh, he said, "We all became good at riding and started traveling around to different racetracks. Then he told her James met Ann and soon afterwards they were married and settled down to raise their family." He stopped speaking again. Then he's telling her, "Tom and I continued to travel together. We enjoyed what we did. But after a year or so, Tom met a woman, her name was Susan. Tom fell hard for her too. But she didn't care for his traveling. So when they married, Tom left with her." Noah is telling her about how Tom bought a farm and was doing okay. "I was still riding the racing circuit and having a great time, till a letter came from Susan when it caught up with me. She wrote that Tom had been hurt working a horse and asked her to write. He wanted me to go there. So I left immediately. But when I reached Tom, he didn't have long to live, and knew it! He asked me to promise I would see that Susan and their little girl was taken care of. I didn't think about what I was doing, so I agreed."

Noah is saying, "Of course, Susan was having a hard time, and it was hard for me to watch my friend in such pain. Whom I remembered as this robust man full of life is now struggling just to draw a breath. Tom died later that same night, so the next day, we buried him. Afterwards, when I asked Susan if she wanted me to get in touch with her family, she informed me that she has no family, or anyone else she can ask for help. So I stayed to do what needed to be done. I worked hard to get the farm to a place where a hired man could be brought in, so I could leave again."

Noah is again having trouble going on with his story, but finally he was able to continue. "Susan was no help at all. She wasn't taking care of herself or the little girl, who was as cute as a button too. One day, I came in after a day's work and Susan was hysterical. As I was trying to calm her, she put her arms around my neck. I tried to get away, but she had a death grip and started kissing me. Believe me, I'm not making excuses for myself, but she pretty much forced herself on me, but I still blamed myself afterwards. I was so disgusted; I felt that I had allowed it to happen. Therefore, it was my fault. I left her crying again. But I went into town and was able to find someone I felt was competent to do chores and look out for Susan and the baby. Then I went back to my life."

But three months later, I received another letter from Susan telling me I am to be a father. I can tell you, Elizabeth, I was stunned! But I had no other choice but to return and found Susan very ill and the little girl ill kept. But I took her with the little girl into town. I found a minster to marry us. So I went to work to do what I could to help the situation. Unfortunately Susan's condition didn't improve. So again, I went into town to find a doctor and brought him back with me to examine Susan. He did what he could, but with a deep sigh he told me he didn't believe Susan had the will to live. I took care of the little girl, Susie, and fell in love with her. She was such a sweet little thing. But nothing seemed to matter to Susan. So months later, she went into early labor. I brought the doctor back to treat Susan. After he did the examination, he came to me to say it's too soon for the baby to come and she doesn't have the strength, and he said, 'As I've told you before, your wife doesn't have the will to live.' He said, 'I'm sorry, sir.' So later that night, Susan died in labor, and my son died with her!"

Noah sat there as he told the story, with tears running down his cheeks. Elizabeth had sat quietly while he told his story, but she couldn't keep from putting her arms around him now. She pulled him to her and let him cry. It hurt to see such a strong man cry. But then it made him more human, and she loved him more for it. Finally, Noah sat up. He wiped at his eyes as he said, "How you must hate me, Elizabeth. I've put off telling you about this story with Susan and little Susie, so afraid of losing you. I had decided not to ever remarry, till I met you. But when you came into my life, Elizabeth, it was like being reborn. Now if I lose you, I don't know if I can survive it."

And she could tell he meant it too. Elizabeth said, "But Noah, you won't lose me, unless that is what you wish. The story I just heard has made me love you even more, not less. You could have just walked away, but you didn't. You took responsibility and did your best to deal with the situation."

Noah reached out to pull her to him. He kissed her lips, her face, then her lips again. "I knew the minute I met you, darlin', that you're special."

They held one another for a while, then Elizabeth asked, "Noah, where's Susie now?" He laughed and pulled her to him and again hugged her tight. Then he said, "Darlin', she lives with me, of course, on the same farm Tom owned, since James and Ann live there too. Ann has been more or less a mother to her. Dare I hope you'll want that job yourself?"

Elizabeth said, "I'm sure I'll love her, Noah. Yes, I want to be her mother," Elizabeth asked, a little uncertain, "but what if she doesn't want me?"

Noah said, "Oh, honey, how could Susie not want you to be her mother? I'll be willing to bet she'll take to you like a duck to water, you'll see."

Elizabeth asked, "Noah, you really think so?"

"Yes, darlin', I do. Now, my dear girl, let's get going so I may introduce you to my family." With renewed enthusiasm, he's telling her more about his family, how Susie had changed his life, in a good way, so she became the new focus in his life. "And now, I have you, too, so I feel blessed."

Chapter  11

Finally, after more miles of traveling, Noah told Elizabeth, "We're getting close to my home now."

When she noticed this huge white house which has two stories with black shutters, a front porch with a swing, and pretty flowers all around it, she said, "Oh my, I wonder who lives in such a large house. It's beautiful!" She turned to ask Noah, "Do you know the people who live there?"

Noah said with a grin, "Yes, darlin', I do," as he pulled the buggy to a halt in front of this beautiful house. He tied reins and jumped down.

As he's helping Elizabeth out, she said, "But Noah, who lives here?"

Just then this handsome couple with two small boys came out the front door. The boys came running to Noah, jumped at him, and if he hadn't caught them, only the Lord knows what would have happened. Noah laughed as he set the two boys down again. "You two are getting too big, or I'm getting too old for this rough stuff," he said laughingly.

"A bit of both, I say," the other man teased.

He looks remarkably like Noah, Elizabeth was thinking, *though his hair is darker.* When he looked her way, she could see his eyes are blue where Noah's are a brilliant green. *Irish eyes,* she thought to herself.

He's dressed as is Noah in white shirt, with the top button undone and the sleeves rolled up, and dark-colored pants. He seems to be lighthearted and teasing too.

Noah, who turned to put his arm around her, said, "James, Ann, this is Elizabeth. These two little scamps here"—he put his hands on each of the boys' heads—"are Bobby and Jimmy."

They both said, "Uncle Noah, we ain't no scamps."

Everyone laughed, and James stepped forward to take Elizabeth's hand "It's good to finally meet you, dear girl. Noah has talked of little else since he met you; and if you hadn't accepted his marriage proposal, I don't even want to think about what would have happened." Of course, James is teasing, but Elizabeth now knew there was a thread of truth to his statement.

Ann said, "Will you leave the poor girl alone, James. You'll learn these two love to tease each other." She reached out her hand. "I'm so happy to meet you." Ann shook Elizabeth's hand and said, "Noah described you perfectly, and you certainly are beautiful, Elizabeth. But we wouldn't expect anything less for Noah. He knows beauty alright."

"From what he has said, you're a special person too, dear girl," James is saying seriously.

Elizabeth thought Ann to be beautiful too. She has the same hair coloring as her mother, Ellen, but her eyes are brown. She still has a slim figure after having her two sons. One can tell she's neat with her appearance also. She's wearing a beautifully made green dress but simple design with a white collar and cuffs to the sleeves. Ellen has one very similar, and as is with her mother, the dress goes so well with Ann's red hair. She's just an all-around pretty woman and seems to be good-natured too.

Noah asked, "Why don't we take Elizabeth inside? But first, here comes that other little scamp," Noah's saying and laughing as this little bundle of blond curls came out the front door. She is wearing a pretty blue dress. She came running and threw herself at him.

She's calling, "Daddy, daddy, you come back."

Noah's right too, Elizabeth's thinking, *she is the cutest little girl with her blond curls and button nose.* It isn't hard to tell Susie loves Noah as much as he loves her. She's talking and asking questions faster then Noah can possibly answer, so he just smiles and let her talk till she finally ran down.

Then he asked, "Have you been a good girl for Aunt Ann?"

Susie answered, "Yeah, Daddy, I be good." She gave him a cute grin as she's pulling at her dress with both hands.

Noah hugged her then said, "Do you see this pretty lady here?"

"Yeah," Susie answered again.

He said, "Well, her name is Elizabeth. She's a very special person. Could you say hi to her?"

But the little girl hid her face against her father's neck. Noah looked over at Elizabeth to smile and said, "She'll be fine in a minute, honey." Susie did finally start turning her face toward Elizabeth, using her hand to cover her little face, but she would raise her hand to take a peek. She did this a time or two more, then Susie took her hand away and finally looked at Elizabeth to say with a cute smile, "You pretty."

Elizabeth smiled back and said, "Thank you, Susie. You're pretty too."

Noah asked Susie, "How about I put you down now, sweetie, then we walk with Elizabeth in the house?"

Susie said, "But me go play with the boys, Daddy." She's already wiggling and trying to get down. Noah is laughing as he's trying to say, "Wait a minute." He set her down then gave her a pat on the bottom. She's running after the boys.

Noah's watching her, then with a deep sigh, he said, "She's growing so fast, I feel as though I'm missing out on too much by being away so often."

James said teasingly, "Oh, but look on the bright side, Noah." When Noah looked at him questionably, James said, "No, seriously. Just think you'll be staying home more now that you'll soon have a wife, right?"

Noah looked toward Elizabeth, thinking again how blessed he feels and said, "Well, I'm sure you're right," and his face lost the look of concern as they walked inside the house.

Elizabeth is in awe as she said, "Oh, Noah, how grand this house is."

Noah said, "Thank you, darlin'. It pleases me that you like the house, since this is where we will live. Do you think you could be happy here?"

Elizabeth said, "Oh, yes, Noah. But I want you to know that I will be happy living wherever you are. But how could I not be happy here?"

He put his arm around her to pull her close. "That pleases me even more, darlin'," Noah said with a heart-stopping smile. It made Elizabeth's knees go weak, her heart is in her eyes, so Noah couldn't help groaning.

"Oh no, Ann, close your eyes," James teased. "They're getting lovey dovey here. Best keep the kids outside."

"Oh will you stop brother of mine, when I have to be careful about walking into a room unannounced at any given time of day with the two of you. I'm right and you know it to be true," Noah teased then asked Elizabeth, "Would you like a tour of the house now, honey?"

"That would be great," she answered.

"No way," James said, grinning. "I remember that trick too, brother."

Ann offered, "Why don't we go in the kitchen instead and Elizabeth can start the tour there?"

Noah took Elizabeth's hand and he said, "Good idea, Ann. Come in the kitchen, honey. See if you like how I built it."

Elizabeth asked in amazement, "Really, Noah, you built this house?"

James said, "Noah rebuilt every stick of this house, and he didn't tell you? But then, I'm not surprised. You will find that this brother of mine can do pretty much anything he sets his mind to. But you won't hear him talk about it."

Just then, Jimmy came running in the kitchen door, calling "Uncle Noah, Susie is stuck in the big tree."

James asked, "What are you saying, son?"

"Susie is up in that big tree, you know which one. She followed us up there, now she's afraid to come back down."

Noah's already out the backdoor before Jimmy is finished speaking. As he's looking up the tree, he asked, "Susie, honey, are you okay?"

" I afraid, Daddy," she cried.

"You stay where you are, sweetie, I'll be right there." He's trying to get his boots off.

While James is already climbing the tree, he's telling Noah, "You keep talking to Susie. You don't worry, Noah, I'll get her down, okay."

When James reached the little girl, she's shaking like a leaf; the poor little thing is so afraid. James said, "Susie, honey, you're a brave little girl, and Uncle James is proud of you, and I will get you down safely to your Daddy, okay? So you put your arms around my neck."

She said, "K," did as James asked, then they started back down to the ground. When they were safely down, James handed Noah his daughter.

Noah took Susie, hugged her so tight that she said, "You hurt me, Daddy." Noah held her away, looked at his daughter questioning, "What did you say, honey? What do you mean 'I hurt you'?"

Susie said, "I say you hold too tight, you hurt me."

"Oh, I'm sorry, honey." Noah was so relieved. "I'm just so happy that Uncle James was able to bring you back down from that tree safely. Now, you do understand, don't you, that you are not to follow those boys up a tree again?"

Susie said, "K, Daddy," as she's holding her little hands together.

Noah said, "Alright now, you need to thank your uncle," as he put her back down. Susie looked up at James and she said, "Thank you, Uncle James. I love you," as she's already running after the boys.

"Now, you come back here, little girl, to give me another hug." When the little girl turned around and ran back to him, James reached down, scooped Susie up, hugged her, then said, "You did hear what Daddy said, right?"

The little imp said, "Yeah. Can I go play now?"

James looked at Noah as he set her down. His brother said, "I guess we can't wrap her in cotton, can we?"

James replied, "No, we can't be too protective. Now let's go back inside to help get our dinner."

Ann cried, "Oh no, I forgot the chicken! It's still on the stove and will be burned by now," as she was running back to the house. The others followed, but of course the chicken was ruined. Ann wanted to cry for real, but James put his arm around her to say, "It's okay, honey. Let the boys take over here."

So the men took charge. James said, "My job is frying bacon."

Noah asked Elizabeth, "Will you go with me to gather eggs to fry?" and they found plenty of eggs in the hen house.

Ann said with a chuckle, "You know, my potato salad isn't going to go with bacon and eggs."

James said to placate her, "Oh, but it can be put in the spring house for supper, honey."

"I suppose, so I could fry more chicken for supper then."

Noah said, "Don't count on us, Ann, we can't stay for supper. I need to get Elizabeth back home. To stay in good standing with her parents." He's smiling at her as he asked, "Right, honey?"

Laughingly Elizabeth said, "You're kidding, right?"

He said, "Yeah, partly, but I don't want to take any chances where you're concerned. You and Susie are my life now."

James knows his brother is being serious, but he had to tease him anyway by asking, "What about us, Noah?"

"Don't be funny, James. Besides we're trying to be serious here," Noah returned his teasing.

After they had eaten the bacon and eggs with the biscuits Ann had made to go with the chicken, which the children thought of as another breakfast, Ann brought out this three-layered chocolate cake.

Ann said, "Elizabeth, I'll give you a tip. Noah has a sweet tooth." The men had coffee, but Ann made hot tea for herself and Elizabeth. Of course the children had milk to drink.

Elizabeth said after taking a bite of cake, "Ann, this is really good cake. What's your secret?"

Ann told her, "It's a recipe handed down from my mother, and the secret is buttermilk with extra cocoa. I'll give you the whole recipe later."

Elizabeth helped Ann clean up the kitchen while Noah and James walked to the stables to check on a mare James had some concerns about. When they returned, Noah told Elizabeth he would give her a quick tour of the house before they leave, so he showed her all the up-to-date conveniences in the kitchen, which are many: Lots of cabinet space and such, as a pump set on the sink so one can pump water in the sink, with a drain, no less, so after washing the dishes, one just lifts the stopper, which she had noticed earlier while helping Ann do dishes. It lets the water drain outside through pipes into an unheard-of soak-away tank. Noah had also built inside toilets, one off the kitchen and the other one off the living room, which drains into the tank as well. He chose most of the furnishings, also did most of the decorating, Ann told her. Elizabeth's having trouble taking it all in. The man that she has come to love so dearly seems to be able to do most anything.

She said with uncertainty, "Noah, how can I possibly compete with you?"

He pulled her to him for a hug, then he held her at arm's length to say, "Please, honey, just always be yourself, the woman I fell in love with, okay? Now, we should get going," he told James and Ann, "but first, where is my daughter? I would kinda like to say bye to her too."

"I here, Daddy," he heard her say.

"Where is here?" he asked teasingly.

Susie was sitting on the stairs, third step up. "I here, Daddy," she said again with a giggle.

Noah walked over to the stairs, leaned over, scooped his daughter up, and sat on the steps with her in his lap. He told her, "Now, Daddy needs to leave for now, but I will be back soon. You know I love you, right?"

Susie said, "Yeah, Daddy." She's playing with her dress, as is her habit.

"Well, I want you to know, soon we'll spend lots more time together, I promise." She gave a nod of her head. He hugged her again then set her back on the stairs. He said, "Now you be a good girl as I know you will."

Susie answered, "I will, Daddy, bye. You too, Miss Elizabeth."

Then Elizabeth couldn't help but smile and bent over to give Susie a kiss on the cheek. She said, "See you soon, honey." The little girl put her fingers up to her cheek then smiled. Ann handed the recipe to Elizabeth. She had written it out while Noah gave Elizabeth the tour. Elizabeth thanked Ann, and they said their good-byes.

* * * * *

Noah and Elizabeth were on their way now so they could get back to the Steele farm before dark. Elizabeth is reading the recipe Ann had written out.

Chocolate Cake

    3 cups flour
    2 cups sugar
    2 teaspoons soda
    2/3 cup cocoa
    1 cup butter, soften
    1cup buttermilk
    2 eggs
    1 cup hot water

Sift together all dry ingredients. Add beaten eggs with butter and buttermilk. Mix well. Add hot water and vanilla. Mix all ingredients again. Makes three 8-inch layers.

Chocolate Fudge Frosting

Mix in saucepan 1-1/2 cups sugar, 6 tablespoons butter, 6 tablespoons milk, 1/2 cup cocoa. Bring mixture to a boil, stirring constantly for 1 minute. Remove from heat. Beat till thick and smooth.

Elizabeth is pleased that Ann gave her the recipe, but Ann knows how well Noah loves the cake.

He said, "That was good of Ann, don't you think, honey?"

"Yes," she said, "and I will try to make it as good as hers."

"Don't worry, honey. I'm sure you will do just fine. You are your mother's daughter, after all," Noah told her with a wide grin. That statement gave Elizabeth a warm feeling, so she lay her head on his shoulder. She's thinking how wonderful this whole day has been. Meeting Noah's brother, James, and his wife, Ann, who are such loving people, with their two sons, Bobby and Jimmy. Then there is little Susie. She is so cute. It's not hard at all to see how much love there is between Noah and his little girl, well, and the rest of the family.

Chapter  12

When they reached the Steele farm, Noah pulled the buggy in back by the stable, tied off the reins, and he turned to say, "We're back in good time, honey," with a grin, and leaned over and gave her a quick kiss. Then he jumped down and walked around to help Elizabeth step down. They had started walking toward the house when they noticed David coming out of the stable.

Noah called to ask, "What's going on in there?"

David answered "We have a mare trying to foal, but she seems to be in trouble."

Noah turned to Elizabeth, "Ask honey, do you mind if I go see how the mare's doing?"

"Of course not," Elizabeth told him. "I'll go with you." When they arrived at the stall, Harrison, Joel, and even Ellen are there working with the mare.

Noah asked, "What seems to be the problem?"

Harrison replied, "She's in trouble, Noah. We believe the head isn't in the correct position to come down in the birth canal so the mare can bring this foal into the world."

Noah replied, "Then we need to turn the head, right?"

"Yes, that would be the thing to do," Harrison answered, "but I've never done it. Have you, Noah?"

"Yeah, I have, but it isn't an easy thing to do." He turned to Elizabeth to say, "Honey, it's not a pretty sight, either, so maybe you shouldn't stay." He asked Ellen if she's staying.

Ellen said, "Someone needs to calm the mare."

Joel said to Noah, "Since that's something you could do, if you tell me what to do here, maybe I can help this mare foal."

"Okay," Noah said, "we can try." After making sure the women are all outside, he told Joel, "I'm going to put my hands up inside the mare to literally turn the head and hold it down. It will take all of you to get the colt out."

Then Harrison said, "If you can keep the mare calm, let's do it." So he and Joel went to work, did exactly what Noah's telling them they need to do. Once the head had been turned, Joel held it in place, while Harrison, with David's help, pulled, and the little colt is out safely. As soon as they were finished with her, the mare's on her feet to go clean her baby.

"The little thing is cute," Joel said. "King's its daddy, you know."

"Really!" Noah asked incredulously. "That will be good to know if King is as good as we believe him to be." But as soon as the mare has the foal cleaned, she's back lying down again. Noah said "Now that isn't a good thing, is it?"

"No!" Harrison answered. "She can get congested. Joel, could you ask your mother if she can do something to help the mare get back on her feet?"

When her son told Ellen the situation, she said "Yes, I believe I can help by making a mixture of herbs for the mare. Just let me go in the house and go through my basket of herbs." Soon, she's back at the barn with a mixture. She said, "We need to somehow get the mare to drink this liquid mixture."

Noah took the bowl to say, "I'll try." He walked over to sit at the mare's head, started talking to her as he put a spoonful of the herb liquid in her mouth. She swallowed it. He continued till all the mixture's gone.

Now Ellen told them, "We will need to keep watch on her till she shows signs of improvement." Then she said, "I will stay for a while."

Harrison told the others, "I will be staying with Ellen."

But first, he and the others needed to get washed up. Afterwards, Joel with David went to do chores. Harrison headed back to keep watch over the mare with his wife. So it was decided everyone else would do what is needed to get the evening chores done. Noah did the milking then helped Elizabeth get the milk prepared, then the two of them took it to the spring house. When the milk's safely in the cool water, she told Noah "We need to take a jug of the cool milk back to the house for our supper."

While Ellen and Harrison are still in the barn, Elizabeth told Noah, "I'll need to start supper, although I'm not sure what Mom had planned."

Noah told her he could help with the meal. "We can do the bacon and eggs, same as James and I prepared for our dinner. We could also fry some potatoes to go with them."

Elizabeth asked, "Really? I don't recall mom ever frying potatoes."

Noah said, "When I was traveling around, eating in different places, one eats things one is not used to and learns to like them. If the potatoes are fried correctly, they're good, honey." He touched his finger to her nose. "Trust me."

Elizabeth said "always" with her smile.

"Now don't smile at me like that, or we'll not get this meal finished in time," Noah teased her with a grin.

"I could say the same for that grin of yours, sir," she said smartly.

"Is that so?" Noah said with another grin."

"Now stop that!" Elizabeth scolds, but she's smiling too.

Noah said with a groan, "We'll just have to grin and bear it, so to speak." They are both laughing now. Finally, Noah said, "We need to get serious here." They did get back to work and well on their way to having the meal done, when Joel and David came in from feeding the animals.

Since Noah's helping Elizabeth, they asked, "Can we help too?"

Their sister answered, "Please." She asked, "David, please set the table, and Joel, if you will get a pot of coffee going, that would be great, I'm sure Mom and Dad can use some."

After setting the table, David told them, "I'll go check on the parents. I will try to bring them back with me."

They did come to eat and were pleased with the meal.

Noah asked "How's the mare and her colt doing?"

Ellen said, "The mare still doesn't show any signs of improving yet. If she isn't well enough to feed the colt, it isn't going to survive without help, you know. So I was thinking maybe we can make a bottle with a nipple and try to feed the little thing some milk that way."

Noah said "If you can get a bottle prepared, I'll help with the feeding and stay for a while too." He looked Elizabeth's way to ask if she would stay with him. She gave him a nod yes.

Harrison's saying, "This food isn't our usual fare for supper, but I have to say it's quite tasty"—he turned to Ellen—"don't you think so, dear?"

"I do," she answered and asked, "whose idea was it to fry potatoes?"

"Wouldn't you know, Mom, it was Noah's idea," Joel answered with a grin. "The man just never ceases to amaze me," he teased. "But they're very good; I'm always ready for something new, you know."

Now what about cleanup duty? Noah's idea, "Why not everyone pitch in while Ellen's doing the bottle?"

"I'm okay with it," Joel said.

"Me too," David offered.

So with everyone helping, even Lily, which was a surprise to all, but no one let on, before long, the kitchen is cleaned, just the way Ellen likes it done. Just in time, too, 'cause Ellen has the bottle ready. So everyone made the trip out to the barn to see how it will work. Noah is holding the bottle, and once the little colt got the hang of sucking it, then everyone had a good laugh watching him go after it. After the colt has been fed and it's back lying down with its mother, Noah and Elizabeth were left to their vigil with the mare and her colt. So they settled down with a blanket she had brought along for the wait. Noah's very pleased to have this time alone with Elizabeth, but after a while, to his way of thinking, it's a bittersweet time. He's happy to be with her but he's afraid he'll go out of his mind from wanting her, but knowing he can't till they are married. So he said, "Honey, we need to talk about not waiting to marry. Will you agree to go with me over to ask James and Ann to stand up with us tomorrow? I just do not want to wait another day to marry you. I want you to be my wife now so we can be together at bedtime, wake up together in the mornings."

Noah asked, "Elizabeth, darlin', how does that sound to you?"

"Oh, Noah, it sounds wonderful to me. I agree and want to be your wife, to spend my life with you," Elizabeth told him. "Don't you realize that, sweetheart?"

Noah looked so pleased, he asked, "Do you realize you just called me sweetheart?"

"Noah, I love you. Why are you so surprised?" Elizabeth leaned over to kiss him lightly, but Noah didn't let the kiss stay light. When it's over, breathing hard, he managed to say, "That's another reason, honey, not to wait," he said with another groan. "It's becoming increasingly difficult for me to keep my hands off you."

"I agree with you, Noah."

"Then tomorrow, we'll let your parents in on what we have decided. Leave early for the trip to my house." Elizabeth agreed.

"Then you best go in the house now. I'll stay here the rest of the night." He kissed her one last time, thinking, *Ah,* he breathed, *she'll be my wife tomorrow, then my life will be complete.* Noah didn't believe he could sleep, but he did, then was awake early. He was pleasantly surprised to see the mare's up tending to her baby. So Noah feels certain now that the mare's going to be okay.

Elizabeth went to sleep almost immediately. She is surprised, too, that she felt refreshed, so after washing and getting dressed, she made her way downstairs. There sat Noah at the table with her father and brothers. Of course, he's so pleased to see her too. He stood to walk to her. He asked "Shall we tell your family now, what we decided last night?"

Elizabeth said, "Yes, let's do it." So they ask Ellen to hold breakfast and sit at the table with them. Noah started by saying, "I want you both to know, I love Elizabeth with all my heart. I didn't think I was ready for marriage till I met her; now that's all I think of. And I thank God that I met her. So we have decided to go back to my home, have James and Ann stand up with us to get married today. We didn't get a chance to discuss any plans but we can still have family and friends for a social gathering later if you would like, neighbors included. We can also have it here if that is what you wish. But Harrison and Ellen, do you have any objections to us getting married today?"

"Just one question," Harrison said, "is this what you want, Elizabeth?"

She looked at her father's dear face, then to her mother's. She smiled brightly to say, "I love Noah with my whole heart, so yes, I want to be Noah's wife, and for us to marry today."

So Harrison looked at Ellen to ask, "Do you have any questions or objections, dear?"

Ellen answered, "But Harrison, how could we object to them wanting to get married within days of their meeting. If I remember correctly, that's exactly what you and I did." She's looking at her husband now with a gentle smile, leaving no doubt that the feelings are still there, and Harrison's returning the look.

Harrison turned back to Noah and Elizabeth. "Now then, the only other thing I would add," Harrison finally said, "is that we are invited, that is, maybe we should all go for the wedding. You know your mother and I would like watching our daughter get married. But first I would like to say—and these are important things to remember—you both will need three things in your marriage: One is patience, another is understanding, and if you will allow it, wisdom can be an excellent gift from God."

After Harrison finished speaking, Ellen said, "I agree with everything my husband has said."

Noah looked at Elizabeth. There is no doubt she's pleased at what her father and mother had to say. So Noah said, "Harrison, Ellen, that is the best advice we could possibly get from anyone. And as for all of you coming with us, I believe we can agree by the smile on your daughter's face she's pleased and in agreement, and so am I. Now, it's settled. But I would like to leave as soon as possible so James and Ann will have time to get ready. This will be a surprise for them as well, you know."

Harrison said, "Then we need to make arrangements for our neighbors, the Boggs family, to come do the evening chores. David, you take care of that, while we finish feeding the animals now."

"But first, breakfast is to be finished and eaten," Ellen reminded them, something they all had forgotten except Ellen, of course. They ate the meal and afterwards the kitchen is cleaned. Then the women can change into their best clothes.

"Elizabeth," her mother said, "A bit of advice, you should wear the blue dress trimmed in white with the cape sleeves, it's so pretty on you, and your wedding day is special, you know."

When the ladies, including Lily, are all dressed, they came downstairs to find the men were waiting to leave.

Chapter  13

Harrison has Ellen with Lily in his buggy; Elizabeth is riding with Noah in his. Joel and David are riding their horses, as usual. When Noah pulled his horse and buggy to a halt in front of his house, Joel brought his horse up alongside to ask, "Why are we stopping here, Noah?"

"This is where I live," Noah answered.

"Surely you're kidding."

Elizabeth said, "No, Joel. This really is where Noah lives. And he built this house too."

"Well, I'm certainly impressed," Harrison told Noah.

"Me too," Joel responded. "But at the risk of repeating myself, Noah, you never cease to amaze me. I'm pleasantly surprised though."

"Good," Noah said. "I'm pleased you like our home. This will be Elizabeth's home too. Ann and James has made it a home for me. Now come in to meet them."

Ann's at the door ready to greet them. Noah made introductions.

Ann said, "I'm so pleased to meet all of you. We have heard so much about you from Noah. But before you ask, it's all good," she said with a chuckle.

"Thanks for that comment. As you can tell, Ann has a sense of humor. Now, Ann, where's that brother of mine?"

James answered, "Right here, boy," as he's coming in from the kitchen. "I've been out since early this morning. Looks like you're a loafer," he said with a teasing grin.

"I will have you know, brother, I have good cause for not working today. It happens to be mine and Elizabeth's soon-to-be wedding day."

James has a pleased smiled as he said, "You're a smart man after all. I was afraid you may let this beautiful girl get away, and that would surely be a crime."

"Not a chance, brother," Noah said with a wide grin. Putting his arm around Elizabeth, he said, "Her family are all here to see the deed is done. This is Harrison, my soon-to-be father-in-law; Ellen, soon-to-be mother-in-law, the best cook you'll ever have the pleasure of meeting; brothers-in-law Joel and David; their sister Lily. Now, you two need to get yourself plus the children dressed. By the way where are they?"

"Out back, playing," Ann told him.

"Okay then, I'll go look for them while you two start getting dressed. I would like to be at the church shortly." He went out the backdoor and called for the children. The two boys came running.

Noah asked, "Where's Susie?"

Jimmy answered, "Oh, she's in the shed there, Uncle Noah." He didn't stop to ask what she's doing; he went looking for her. There she is up on a work bench.

Noah asked, "Susie, didn't you hear me calling for you, sweetie?"

"Yeah, Daddy, but me no can get down."

"What are you doing up there, little miss?"

"I do what Jimmy do, he climb here"—she put her hand on the bench—"he help me up."

"Well, I believe I need to have a talk with those boys."

"No talk to boys, Daddy." Susie is saying and shaking her little head no. "I like play with them."

Noah groaned. What choice did he have but to forget it for now? "I know," he said and scooped her up. "Come with me now, little one."

When he brought Susie back in the house, he looked at Elizabeth to ask, "Honey, I don't suppose you could help get these three scamps washed up while I get washed up and dressed myself."

Elizabeth said, "Sure, you go do what you need to; we'll take care of the children." She asked the children, "Can one of you show me where we can get you three washed up?"

So Jimmy led them to the back porch built for washing. She found washcloths and soap and a pan there too. After getting water and helping the boys wash up, she sent them inside to get dressed. She set Susie on the table. Lily had come out with her, so she's helping to wash the little girl and said, "She's really cute, isn't she?"

"You say I cute, I say you cute," Susie said to Lily with a cute grin. She turned to Elizabeth to say, "you pretty." Both Elizabeth and Lily laughed. Susie laughed, too, and clapped her hands. When she's all clean again, they asked if she would show them her room to find a pretty dress to wear to a wedding. Susie clapped her hands again. "I go to wedding." She took them to her room.

"Susie, your room's so pretty," Lily said in awe.

"Me think it pretty too," and smiling brightly, Susie said, "Daddy make it pretty for me." She pointed to herself and clapped her little hands again. The two sisters smiled and Elizabeth went in search of clothes. She found underclothes, a pretty blue dress which will match the little girl's eyes, a pair of black buckled shoes and white socks.

After Susie is dressed, Elizabeth brushed her curly blond hair. *It's so pretty*, she's thinking, and told her "You look pretty,

Susie. Daddy will be pleased." So they took her downstairs where the others are waiting.

Noah said, "Would you look at the three pretty girls?" He had included Lily; she's pleased and smiled. Noah looked at Elizabeth with a look that made her knees go weak. "Are you ready to do this, sweetheart?"

"I believe I am," she answered, and she's thinking he's even more handsome in his suit of black, a white shirt with a pearl-grey tie. She isn't used to seeing him dressed this way. *His eyes are shining, too, so he must be as happy as I am.*

Noah's saying, "Okay then, people, let's go." He reached down, picked up his daughter, and held her in one arm and put the other one around Elizabeth. They walked out to the buggy. He put Susie on the seat and helped Elizabeth up to sit beside her. He walked around to climb in himself to lead the way to the church. When the others arrived, Noah and Elizabeth with Susie were waiting for them so they could all go in the church together. The Steele family walked in to sit down in the front pew with James and his family. Noah handed Susie to James. He took Elizabeth by the hand and said, "Honey, let's go talk to the minister." They found him in his office. Noah knocked on the door. When the man looked up in surprise, he said, "Why hello, Mr. Bennett, it's good to see you."

Noah shook hands with the man and he said, "Good day, sir, this is Elizabeth Steele. She has agreed to marry me, and we have come to ask you to marry us today—now, as a matter of fact. Elizabeth's family as well as mine are here to be part of our wedding."

"Well, I suppose I can do it, though normally weddings are planned ahead, you know."

Noah informed him, "We just decided last evening we wanted to get married today. So, do you want to marry us, or do we need to go somewhere else, sir?"

"Now, Mr. Bennett! Of course I will marry you to this pretty young lady. I didn't mean to imply I wouldn't."

"Good then," Noah said. "Let us take care of the necessary paperwork now—a marriage license for us to sign after we are married, isn't that all we need?"

"Yes, that's it, sir. I have the document right here. So if you are ready, then we could start the ceremony."

He followed them out where their families are waiting for the ceremony to begin. So when James set Susie beside Lily, he and Ann then walked up to stand with the couple to be married.

Susie stood up. She said, "But Daddy, you forget me."

Noah was surprised but looked at Elizabeth, who said, "Yes, of course, Susie should be part of this wedding too." So Noah reached out his hand to Susie. She came running to him. Noah and Elizabeth let her stand in front of them during the ceremony.

While the minister is doing the ceremony, Noah's letting his mind wander and thinking how full of happiness his life is now, and it all happened in a matter of days. Elizabeth, whom he loves more then life itself, and his daughter who adds to his happiness. The minister is asking him, "Will you take this woman to be your wedded wife?"

Now he came to attention; he almost missed hearing that part by his wool gettering but Noah said yes loud and clear then listened to the rest of the ceremony. When it's over, everyone is happy for them.

Susie said, "Me happy too."

"Well, I am glad you're happy, honey," Noah said. He and Elizabeth thank the minister and introduce him to everyone, then Noah gave him money for doing the ceremony and he said, "Good day, sir."

"Now, why don't we all go somewhere to eat?" he told Harrison and Ellen. "That will give you two a chance to become better acquainted with James and Ann. He asked, "Does anyone know of a place where the food is good?"

Joel answered, "Yeah, I have eaten at the hotel dining room. The food is good there."

"Is it okay with everyone then if we go eat at the hotel?" Noah asked, and everyone agreed.

"Do you expect them to say no, brother? They're all hungry," James teased.

Joel was right, and after Harrison asked the blessing and they have tasted the food, it's good, everyone agreed, and they enjoyed themselves visiting. Ellen asked Ann and James to come visit them at the farm. They promised they will.

Noah said, "It's time to go. But Ann, if it's okay with you, I would like to take Susie back with us now, but we need to get some of her things first?"

Ann said, "You should know it's okay with me, Noah, but thanks for asking."

When they were back at the house, Ann went along with him to Susie's room to pack some of her things.

"We can't forget her Dollie, of course," Ann reminded him."

Noah went to his room then to pack some of his own clothes with other things. He said to James as they were ready to leave, "Come see King run, you'll be amazed." They all said good-bye then started the trip home.

Chapter  14

It's late when they arrived back at the farm. They needed to decide on sleeping arrangements.

Lily said, "Susie can sleep in my room." Since the little girl had fallen asleep on the ride home, Noah's carrying her. Lily is leading the way with a lamp.

He asked, "Are you sure about this, Lily?"

She said, "Yeah, it will be okay, Noah."

He looked at her, uncertain for a second, then said, "Thanks, Lily."

Noah had taken Susie into Lily's room. He said, "I'll undress her, Lily, if you wish."

"No, Noah, let her sleep."

"Then I will bring in her things. Good night and see you in the morning."

Noah made his way back downstairs to get his and Susie's things, but Joel is just bringing them in the house.

Noah said, "Well, thanks, Joel. I was just coming to get them."

"That's okay, Noah. I'm sure you're in a hurry to get to bed." Joel replied with a wide teasing grin.

Noah returned the grin and said, "Thanks again." He took the things with a lamp to light his way back upstairs. He climbed the stairs then stood there in the hall, uncertain as to which bedroom he will find his wife.

Joel is there once again to rescue him. "Noah," Joel asked laughingly, "is this by chance the first time you're having a problem finding a lady's bedroom?" Of course Joel's teasing again.

"I believe you're enjoying yourself a little too much, brother-in-law," Noah said with a chuckle. "Now let's get serious, Joel. Just tell me in which room I'll find my wife?"

Joel decided to give him a break. He said, "It's the room on your left there. Sis and I have the rooms with the front view."

Noah's thinking with a smile. He had been standing that close to her all the while. He opened the door, stood for a second watching his wife as she's brushing her hair and humming happily. He asked in a husky voice, "Are you really happy, darlin'?" She turned toward him, smiling. "Yes, Noah, very happy. How about you?" Noah dropped his things, set the lamp on a table, closed the door, walked toward his wife as she stood waiting. He said, "Elizabeth, I had no idea a person could possibly be as happy as I am." He took her in his arms and kissed her in the way he had wanted from the moment he had looked in her beautiful face. Then Noah felt as though he had fallen off a cliff. Finally he's able to drag his mouth from hers. He said, "Honey, here, let's get in bed so I can love you in the way I have been dying to do.

And it was heaven for both of them. Noah couldn't get enough of kissing his wife. She is surprisingly responsive, too, for the innocent she is. She went to sleep immediately though after their loving. Noah had to smile to himself. He didn't believe sleep would come to him so easily though, but he was wrong.

He came awake, early as usual but refreshed. He looked over at his sleeping wife. He would like nothing more than to wake her by making love to her again, but he wouldn't. He decided to go give King a run instead, which will be good for the two of them. When Noah made his way to the stable, he's not surprised that the little dog was right there watching as if he is King's protector. Noah had to smile again and thought what an unlikely pair they are. It's still early and there is a chill in the air because the sun is still hiding for now, but there is enough light to see the mist hovering over everything in the distance. There has been a heavy dew overnight, so when the sun comes out, it will sparkle on the grass and look like teardrops where it has settled on the tree leaves. He has always loved this time of day though, when it's quiet time, before the birds and other creatures begin to stir. Noah headed King up to the track that had been made to run him. He set his watch and he's now having a good run too, but Noah's thinking he wished he had had the foresight to bring a jacket with him. There was a little chill in the air, and King was running fast, as though there were a strong wind blowing behind him as he ran the full length of the oval track. It's time to get him back to the stable and cooled down. But Noah is well pleased with this morning's run.

When Noah returned to their room, Elizabeth is still sleeping. He knew it's too much of a temptation not to wake her and make love, even though she looks so adorable while she's sleeping. He undressed quickly. As he's pulling the covers back, she opened her beautiful eyes. "Noah, where have you been?" she asked, still sleepy, but as he reached out to her, she did say, "Oh, you're cold."

Noah chuckled as he crawled in bed to lie down beside her. He put his arms around her and just held her close for a second or two then said, "I woke early, as usual, and took King for a run. I thought it better that than wake you, which is what I would have rather done, but I forced myself to let you sleep. Now that you're awake, honey," he said, grinning, "that is no longer a problem."

He went about loving his wife, then they both had a nap. When they woke again, it's almost too late for Elizabeth to help

Ellen with breakfast. Everyone's smiling at them when they walked in the kitchen. Noah expected the teasing looks, but Elizabeth didn't have a clue as to why. She was uncertain as to the cause and for the wide smiles. Noah whispered, "They're happy for us."

"Oh," she said, then she smiled herself.

After Noah sat down at the table, Joel asked, "Did you remember tonight is when we take King to the Jones's farms to run him against their horse?"

"Yeah, I remembered," Noah replied. "But I took King for a run already this morning, and the Jones's horse better be fast, or King will leave him in the dust. I swear that horse is getting faster each time he runs," Noah told them with a wide smile. "That reminds me, Harrison, how did you come by King? If he wins the derby, he will be worth a lot of money, you know."

"Well," Harrison replied, "I hadn't thought about that, but there's a story to it." He looked Joel's way, then he continued with the story. "I happened to go to a horse auction in London, you know, up here west of us. Joel was with me, and there was this mare. I liked the look of her. I decided to bid when they brought her up, but when I made my first bid of twenty five dollars, this hairy-looking character bid just one dollar more, so I bid five more, my next bid. And if looks could kill, I would have died on the spot. Right, Joel?"

"Yeah, he was scary-looking alright, so was the other characters with him, like a pack of wild dogs. Honestly, they looked to be straight out of the hills. Anyway, they were not happy that dad was bidding. I have wondered, I'm sure you have too, dad, if those people were aware the mare was with foal and knew who the sire was."

When Harrison continued, he said, "It became obvious to everyone there, how obnoxious they had become. I bid two more times, five dollars each time; this guy would only bid one dollar and he's trying to intimidate me by staring at me, hoping I will back down. So the auctioneer asked them to leave, but they didn't budge, so he said, 'Well the next bid has to be at least five dollars or more than the last bid,' So my bid was five dollars, there was no answer from those men, so my bid was accepted. I bought the mare for forty dollars. I would have paid more, but because of those people, there wasn't any other people making bids. When we were leaving with the mare, Joel and I both became concerned the way those people were watching us, like a cat watching a bird, so we were told to go talk to the sheriff. We did, and he sent two men to travel with us on the trip home. And I have never been more concerned before or since that time. I worry, Noah. If you do enter King in the derby, they may come after him. They seem to be under the allusion that King is theirs and I have stolen him. The sheriff told us they are a bad bunch out of Harlan County, rough as they come, so be forewarned!"

"That's an extraordinary story, Harrison. Did you two have some sleepless nights after that ordeal?" Noah asked seriously.

"Yeah," Joel said, grinning. "I could see in my mind, for a long time after that, what those men looked like. You would need to see them for yourself, Noah, to believe it."

Elizabeth set a cup of coffee in front of her husband. He grinned up at her. Harrison made mention that, "It's past time, boys, that we get started working ground for the corn crop." "Mind you, I'm not saying I regret the time we have spent with King. But now, we need to do catch-up work."

Noah spoke up to say, "I'll help with the work and maybe we will get you caught up." He turned with a grin to ask Elizabeth, "Do you have plans for the day that included me?"

"Since this is wash day," she answered, "I will be busy helping Mom, so feel free to do whatever you need to."

"Okay then," Noah said laughing. "I'll help with the farm work to earn my keep."

After they had eaten, the men were ready to finish the chores. Before going to the field, Noah came to Elizabeth where she's helping Ellen clear the table of dishes. He gave her a kiss and said, "I'll see you at dinnertime, honey." But as Noah is ready to follow the other men out the door, this little ball of energy came running into the kitchen, calling, "Daddy," and made a jump for Noah to catch her.

Susie asked, "Daddy, where you go?"

Noah laughingly said, "You little imp, what if Daddy isn't there to catch you?"

"Me fall, but Daddy, you always there to catch me."

"Yes, I am for now, sweetie, but you're getting a little old for it, you know."

"Yeah, K," she said.

Noah told her, "Now Daddy's going to work with grandpa and your uncles outside in the field today. You stay here with Mommy, so be good."

Susie had this delighted look on her face as she asked, "Elizabeth is my mommy?"

Noah laughed again. He said, "Yes, sweetie. Does that make you happy?"

Susie looked at Elizabeth to ask, "You wanna be my mommy?"

"Yes, darling, I do. This is your grandma Ellen and aunt Lily. We are all happy to have you here to live with us."

The little girl clapped her hands. She said, "That good, Daddy?"

"That's great, sweetie," Noah said. "Susie's a lucky little girl, and I am a lucky daddy. Now I must go. I'll see you at dinnertime," and he's out the door.

Ellen, with Elizabeth's help, did the wash and cooked dinner, while Lily played with Susie. The men were getting a good start toward working the ground in preparing it for planting corn. With all four men working together, they will be able to get the corn planted in time to get a good crop, so that is all that really matters. Noah's enjoying working with his hands, so he feels he is doing his share. He and James usually hired men to do the farm work. But Harrison and his sons are hardworking people who enjoy their work, so it spurred him on to do his best work too, although Noah has always been a person to do his best at whatever job or building he starts. They quit work for the day, which was early because they will be taking King to the Jones's farms to compete against their horse, but they did feel good about what they had accomplished this day.

After supper, while the other men were getting chores done, Noah did the milking; David brought the milk in for the women to get it ready and taken to the spring house. Noah and Joel are getting King prepared to go compete against the Jones's horse. Harrison stayed at the table to read his Bible; he has always tried to read, at the very least, a chapter each day, while the women were taking care of their chores in the kitchen.

Now the ladies go to their rooms to change into more presentable clothes to be ready to leave. So after David hitched a horse to the buggy, he came in to tell them Noah and Joel are ready to leave with King.

Elizabeth called to Susie, "Come along, honey, let's go see Daddy."

When the two of them walked out to the buggy, Noah is there to help them be seated, but he will be riding King, along with Little Jo, of course. Joel and David are riding their own horses as well. When they reached the Jones's farms, the three men on horseback were already there. Harrison brought the horse and buggy up to a halt. Noah had already dismounted and walked King, with the dog trotting along, over to the buggy. David and Joel were also there to help the women, with Susie and Lily, to step down.

Noah was leading King but used his free arm to put around Elizabeth. He told her, "I'll see you after this is over." He gave her a quick kiss. "We haven't spent any time alone today, but there is still this evening," he said with a smile that left no doubt what he's thinking.

She returned his smile and said, "We both have been busy, but I will look forward to later."

"I will count on it, honey," he said with another quick kiss. He led King and Little Jo over to where the other men were greeting William and his father, after greeting them himself. Noah stood looking around at the Jones's farms and has to admit Joel was right; this is a very nice setup. Bob Jones noticed the little dog trotting along so closely beside King. He's curious and asked, "Where did the dog come from, and are you not concerned with him being so close to the horse?"

" No," Harrison told him. "Joel and David found the dog in King's stall one day, and he has been King's close companion ever since. He and King seem to have a need of one another."

Bob laughed, "I have never heard a story to top that one. Really, it's amazing."

Noah said, "Bob, I'm impressed with your track and setup here."

Bob said, "Thanks, but you see, we have been in this business of raising thoroughbred horses and training them to run for many years, so we have hopes for our horse here." He ran his hand down the horse's neck.

Noah said, "Well, he's a beauty. May the best horse win. But I am in a good mood anyway, since Elizabeth and I were married yesterday."

"Well now, that is something to feel good about. Congratulations," Bob said. William could do no less than congratulate Noah, but he isn't at all happy about it but didn't let on; he just excused himself.

Susie, who had been standing with Lily, where Ellen is visiting with Sara Jones, came over to Elizabeth now to ask, "Where Daddy go with that big horse?"

Elizabeth said, "Oh, honey, that horse is King. He is big and as black as midnight, isn't he? But he has to be the best-looking horse ever, don't you think, honey?"

"Yeah, he big," was Susie's answer. Elizabeth said, "Well, Daddy is going to ride him to race against that other horse there. Do you see him? But I believe your daddy will win with King, because King doesn't like to lose, you know. He knows he is special too. It must be partly because of the name 'King,' it suits him so well."

Susie said, "Yeah, Mommy, he pretty too."

"Yes, honey, you're right. He's beautiful," and Elizabeth is thinking so is Noah.

William is now walking over to her. He's looking serious as he said, "Elizabeth, Noah just announced that you and he were married yesterday. I missed out with you, which I will forever regret, but I wish you happiness, my dear."

Elizabeth answered, "Thanks, William, that is kind of you."

"Well, take care now," he told her and turned to get this good-looking horse to start walking to the track.

Noah did the same with King; and as they were walking to the starting line, he said, "William, this really is a great track. It will make for a better run, don't you think?"

"Yes, the track is great. But Noah, I would like to tell you, I will always regret the fact that Elizabeth chose you instead of me, but my wish is that you will be good to her."

Noah gave William a steady look as he said, " William, there's no need for you to worry about that. I will always love and treasure my wife. I also would like to reassure you that Elizabeth never meant to hurt you. I can tell you from mine and Elizabeth's experience, a person can't always choose the person whom they fall in love with. It happened at first sight for both Elizabeth and me, but it may not always happen the same for others."

"Thanks for telling me," William told him. "It helps a little anyway and gives me a guide as I go by in my own life."

When everything is set for the race, David reached for the dog. The two horses with their riders are ready. When they were given the signal to start, King is off and running fast as usual. He is way ahead of William and his horse. He came across the finish line with a good lead. Little Jo is barking up a storm.

Bob Jones looked at his watch in disbelief. He said, "Well, Harrison, it's a good thing I am looking at this watch and see the time for myself, or I wouldn't believe it!" The two men compared their watches and the time. Both had two minutes and thirty-four seconds.

Harrison said with a grin, "That is a good run, but he keeps improving with each run, you know."

"Well," Bob said with a sigh, "I see you people have a right to be excited about that horse. I can see there is no reason for us to take our horse to the derby." As William rode up with their horse, Bob said, "Right, son?"

"I think not, Dad. I followed him all the way and there were times when I had trouble keeping King in sight," William said with a chuckle. "I suppose we will be going to the derby to watch King run."

So Noah and the Steele men were pleased with King, and happy Bob and William is willing to take it all in the spirit of horseracing.

* * * * *

On the trip back home, Susie fell asleep; and since everyone else is ready to find their beds as well, Noah carried his daughter upstairs to Lily's room again. Lily walked ahead with the lamp and turned back the covers so Noah could lay the little girl in bed. He pulled off her shoes.

Noah turned to Lily to say, "I hope you know I appreciate this, Lily."

"I know. But you should know I like having Susie here," she told him with a rare smile. *A smile,* Noah thought, *Lily doesn't smile nearly enough.*

He continued to their room to find Elizabeth's waiting for him, and he thanked God again for allowing him to have her for his wife. As he had told William earlier, he will always love and treasure Elizabeth. He walked to her now and took her in his arms and just held her for a few seconds. It felt so good to hold her like this.

"Darlin', do you have any idea how much I love you?" he asked.

"I hope at least as much as I love you, Noah." She's smiling up at him.

He took her face in his hands. "I love you more, you know, but let's go to bed so I can prove it to you."

And he did just that, and it was very late before either of them was able to sleep.

Next morning, Elizabeth is waiting for her husband to return from his run with King. As Noah walked in the room to see his wife sitting up in bed, he was pleasantly surprised and pleased beyond words. Noah came to the bed and started undressing.

"Why are you awake so early, sweetheart?"

"Waiting for my husband, sir, to let him know how much I appreciate him."

"Is that so, wife?" he asked with a tender smile and asked softly, "Do you wish more loving, honey, or just to cuddle?"

"I just wish to feel your arms around me, husband."

"My pleasure, sweetheart," and he sighed deeply as they both fell asleep with her wrapped in his arms, her head cradled between his chin and shoulder.

When they came awake, the sun's up. It was later than usual for them to go downstairs.

Elizabeth groaned, "Oh no, we'll get those looks again this morning."

Noah laughingly asked, "Does it really bother you, sweetheart? It's all good-natured teasing, you know."

"You're right, of course," Elizabeth replied. So when they were dressed, she turned to her husband to say, "Okay, sir, I'm ready now to go face the music."

Noah's still laughing as they came into the kitchen, and when asked why he's laughing, he replied, looking at his wife, with a tender smile, "Oh, it's just a private joke. Right, honey?" Elizabeth returned the smile. Noah grinned, then turned to Harrison to say, "Sorry I'm late, sir. I must have been more tired then usual after King's run this morning."

"How early do you get up to run King?" Harrison asked?

"At four, while it's still cool out, but I still need to cool him down afterwards," was Noah's reply, as he put another forkful of eggs in his mouth.

"Well," Joel said, "in that case, I will be up to help with King in the morning. It shouldn't be all your responsibility, Noah, to train him then cool him down as well."

"I can help too," David offered. "It's a family affair, isn't it?" Everyone laughed at David's little joke.

Then it was time to start the day's work. The men would put in a longer day now. Ellen has a lot planed for today as well. They had been neglectful of the garden. She remarked that there's weeds to chop and more seeds for late planting. So when the inside chores were done, Elizabeth went with Ellen to do the garden work.

They were just finishing up when they heard the sound of a buggy arriving. It was James and Ann with their boys. Lily and Susie had been around front. They came running to the backyard to see who their company is. Susie's clapping her hands when she realized who it is.

James came to pick her up in his arms. He said, "Well, pumpkin, we're happy to see you too. Although I would imagine you're more happy to see the boys, right?"

"Yeah," was Susie's answer. With her arms around James's neck, he gave her a tight hug then put her down. She's already running away. "I play with the boys."

"Well, that never seems to change," Ann said laughingly. Then she turned to Ellen to say, "We just decided to take a chance it will be okay for us to drop in on you all."

Ellen said, "Oh my goodness, yes, Ann, we're happy to see you. Come inside. James," she said, "the men will be in from the field anytime now, so I need to finish up dinner, but Elizabeth can take you out to the front porch if you like."

"We're not here to be a bother," James told her. "I'll just go on the hunt of the men, maybe I can help."

"I'd be happy to help with dinner too," Ann told them. "If you're like me, you can always use an extra hand in the kitchen."

So by the time the men were in for dinner, it's ready to be set on the table. It's a happy time for everyone but especially for Noah. He's pleased to see his brother, James, and the family, and have them here with his wife and her family, since he has been lucky enough to become part of it.

James is telling them how Susie had greeted him. "The little imp couldn't wait for me to put her down after my hug so she can go play with the boys."

Everyone else laughed knowing he's telling the truth, but the way he tells it is funny.

After the meal, the dishes were left for a bit as usual so the ladies could enjoy a rest on the front porch with the men before they return to the field.

James said, "One thing I ask is to see this horse, Noah, you were telling me about and then I will help when you return to the field."

"Well then, let's go see him now. King is his name, by the way, but you need to be respectful of him or watch your step," Noah said as they walked out to the stables. Joel and David walked with them.

Noah said, "You know, James, actually King belongs to Joel here. Because of his unfriendly nature though, Harrison wanted to sell him, but Joel wouldn't give up on King, so Harrison gave the horse to Joel who had taken care of him since he was foaled."

By now they had reached King's stall. As usual, King is being his unfriendly self, so James whistled. "That's a horse that demands attention, alright."

"Yes," Noah replied. "Seriously, yes, I'd say so, and like I told you, don't ever just walk up to him, because he doesn't like it, so be forewarned!" As Noah reached out his hand to let King smell it, the horse walked up to rub his nose against the hand. Noah's talking to the horse all the while.

James said, "I have watched him do this since he was still just a kid, it still gets to me. It always seems to work too."

"Well, I can say for sure that it works with King," Joel told him. "I fed him every day after he was weaned from his mother, but he would never let me near him no matter how I tried. That's the reason why I named him King."

"Well, he certainly is a magnificent horse, no doubt about it," James declared. "You'll get a chance to find out just how magnificent he really is, if you wish,"

Noah's telling James, "We've decided to enter King in the Kentucky Derby. We will need all the help we can get, too, to make it there."

Noah's thinking to himself that he would relay the story Harrison and Joel had told to him this morning at another time. "For now, it's time to get back to work," he said aloud. "But before we go, I wish to show you something that you'll not believe unless you see for yourself, so come to the door where you can see inside the stall."

James was still wary of King but looked over the door to see the little ball of black and white fur curled up on its bed of hay in the corner.

"Well, I agree; I wouldn't have believed it. If King is as unfriendly as you all say, how did the pup get in there?"

"Oh, he just showed up in King's stall one day," Joel told him, "The thing is, King has never had a problem with the dog being in his space. So when we're done in the field," Joel told James, "then we can turn our attention to the training of King."

"Well, if it's okay, I would like to take an active part in the training."

"Sure," Joel replied. "We can use the help."

Chapter  15

J ames and Ann stayed on so James can help with getting the corn planted. Then they can all get serious about getting King groomed for the derby. They also needed to register King, getting a document to certify him—an official record then entered him in the derby.

"I assume we'll need to go to Louisville to do this," Noah's telling everyone at the supper table.

James is too busy eating to follow the conversation though. He said, "Ellen, this has to be the best fried chicken I have ever eaten. Ann, did you watch her while she was frying the chicken?"

Ann laughingly answered, "I did James, but I didn't see her do anything differently than I do, or anyone else I know, as a matter of fact."

Elizabeth said, smiling, "Don't feel bad, Ann. I have watched Mom make biscuits since I was old enough to understand what she was doing, and I still can't make them to taste as good as hers. I firmly believe that Mom just makes everything she cooks with the love of doing it for her family. But I believe I can safely say that's how she does any job, cooking or otherwise. Right, Mom?"

Ellen answered, "I enjoy doing it for my family is all."

Noah responded with, "I believe I told you, James, that Ellen is the best cook you'll ever meet. Now maybe we could get back to what we were discussing, that is, getting King registered for the derby, although it's really a decision for Harrison."

"Noah, you have experience in the horseracing world, so whatever you say we need to do, let's go ahead with it," he replied.

"Well then, who do you suggest goes to Louisville? I'll go if you wish, but I'm not the owner, so we want this all to be legal. So either you or Joel needs to go as well."

"Both Joel and I will go," Harrison told them, "just to be on the safe side. I still have the bill of sale to take with us, and Joel, we can transfer ownership later if that is okay with you."

"There's no hurry, Dad," Joel assured him." Let's go get this business taken care of tomorrow. Then we can get back to training King. But how will we transport him to Louisville?" Joel wanted to know.

Noah is telling them, "We can just take the train from Corbin to Louisville. More than likely, I will need to ride with him. But I think we should all go to the races as a family. And now, the time for the race is getting closer." "James, do you and Ann plan to go with us and take the boys too? Let's make it a fun time."

So the next day, Harrison decided that all five of the men should go to Louisville for the experience. It was that, and more though, while they were at the registry's office to register King. Harrison and Joel recognize the men from the auction in London. So the other men also got a good look at them. When they were finished there, they decided to go get a bite to eat. Noah took them to the hotel dining room where he's in the habit of eating when in Louisville. They had just been seated when it wasn't hard to notice the group of men that came in next. They stand out like a sore thumb.

Noah said, "I have to tell you, boys, those people look like what I've heard mountain men described. They are uncivilized and rules do not apply. So I believe we will need to be on the alert. And I would say they have been watching you all along, Harrison. I realize that's not what you want to hear, but I'm afraid it's true. They must have information on who King's sire is."

Everyone did stay on the alert but was sure those men followed them back to the farm. And that was definitely a concern.

Harrison said, "This is a time I have dreaded for the last three years."

"But Dad," Joel's telling him. "You're not at fault. How could you know how far these men are willing to go to get King? I do believe, and I'm sure you all are aware, we need to stay on guard. So, about the women, should they be told?" Joel asked.

"Yes," Noah replied. "I, for one, think they should. Harrison, James, what do you say?" They both agreed then to tell their women as soon as they reached the farm. But when the men did return to the farm, they found these mountain men had gotten there ahead of them.

When the women were told by the boys, there were strange-looking men outside at the stables.

Ellen turned to the other ladies to say, "Hunt for all the firearms we have in the house." They found one for each of the women, with two extra. Ellen told Lily to keep the children inside the house and not to come out. The three women walked out to ask what these people wanted. But they could only see one of them, so they had to assume the others were already inside the stable. Ellen asked the man left outside, "What are you people doing here on our property, and who is inside the barn?"

"You jest stay outta' this, woman. You have no say in what we do here."

"I believe that I do, mister. This is my home," Ellen told him smartly. "I intend to find out what's going on in the stable!"

She turned to Elizabeth and Ann, and she said, "I've had some experience with men trying to take what they wanted during the war. Now, Ann, you hold that gun on this man. Shoot him if he gives you trouble. Just aim below the stomach to what he holds most dear."

The man's eyes widen. "You's won't shoot me," he said to Ann.

"Don't bet on it, mister," Ann told him. "Now you just sit there on the ground, and don't try anything."

Ellen with Elizabeth made their way inside the stable. They could hear the men talking. They were trying to decide which horse in there is King. When the women could see the men better. *They are a scary-looking bunch alright*, Ellen's thinking. There are three inside the stable, the most mangy-looking men she has had to deal with before, and she doubted they know that soap is used to bathe with. Their hair is too long and stringy. "They are just a dirty bunch of men," she's whispering to Elizabeth.

But then, Ellen spoke up to ask, "What are you people doing on our property?"

"We have a right to be here, woman. You put that gun down now! We'll take what we come fer, and you can't stop us!"

"You, sir, have no right here"—Ellen raised the gun—"now leave!"

The man who seems to be their leader said, "Now, Willy, take that gun away from her."

"Stay where you are!" Ellen warned. "Unless you wish a hole in your stomach."

The young man stopped walking, looked around at the other man to say, "Larry, I think she means it."

So this Larry pushed the other man aside then started walking toward Ellen. She shot at his feet. He stopped, and with a snicker he said, "I knowed you couldn't shoot straight."

"Believe me, mister, if I had wanted to hit your stomach, I would have aimed at your stomach. Now take one more step, you will find that out for yourself!"

The man must have realized Ellen is serious, so he said, "Okay! But I tells you women, we be back, you can count on it." So the three men were leaving, but as they were walking outside with Ellen still holding the gun on them, Harrison, with the other men, rode up. Ellen didn't dare let it show, but she's certainly relieved to see her husband.

Harrison's off his horse quickly as a much younger man would do and is at his wife's side. He reached out to say, "Here, let me take the gun now, dear," but Ellen is holding on so tight. He said, "You're so brave, my dear, but you can let go of the gun now," but he still had to pull the gun loose from her hands. "I'm proud of you and the other women." Ellen is so relieved and was able to smile at her husband.

When they had these mountain men tied up, Noah and James left them to Joel and David then rushed to their wives' side to ask, "Are you two okay?"

"We're fine," they both said as one.

Elizabeth is now telling Noah, "You should have seen Mom, Noah. She made those scary men back down."

Noah said with a chuckle, "I can believe it, honey. Ellen Steele is one of a kind. Now why are you whispering?"

Elizabeth said quietly, "So those nasty men can't hear me."

Noah pulled his wife close. He wanted to laugh but didn't dare. James was asking Ann the same questions. Ann told him pretty much the same as what Elizabeth had said.

James smiled at Noah. "You know, brother, I say we have some scrappy women here."

"Yeah," Noah replied. "They did good, but seriously, James, we have to do better ourselves, to be more protective of them."

"You're right about that," Harrison spoke up. "Our women and children need to feel safe in their own home."

"But Dad," Elizabeth is saying, "Mom told us that she had to protect the farm during the war."

"Well, that's true enough, honey," Harrison is telling them. "This kind of thing happened to people during that time, but that was a different situation and one couldn't always tell who to be more concerned about, the union soldiers or the rebels of the south after food. But the deserters from both armies were the worst. We had to deal with it then. We had no choice in the matter. But this business of these people, we shouldn't have to deal with them! So we need to take them into Corbin and let the law take over. We need to decide who goes and who stays here at the farm. We are not leaving the women and children on their own again."

Ellen is saying, "I do not believe they were able to determine which horse is King."

"That's at least some good news," Noah replied. "But they will not give up on their quest for the valuable horse. They believe in their minds that he was stolen from them. So they will be watching everything we do now."

"Harrison, shouldn't you and Joel go take them in to the sheriff so you can tell your story about what really happened and show your bill of sale?"

Harrison sighed deeply and said, "Yeah, Noah, I suppose you're right. Then you and James stay here at the farm. The boys and I will take care of this group of nasty men"—he chuckled—"as Elizabeth appropriately called them."

"You all deal with them. James and I will hold down the fort here. But first, we'll help you get these men tied up. I believe maybe we should tie them on their horses too."

Joel and David both laughed out loud, they think it's funny, and Joel said, "That's a good idea, Noah, and one I'll remember. Something else I just remembered, where's that little mutt of a dog? He hasn't made a peep." So Joel walked inside the stable on the hunt of the pup and found him on his bed of straw in

King's stall, unhurt. *He must not have felt King was threatened,* Joel's thinking with a smile.

When Harrison and his two sons made it to Corbin to turn the men over to the sheriff, they had the chance to tell the story from the beginning, with the auction, till what happened today.

The sheriff said, "Well, you know, since this isn't the first time we've had problems with this Howard bunch, it won't be the last. They're a clan of people that don't abide by the rules. Their leader, Larry Johnston, doesn't recognize the law either! When he wants something, he will do whatever he needs to do to get it. I have to tell you that Larry being in jail isn't going to change anything either. His followers will continue to try and steal your horse. So stay on the alert! When you go to Louisville, if I were you, I would check in with the sheriff there."

Harrison thanked Sheriff Wilson said good-bye, and they were on their way back home.

Chapter 16

They arrived back at the farm just as Noah and James were finished with the evening chores of milking and feeding and bedding down the animals. Afterwards, they all went in the house for supper then relaxed. After the day they have had, eating and just relaxing is a good thought. But they were all tired, including the children, and ready to make an early night of it.

In the following two weeks, it was a busy time for everyone in different ways. For the men, it was getting the tobacco crop laid aside so it will not perish while they're in Louisville. They didn't have an easy time with it, though, after the rain set in for the next two days. But finally, they were able to get the tobacco patch taken care of. The corn crop will be okay too. Tom Boggs will keep an eye on things along with two hired men. Then they can concentrate on preparations for getting King to the derby. After finding those men here. and the women had to deal with them, when they returned from their trip to Louisville, Noah had decided to write a letter to a racing buddy living in Louisville to make him aware of the situation and let him know he can use his help at the track.

The women need to keep all the washing done up the garden weeded any canning done also. Connie Boggs will come along with her brother, Tom. She will help take the milk home with them or let the hired men have some of it, if they wish. So the day before they were to leave was spent packing. Lily's keeping Susie occupied, which is a big help. So everything that needed to be taken care of was done so everyone had an early night. James and Ann had taken the boys home the day before to do their own packing and make sure everything at their place will be okay while they're gone. The plan is for them to be at the train station early to meet up with everyone else there.

Next morning, as the men were getting King ready to walk out of the stables, here is something they had all forgotten to take into consideration: The little dog trotting along beside King.

Noah climbed in the saddle. He said with a sigh, "Give him here to me. You know he isn't going to let us leave him behind."

Joel reached down to pick the little mutt up and handed him to Noah.

Then Joel and David mounted their own horses and they started the ride to the train station. The little dog was sitting in front of Noah, as if that's where he belongs. When Noah arrived with King, Jo is handed to David.

Harrison is bringing his womenfolk with Susie in the buggy. The Howard bunch, who's easy to spot, are there also, watching King as the horse is being loaded on the train. Noah and Joel will stay in the train car with King, and the dog with them, of course. Harrison, along with James and David, are to stay with the women.

But Susie decided at the last minute she wanted to go see daddy, so she is running toward the train car where Noah is. Elizabeth ran after her to bring the little girl back. One of the clansmen made a grab for Susie. Elizabeth, still carrying the bag with some things for Susie to play with, made a swing at the mangy-looking man with it and hit him full in the face, which startled him so he dropped Susie. The man put his hand to his face. Then Elizabeth reached out pulled the child back behind her, just as the sheriff's deputy walked up. He told the man, "Stand still. You're under arrest, mister. So put your hands up where I can see them."

The man asked, "Why did she hit me?"

The deputy took away the man's gun as he said, "Could be 'cause you grabbed the girl, don't you think?"

"I ain't gonna hurt her, I jest wanted to get her pa's attention."

"I believe you have it now!" the deputy said as Noah came running up. The deputy told him "The woman and child are safe for now, sir. But if I were you, sir, I would keep an eye on these hoodlums. They're a bad bunch. So if you will excuse me, I need to take care of this one."

"Elizabeth, honey, are you alright?" Noah asked, still short of breath. "Susie, are you hurt, sweetie?"

"No, Daddy. Mommy hit the bad man."

"Yes, darlin', I could see that as I was trying to get here." He told Elizabeth, "I heard Susie calling to me. I turned just in time to see the bad man, as Susie called him, grab her. My heart sank then, but you, sweetheart," he said to Elizabeth, "came to the rescue. You were wonderfully brave, honey. But I have to tell you both I aged ten years," Noah told her seriously. "Now," he said, "I will take the two of you to your seat on the train." Then he gave his wife a quick kiss. He picked Susie up. "Now let's find your seats with James and Ann. Of course, Susie will love being with the boys," he said as he tweaked her nose lightly.

"Daddy, you funny. Will you ride with us?"

"No, sweetie," Noah told his daughter. "I need to stay with King, to keep him calm and Little Jo, you remember, the little dog who's attached himself to the horse?"

"Yeah, Daddy. He cute."

"I suppose he is, but now you and Mommy will be safe here, with all the people who love you."

Noah set his mind at ease by taking his wife and daughter inside the train and finding their seats with the rest of the family. Before leaving though, he looked at his brother, James. He said, "Do not let them out of your sight, please."

James gave his brother his solemn promise then said, "Don't worry, Noah. We could see what happened out there when that man grabbed Susie. He's one of that Howard clan, isn't he?"

"From what the deputy said, we have to assume he is. So we now know how far they will go. The only hope is that they're not very good at what they're trying to do. But we need to stay on the alert."

Noah's on his way back to the boxcar where they had loaded King. He's checking out people on his way, but the rest of the Howard clan are easy to spot, so they must already be on the train. But he isn't taking any chances. He returns to where he and Joel will keep watch with King and Little Jo.

Chapter  17

When the train pulled into the station at Louisville, Noah told Joel that he's going to make sure Elizabeth and the rest of the family get off the train safely. When he felt confident that they were all safe, he walked back to help unload King. David has come to help, so again he gets the job of looking after the dog, who he reminded could have stayed at the farm, for which he was totally engaed, for the dog only has eyes for what's happening with King. Since he isn't the only horse on the train, it will take some time to get King off. Meanwhile Harrison will see to hiring transportation. They will need at least two of the large buggies to get them all to the hotel.

King was unloaded, finally, without a problem, for which they all gave a sigh of relief. When Noah had a chance to look to be certain the family is still okay, he noticed a familiar face in the crowd, a good-looking man, and he is so pleased.

Joel asked, "Why are you smiling, Noah?"

"Oh, I see more help for us, someone we can depend on."

Noah, Joel, and David, with Little Jo, walked King over to where the family is waiting for their ride to the hotel. He motioned for his friend to come over. Noah introduced him.

"This is Toby Tyler." All the men shook his hand, and the women told him they were pleased to meet him. Noah had felt certain the fact Toby is black would make no more difference than if he were white, and he was proved right.

But Toby has a surprise for Noah as well. He reach out his hand for this good-looking black woman and a boy of maybe twelve. He introduced them as his family.

He said, "This is my wife, Tansy, and son, Johnny."

Noah laughingly said, "You old dog, Toby. All the time we rode together, you never once told me you have this good-looking woman for your wife and a son this big."

Toby said with a wide smile on his handsome face, "I don't tell everything, I know. You being good-looking yourself, Noah, I didn't want you anywhere near my Tansy. But now you have your own pretty wife, then I guess Tansy's safe with you."

Noah is bent over laughing. He then stood to say, "You old fraud, you're joking and you know it. Now tell my wife it isn't true. I will not have her worried that I'm a womanizer."

Toby grinned then he looked at Elizabeth to say, "I never really expected Noah to remarry. But if you don't already know this, Mrs. Bennett, once Noah asked you to marry him, that meant you're the only woman in his life, and that's for certain." Toby looked at Noah. He grinned again. "Better?" he asked.

Noah laughed, "At least it's the truth," as he gave Elizabeth a quick kiss.

He said, "We best get going now. I see the buggies are here to take you all to the hotel." He turned to Toby to ask, "What about you and your family?"

"We need to find a place."

"Come along with us then," Noah told him. "We have things we need to discuss anyway."

So everyone piled in the buggies, except for the men riding their horses. Of course, Noah's riding King, with the little mutt.

Noah said they would go to a hotel near the track. He's in the habit of staying there in the past. So it was like a parade with the two buggies and four men on horses.

When they arrived at the hotel, Noah said, "I'll get the rooms lined up. Then the women and children can get settled in while we men take the horses to the stables."

For now, Joel and David are out front with the other horses and King. Again, David gets the job of holding Little Jo. Noah rented rooms—one for he and Elizabeth, with a small side room with a curtain for Susie; the same accommodations for all the couples with children, Toby and Tansy with Johnny as well; one room for Joel and David.

"Now, does that take care of everyone?" Noah asked.

"I believe so," Harrison replied. "It's a good thing we have you with us, Noah, to make these arrangements. I haven't traveled enough to know what to ask for."

Noah laughed as he said, "Just remember, you ask for what you want and hope you get it."

After helping his wife and daughter to their room, he was telling Elizabeth not to open the door unless the person gives their name. Then he said, "On second thought, I believe all of you women should stay in one room." After discussing it with the other men, it was decided that it was the best solution—against the wishes of the women, of course, but they would make the best of the situation for now and take it up with their husbands at a later time. Then the men go to take the horses with the two buggies over to the stable, which is just across the street. They would make arrangements for King to have a stall where they will be able to keep watch on him.

But as they arrived at the stables, sure enough, there are four members of the Howard clan already there.

"How many can there be of them?" Joel asked in amazement at these people.

"Who knows?" Noah replied. "We can't let our guard down though. Just try to keep every one of them in your sight, Joel. But really, that goes for all of us."

Noah turned to Toby. "Remember I wrote to you about these people in my letter? There was an incident at the train station in Corbin. One of these men grabbed my daughter, Susie. Luckily, Elizabeth, bless her heart, was carrying a bag. She hit the man with it, and he let Susie go. Thankfully, one of the sheriff's deputies was there, he arrested him. But we do not know what they will try next. These people have been sent to get their hands on King, and there seems to be an endless number of them. But you know, maybe it's a good idea to let them try. Because he would never let them get near him. What do the rest of you think?"

Joel said laughingly, "You know, Noah, that just may be the best way to deal with them. It will serve them right if they get hurt."

So the decision was made to keep watch but make it easy for these men to get to King. They let the stable owner in on their plan. Some of them needed to go take the women and children to get something to eat. Joel and David decided they would stay with King. They had settled him in his stall and made a bed in the corner with straw, just like home, for Little Jo. But the little dog is happy anywhere as long as he is with King.

Joel and David decided to eat later while the other four men walked back to the hotel to take their wives and children to get a meal. And not anytime too soon either, it seems, for everyone is stuck in that room together. When Noah knocked on the door, it was jerked opened without pause!

Noah was saying, "I thought you ladies were told to wait for a name before you opened this door."

Ann was the one to answer. With her hands on her hips, she said, "I would almost pity those men if they were to get in here with these children! Now you men better discuss your idea with us next time."

Noah looked to James, at a loss for words. "She's your wife, James, talk to her."

"Sorry, Noah, but we are all in agreement," Elizabeth told him with an apologetic smile. Ellen and Tansy spoke up to say the same thing. "The only good thing about your idea, Noah, I have to say," Elizabeth told him, "is that we had a chance to get acquainted with Tansy."

"I am not going to be that nice about it," Ann said. "Get us something to eat first, then let us get out of this hotel!"

"Well, okay, that is why we're here," Noah said seriously as he reached for his wife's hand to give it a squeeze. "I apologize, honey. Obviously, we—or I—it was all my idea. And you're right, I wasn't thinking," he said with a tender smile. "Now if all of you are ready, we will go to the dining room to eat."

"Listen to the sweet-talking man," James teased. "Now, Ann, what can I say to get back on your good side?"

"Well, according to Noah himself, he's the one we are supposed to be upset with, but he did apologize nicely. So you, my husband, are still in good standing," Ann told James and she stood on tiptoes to give him a quick kiss.

Noah is still holding Elizabeth's hand and watching his brother's wife kiss him. He turned to his own wife to say, "Looks like I missed out here all around."

"Is that so, husband?" Elizabeth said as she stood on her tiptoes to give him a kiss. He put his arms around her to hug her close.

Susie said, "Daddy, you hug me too?"

Noah smiled at his wife then turned to his daughter. He said, "Come here, sweetie." He picked Susie up, gave her a hug, and said, "Now, let's go eat." Noah set Susie down and took her hand. The others were already ahead of them. He took his wife's hand and asked, "Why was Ann so upset, honey?"

Elizabeth said, "Well, I believe, mind you, it's just my opinion, it was because the boys, with your daughter, were a little rough and tumble."

Noah laughingly asked "When are those two"—he held up Susie's hand—"with this one not playing rough?"

"I don't know," Elizabeth replied. "Maybe it was because we were all closed in that room, Noah. It wasn't fun, you know."

Noah squeezed her hand again. "I'm sorry, honey."

"I know you did what you thought was best for our protection, Noah. I suppose Ann forgot that part."

"I'm so happy you are a more sensible woman, honey," he told her.

"But Noah, you can't always count on any woman being sensible. It isn't in our nature, you know," she said with that cute grin. Noah gave a bark of laughter, and he's still laughing as they walked into the dining room.

But soon, Noah isn't happy at all because the man who came to seat their party said that Toby and his family couldn't be seated.

"Well, in that case, we will all be leaving, and we will all check out of this hotel as well. Am I right?" he asked the others?

Toby said, "Noah, just forget it. We can go."

Harrison said "No way, Toby. We'll all go somewhere else."

The hotel manager came to see what the problem is. He recognizes Noah and came to shake hands. He asked, "Is there a problem here with the seating?"

Noah said, "Yes, as a matter of fact, we were just leaving since our friend here"—Noah put his hand on Toby's shoulder—"was told he and his family wouldn't be seated. If they can't eat here, then we will all leave to take our business to another hotel."

The hotel manager looked at the waiter. He said, "All these people are to be seated, and their meal is on the house. This means you do not get a tip." He then looked at Noah to say, "Sorry, this will not happen again, Mr. Bennett."

They were led to a long table that will seat them all comfortably.

"Okay now," Noah said, "Toby, I can't tell you how sorry I am this happened."

Toby said, "Don't, Noah. You are the best friend a man could have, and we are here together; that is what matters to Tansy and me. We have made new friends and you made that possible."

Ann started clapping, then everyone joined in. She smiled to let Noah know she is no longer upset. Elizabeth reached for Noah's hand and gave him a bright smile to let him know how proud she is of him. The waiter came back with a much better attitude. He's smiling from ear to ear to ask for their drinks order. The women wanted tea, the men ordered coffee, and milk for the children.

Noah said, "The food I have eaten here in the past has always been very good."

The men decided on the steak dinner, the women had mixed orders, and so did the children. But everyone then had either apple pie or chocolate cake. Noah was right, it was good food and good conversation too. It wasn't all talk about racing or farming or women's complaints. They laughed together. Even the children were well behaved.

After they had a good meal and relaxed a little with their wives, Noah said, "If you ladies still wish to get out of the hotel, then you may want to get prepared while we men can go to relieve Joel and David." So that's what they did, but Toby decided he would stay at the stables, "While the rest of you men can spend the day with the ladies," he said grinning.

"Yeah, well I shouldn't be surprised, you wily old fox," Noah teased. "I suppose you, Joel, and David can handle anything that comes up here." So when Joel and David returned, Johnny decided to stay with his father at the stables.

After retrieving the horses with the buggies, Noah and the other men made their way to the hotel to collect the women and children. Then they were on their way to do some sightseeing, maybe even some shopping as well. It's important to keep the ladies in good humor, as they learned earlier today. Noah took them out in the country to see some of the old southern homes and horse farms.

"And the beautiful rolling hills around Louisville is what dreams are made of," Noah is saying, "as Toby can tell you he and Tansy met while working on one of these farms." They were all impressed as they rode around a while longer. Then Noah asked, "Are you people ready to go shopping now?" which, of course, the women all agreed was a good idea.

Chapter 18

They found a place in town where the women can find pretty much whatever they wished for themselves or the children, and there is something of interest for the men as well. Elizabeth had said she would like to find a riding skirt, something her father wouldn't frown on. Noah knew just what his wife is talking about. He took her to where he believes they will find them. They did find the skirts and blouses to match, which Noah was pleased to see. The skirts are in dark colors, so Noah matched a light-yellow blouse with a dark green skirt, the same with shades of blue and brown. Elizabeth is trying to tell him she only needs one skirt, but he isn't listening. Noah is looking around for something more. He found a dress he believes will look glorious on his wife, and he told her so. He insisted she try it on. She finally agreed so they went to ask the clerk to show them the changing room. When Elizabeth had changed into the dress, she has to admit it is a pretty shade of blue, which is her favorite color, of a gossamer light delicate fabric. Also it has a low neckline which she has never worn before, with short sleeves. The fit is perfect though. Noah had said he wished to see her in the dress, so she walked out where he and Susie are waiting. Susie clapped her hands. "Oh, Mommy, you pretty."

Noah said, "She's right, sweetheart. That dress is pretty, but you are beautiful, darlin'. So now we need to find a hat to match. You know, it has become the thing, for women to try and outdo other women with their hats for the derby. So we need to find you just the right hat." He looked down at his daughter and tapped her on the nose. "We need to do the same for you, too, sweetie."

After finding a hat for Elizabeth, as they were looking through the children's clothing, Harrison and Ellen, with Tansy and Lily, are walking toward them.

Harrison said, "We have been looking all over for you people, thought maybe you had left the country, but here you are. So what's up?"

"Noah laughed and said, "As usual, Harrison, you have a way with words." But he told them, "What we have been doing is looking for hats." He looked to Tansy and asked, "Isn't it the thing for the women to choose a special hat to wear for the derby?"

"That's right," Tansy told Ellen. She said, "You ladies really should look for a new hat."

"'That goes for you too, Tansy. My treat," Noah told her with a wink. "And I will not take no for an answer."

"Did anyone ever tell you, Noah Bennett, that you're bossy?" Tansy said to him with a grin.

"Yeah," was Noah's reply, smiling. "Your husband used to tell me that at least once a day. And I think Toby is a lucky man to have you as his wife, Tansy. I also believe he knows that, doesn't he?"

"You know it, Noah," she said with a smile that lights up her whole face.

Ellen is smiling as she said to her husband and Tansy, "Let's go find the most glorious hat in this store," which is so uncharacteristic of Ellen, but she's enjoying herself, which her husband is pleased to see. Just then, James and Ann came walking up with their boys. Ellen asked, "Ann are you looking for a hat to wear to the derby?"

Ann looked at James to ask, "Am I, Mr. Bennett?"

James looked to Noah questioningly, "Is that what everyone else is doing?"

Noah said with a silly grin, "I believe the women are."

"Oh, you're cute," James said.

Noah grinned again but said, "Seriously, it's something women think they need—is to buy a new hat for the derby to outdo all the other women. You will notice that when we get to the track tomorrow."

James turned to his wife to say, "In that case, we need to find you a hat to knock their socks off, sweetheart."

So James and Harrison took their wives, with Tansy and Lily, along with the boys who are in the least impressed, to find the perfect hat. Noah and Elizabeth are still looking for a dress and hat for Susie. They did find a dress that Noah insisted on buying, it is very similar to the one he bought for his wife. All the other women found just the right hat too. James was in the same mind as Noah and bought Ann a beautiful dress that matches the hat they bought her. Harrison told Ellen she, Lily, and Tansy should do the same thing, and, like Noah said, no excuses. So all the women now have new dresses with hats to match.

Chapter 19

When they arrived back at the hotel, the men decided to escort their wives to their rooms. Harrison said he will be staying there while Noah and James take the buggies back and check on how things are going at the stable. As they bring the horses to a halt in front of the stable, there are two men outside the door. Noah looked to James to be certain he's aware something isn't right.

James spoke to Noah in a loud enough voice to carry and be heard by everyone, "I believe I'll go back to the hotel with the wives, brother." So James stepped down from the buggy then starts walking back toward the hotel. He walked in the front and out through the backdoor and makes his way around to the back of the stable, where he found another one of the Howard clan. James walks up behind the man, takes his gun away no problem, and told him to move inside the stable.

Noah walked in the front door so one of the Howard men is following him. When he walked back to King's stall, there are two more men. They are holding Joel, David, and Toby with poor Johnny standing behind his father; all of them at gunpoint.

James is coming in from the backdoor with a wide grin to say, "Look who I found outside here, guys." He told the other two Howards to give Noah and Joel their guns.

The leader, whom Joel called Hank, asked, "You people must want this horse pretty bad to try and take him in broad daylight. Why do you want him so bad anyway?"

"Well," he said, "'cause Larry has wanted that there horse, since his momma was put up for sell. And your pa outbid him."

"Yes, that is correct. Dad did outbid this Larry. But because this Larry didn't want to buy the mare, he wanted to intimidate everyone else to keep them from bidding. And Dad didn't give in to the intimidation and bought this horse free and clear, so this horse belongs to us. What would you people do with King if you were able to steal him?"

"We want that horse to ride him in the race, course," this Hank spoke up to tell them, as if Joel should know that's what their plan is.

"And how would you get around all the rules at the track? King here is registered to run with,"—he pointed to Noah— "Noah here to ride him."

"Then we jest take him, too"—the man pointed to Noah— "with the horse."

Noah said with sarcasm, "Well, I believe I'll have something to say about it. But if you still think you want King, we will let you try to take him. Let's stand out of the way, men. If one of you can get that horse out of the stall, we won't stop you."

Noah and the others moved back. At first they can't believe it, but the man called Hank walked to the stall door. King started snorting and looking wild eyed. Anyone with a lick of sense would have known better, but the man, to his credit, or because he doesn't know any better, continued to open the stall door. As he walked inside, King reared up on his hind legs and pawed with his front hooves, and Little Jo is barking. Then Jo ran at the man, to grab his pant leg, which is such a surprise.

He said, "What's that little old dog doin' there with that big horse anyway? And get him off me," he yelled, and he finally was able to shake Jo loose. He backed out of the stall. He looked at one of the younger men. "You get him, Billy. You ain't fray nothin'."

"Well, jest step back outta my way then." The younger man with a cocky swagger walked in the stall. King did the same as before, but Billy wouldn't stop, he walked toward King, who reared higher this time.

Hank yelled, "Get outta there, man!" But the silly man continued to walk toward the horse. And King came down on the man's head and shoulders. Noah was in the stall immediately talking to King to calm him to give Joel and David time to go inside to pull the man out of the stall. But first they had to get Little Jo off him. The man had been hit in the head.

"He ain't hurt bad, jest a little addled," Hank muttered. When he was pulled out of danger, Joel turned to Hank. He said, "You have to understand that King has a mind of his own. He will not allow anyone he does not want near him in that stall. If you still are determined to take him, you will do it at your own risk. You now know what to expect. Besides, too many people know King belongs to us, that we are here to run him in the derby race tomorrow. And there is nothing you can do to get around that fact. Now David and I will go get the law to come get these men out of our way. But before we go, I would like to know, how did you know that mare was with foal, and how did you know who the sire is?"

"The horse that bred the mare was from Spain, but he was done killed in a rid-in' accident, 'fore his owners could race him here. And they never knowed about the mare bein' bred by that there stallion. So they didn't want to take her back with them. I ain't gonna tell yous how we knowed that."

"I didn't expect you would," Joel answered as he looked at Noah with a grin. Toby went with them to get the man outside to bring in to stay with the others.

When Joel and David arrived at the sheriff's office to explain what was going on, Joel ask, "If they would send men back with us to pick up the Howard clan, hopefully we will be rid of them once and for all." The sheriff's men took the Howard clan away to jail.

So again, Joel and David stayed with King while the other men went back to the hotel to have supper with the family. The agreement was that Noah and James would come back to spare them so they are able to eat then rest for a while. But Noah needs his rest, so Toby decided he would take Noah's turn, "And there is nothing more to say about it," Toby told them. Everything was quiet the rest of the night, so James and Toby rested well enough.

The next morning, Joel, David, and Toby were with Noah when he left for the track with King. Of course, the little mutt wouldn't stay behind. They didn't expect any problem with him though. So everything went great, and since Toby is as familiar with the track as Noah, they both showed Joel and David around. Then Noah wanted to take King for a run while there are a few people around.

When Noah returned, he said, "King is fine, but I have to tell you all that after what happened yesterday, I had my concerns."

"So did I," Joel replied. "That was an unfortunate incident that occurred yesterday." But again they all agree it just proves what a champion King is. After cooling him down, he was put in his stall and given some oats. Now there is time for him and the men to rest before all the commotion to do with the race begins.

Harrison and James let the ladies and children sleep in a little later, before taking them to breakfast. They all had a good night's rest for the first time since that Howard bunch started causing them problems over King. There was no need to start dressing yet for the trip to the track till after the noon meal. But Noah had told them to be at the track by 3:00 p.m. When they were all dressed, everyone looked their best, but all the women, along with Lily, look outstanding, the men thought, in their new dresses, with the hats that had been chosen. Each has a right to be proud. Susie looks adorable and the boys look handsome in their Sunday best.

Harrison and James arrived at the track in good time with their charges. After seeing some of the other hats, the women were well pleased with the hats they had chosen for today. They would hold up against any of the others there. After escorting the ladies with Lily and children to their seats then asking for their wives to save their seats, Harrison and James walked to the stable area to find King's space. When they finally did get there, they found the four men were hard at work getting everything into place for the start of the race.

James asked Noah, "Did you bring your lucky shirt?"

Noah answered, "Course, I did," with a flash of white teeth, with his Irish brogue clearly there. "I always wear it when riding in a race." Noah looked over at Joel to say, "Seriously, its not that I believe King needs luck to win. I don't. It's just something I started years ago and have done ever since."

"I don't have a problem with it, Noah," Joel told him. "You're the one who will be riding King in the race." After Noah had asked about Elizabeth and Susie and the rest of the family, he felt better knowing they are here and safe; now he feels whole again.

James told him that all the women look great with their new hats. "Your daughter looks adorable." Noah had to smile as a proud father.

Chapter  20

N ow it's time for King to be saddled up to start over for the walk in front of the stands. The other men were trying to decide who would be stuck with the dog when Little Jo ran to David and started barking. Joel and Toby had to laugh.

"Aren't you pleased he likes you?"

So with a long surfeiting sigh, David reached down to picked him up. "But," he said, "you are to stay quiet, you understand?" but that part was ignored. The others are trying to hide a smile.

When Harrison and James arrived back to their seats, they told the women that Noah will be riding King past the stands, along with the other horses with their riders. Noah knew before they reached the stands they are to mount their horse and get in line according to their number—six. As he and King are riding by the stands, Noah's looking for his wife. He needed to see her before the start of the race. And then, there he could see her. She is beautiful, standing out in the crowd, with the hat he helped her choose for today. It's black with two pink rosebuds for decoration, not to overdo it. She is looking at him to share a moment, unaware of anyone else. Then he heard, "Daddy, I can see you." Noah lifted his hand to let them know he can see them too. Elizabeth was watching Noah looking for her and Susie. It was as though she could feel him touch her with his eyes. His look is so intense. He is wearing a shirt she hasn't seen before, it's red trimmed in blue and white. He looks so good, but to her he always looks great.

Now they are calling for the horse by number and his rider by name. When King's number, six, was called, then they announced Noah Bennett as his rider, the roar of the crowd is loud. Elizabeth wasn't at all surprised though. Now they were ready to start the race. Joel, Toby, and David with his charge made their way to the infield fence to be sure they have a good view of the track.

When they gave the signal to start the race, the horses were off. The others were jockeying for position while King found a hole and was through it. He was in the lead before the other riders knew what was happening. There is a good distance between King and the closest horse now. The crowd is rooting for him too. So when King came across the finish line, Noah breathed a sigh of relief and said, "Thank you, Lord." The clapping and yelling was so loud it was hard to hear. People were standing up. Elizabeth was having trouble seeing, and poor Susie can't see at all, so James lifted her up to sit on his shoulders, then she clapped her little hands for her daddy.

When Noah made it to the winner's circle with King, Joel, Toby, and David were already there to be on the safe side, since they are all aware King doesn't like crowds. But Noah asked Joel, "Would you get Elizabeth and Susie and bring them back here, please?" Before Joel came back, Little Jo wants down, so David handed him to Noah. Now they are ready to make the announcement of the winning horse and rider.

But Noah said, "My wife is on her way, so just wait a few minutes, please." Then Joel is there with them. Elizabeth and Susie rushed to him. Noah hugged them both and gave his wife a kiss. He turned to the announcer to say, "Okay now, sir." Everyone laughed, then he had to have his picture taken with just King. Then he asked to have his wife and daughter, of course the dog is with him, in the next picture. By this time, the rest of the family are there to take part in the moment, which is great. They also realized that Bob and William Jones with Sara are there as well. So when Noah walked King back to the barn, there's a good-sized crowd to follow. As they reached King's space, Joel and Toby told Noah they would take King to cool him down, and David can put Little Jo in the stall out of the crowd's way. So that left Noah to visit Elizabeth while the other ladies are visiting with Sara Jones. She had decided to come at the last minute, she's telling them. Noah is talking to James and some other men.

When someone called to Noah, he knew that voice. She asked, "You didn't forget about me, did you, Noah?" He turned to look at her. She is still a very beautiful woman with her red hair, but her looks are more flamboyant, while Elizabeth has a flawless beauty inside and out that seems to glow.

"Kate Nelson," he said casually. "How are you?"

Noah is thinking there was a time when just thinking about her could make him want to be with her. But there is nothing now, he hadn't even thought of her again, since he had met Elizabeth.

Kate was asking, "Why haven't I heard from you, Noah?" He turned to look at Elizabeth, then turned back to Kate. He gave a nod toward his wife as he said, "See the blond beauty over there? She and I have been married now for a little over six weeks. It has been the happiest time of my life."

"But Noah," Kate is saying, "you told me you were never going to get married. You didn't think you were cut out for being a husband." She gave a sulky look.

"Yes, that's how I felt before I met Elizabeth. Now it has been good to see you, Kate, but if you will excuse me now, I wish to be with my wife and family." He tipped his hat and walked away.

William Jones had been standing nearby. Kate turned to see him there. She called, "Hey there, handsome, how would you like to show me around the track?"

William was looking at the most beautiful woman he had ever seen, but much too forward for his taste, so he answered, "Sorry, ma'am, but I am with Mr. Bennett and his party." He did as Noah had—tipped his hat, said good day, then walked over to where the others were visiting.

* * * * *

But Joel had just come to bring King to his stall, and when the horse walked in there, the first thing he did was to go to Little Jo to give him a nudge. They both seem to be relieved the race is over.

William called to Joel. He said, "You people sure know your horses."

"Yeah," Joel replied. "Didn't King have a great run?"

"He sure did, and Noah is a great rider too," William said with a wide smile. "I would say the two of them are unbeatable."

"And you would be right," Joel said laughing. "Come on, let's join the crowd." As they walked over to the others, William could see Noah with his arm around Elizabeth. She is looking up at him, laughing; he is looking at her with tenderness. He's thinking, *I can see for myself that Noah really does love her and she loves him.* William is thinking he will just have to accept it as fact. *But I will always love her, because she is such a special person.*

As he walked with Joel up to the group, Elizabeth smiled at him as she said, "It is so good to see all of you here, William. It was a pleasant surprise to see your mother too."

"Thanks, Elizabeth," he replied with a smile. "The fact she knew you folks would be here was the deciding factor," he said with a chuckle. "Well, it's good you all could be here too," she told him.

"You know what would really be great?" Noah is saying, "If you and your parents can join us at the hotel dining room for a celebration dinner."

Joel said, " Noah, that's a great idea. How about it, William? Where are you and your folks staying tonight?"

"We hadn't really decided to stay," William answered. "But let me ask Mom and Dad. I believe they will enjoy being with your family to celebrate." He walked over to where his father and Harrison Steele are talking.

William said, "Excuse me, but Dad, we have an invitation to celebrate King and Noah's win at their hotel."

"Why, that's a great idea," Harrison told Bob. "You and Sara do come, we will have more time for our discussion there."

Bob laughed, "Then said I am sure Sara will be delighted. Let's go ask her," and he led the way to where their wives are.

Sara turned to say, "I am so pleased you talked me into coming with you and William, dear."

Bob asked with amusement in his voice and a twinkle in his eyes as he said, "Then would I be right to say we will be happy to join these good people for a celebration dinner at their hotel?"

"Oh my, yes, Bob, I think that's a great idea," Sara replied.

Chapter  21

So Harrison and James were able to get their charges all together so they can leave for the hotel. William, along with his parents, Bob and Sara, were ready to leave as well. Noah and the others were getting things together to leave with King, but they will wait till most of the crowd has left. So they would all meet back at the hotel. Everyone wanted to wash up. The Jones family, as luck would have it, was able to get a room. The agreement was to meet in the dining room in a short while. Ann was elected to go to the management of the hotel as soon as they returned, which gave them enough time to prepare for a surprise celebration dinner. With wine to do a toast to Noah, Ann chose steak, baked chicken with fresh green beans, mashed potatoes, a choice of salads, a chocolate cake for Noah, but a choice for the others who would rather have pie.

✳ ✳ ✳ ✳ ✳

Noah knocked on the door.

Elizabeth asked, "Who is it?"

"I am the man who is going to show you a great time tonight, sweetheart."

The door opened wide. Elizabeth walked into his arms. "Oh, Noah, I am so proud of you." She kissed his lips then all over his face.

Laughing, he pulled her to him to say, "Have I told you today how much I love you?" as he stepped inside and pushed the door closed behind him then pulled her in his arms again to kiss her deeply. Then he just held her close to him for a few seconds. "I suppose I should wash up and change clothes so we can go meet the others." But he noticed Susie is already asleep. "Oh, poor baby, it's surely a shame to wake her." Noah's asking, "What should we do, honey?"

"Well, maybe Lily will stay with her, and more than likely Bobby and Jimmy are tired too. I'll go to Mom and Dad's room to ask, while you change."

He gave her a quick kiss. "You know, sweetie, I wish we could just stay here ourselves," he said with a sigh. "But go talk to Lily," he said with a smile and with a little pat on her backside.

She returned his smile and said, "Yes, sir."

When Elizabeth asked Lily about staying with the children, she said, "Yes, I wasn't really looking forward to going to the dining room anyway."

"Oh, thanks, Lily. We can have food brought up to our room. How does that sound?"

Lily answered, "That will be fine. Will I need to come to your room then?"

"If you don't mind," Elizabeth said. "Susie is already asleep. It seems a shame to wake her, and Lily," "I hope you realize just how much we appreciate you for doing this for us."

"I know," Lily told her, "I agree we shouldn't wake Susie."

So Elizabeth walked down the hall to James and Ann's room to ask if they wish for their boys to stay with Lily. James looked to Ann for an answer. She said, "They're tired too," so she ask the boys who agreed readily they would just as soon stay with Lily to eat in Uncle Noah's room; sounds like fun. So the food was ordered for the children to be brought to Noah's room.

When James and Ann came to drop their sons off, James reminded them, "This isn't a party, so behave for Lily." They promised they would. Then Harrison and Ellen came with Lily. Toby and Tansy were right behind with Johnny, who had decided to stay with Lily as well.

"So it will be just us grownups," James teased. "Do you all think we can handle it?"

"We are willing to try," Toby said, laughing, as he took Tansy's hand, "Right, Tansy girl?"

"I am willing," she answered.

Everyone else agreed and headed for the dining room where William and his parents are already waiting.

Noah said, "Sorry, folks, if we kept you waiting. But there was a need for us to make arrangements for the children. Now I don't believe you people have been properly introduced to my good friend Toby, who was a great help with Joel and David to handle King, and this is his beautiful wife, Tansy."

William said, "I'm pleased to meet you, Toby," as he was shaking hands with him. Then he turned to Tansy, took her hand, and said, "It's a pleasure to meet any friend of the Steele family."

Bob and Sara were behind him to meet them as well. After they were seated by a waiter, another waiter came to take an order for drinks—as usual, tea for the women, coffee for the men—while other waiters came out with trays full of meats and the rest of their meal.

Noah asked, "What is this?"

Ann spoke up to say, "Noah, this is your celebration supper, so enjoy."

David and Joel had decided to join them, so David stood up and started clapping. Then everyone else followed his lead. The diners at the next table asked, "What's the occasion?"

David announced, "This gentleman happens to be Noah Bennett, who won the derby race today, of course, with the horse King. And this lovely lady here is his wife, Elizabeth." He asked them to stand. "She is my sister, and there are our parents, Harrison and Ellen Steele; my brother, Joel; Noah's brother, James, with his wife, Ann." David pointed to the others. "These are friends." There is a loud cheer and more clapping. Some of the people had been at the race and were pleased to meet Noah personally. But then they let them enjoy their celebration dinner.

After they had finished the meal, the cake had been presented to Noah, "Who happens to have a sweet tooth, everyone should know," Ann teased. Then they all had cake or pie with coffee or tea. Then the wine was brought out to make a toast.

Noah said, "I don't know whose idea this was, but it was a good one. I thank you all though. It really means a lot, you know."

Ann spoke up to say, "I did it at the request of your wife, Noah. Along with everyone else, we wanted you to know how proud we are of you and King."

"James," Noah teased with a grin, "I will let you give your wife a hug and a kiss for me."

"I appreciate that, brother," James said with a crooked grin that's so much a part of him. Everyone else had a good laugh. "But no kidding," James spoke up to say, "that was a great run, Noah, that you and King took."

Noah grinned then said, "King deserves all the credit. He is a true champion. Everyone else agreed King is a champion."

But Joel reminded him, "We know the truth, Noah. You are the reason King ran that race and won today."

"Thanks for saying so, Joel, and I must say the meal—the celebration—was great."

Noah is saying, "But the family and friends are awesome." He gave a toast to them.

After everyone has finished their meal, Noah said, "Now I am afraid it's time to bring this party to a close. The waiters are waiting to clear the table," he said, "and you should know, our day"—he included Joel, David, and Toby—" started early." Everyone had to laugh but they knew it to be true.

So everyone is ready to call it a day. The Jones family went to their room while Joel and David were heading back to the stables to check on King. As for the others, they will go to Noah's room to get their children. They were all following Noah and Elizabeth up the stairs. Just as Noah came to the top step, though, he can see two men standing in the hall near his and Elizabeth's room. He put out his hand to Elizabeth and told her and the others to stay back, and told them about the two men.

"James, would you go back downstairs to come up the back way to the other end of this hall? We will see if they are a threat to us. Come to think of it, Toby, would you mind going to the stables?"

"I'll go with Toby," Harrison told Noah.

"Good," he said. "But first, would you take the women back to the dining room for now and alert the management that we may need help?" With the women taken to safety, Noah felt relieved.

When Noah could see James coming from the other end of the hall, he started walking slowly down toward his room. When he reached the door, the two men came walking toward him.

Noah asked, "Is there something you men wanted?"

One of the two men spoke up and said, "Yeah. You Noah Bennett?"

"That's me," Noah told them.

"You's come with us," the man replied.

"Why would I do that?" Noah asked.

"'Cause we tell you to."

James spoke to say, "But I believe the man is trying to tell you he is not going anywhere with you!"

The other man, who looked to be younger, turned to James. He said, "You mind your own business, man."

"But this is my business, man! This happens to be my brother. You two people are not taking him anywhere, do we understand one another? You two are part of the clan of idiots that have been trying to get your hands on the horse King?"

The two men both looked dumbstruck but said, "We have a right to that there horse. We aim to have him, too."

Noah told them, "We will try again to tell you, people, one more time, the horse King was bought and paid for. He is registered to Harrison Steele and his son Joel. That tops any belief that you people have a right to him. If you happened to get your hands on King, there isn't going to be anyone to take care of that horse or your women folk."

"Well, that there is why we be takin' you," the second man said without a blink of an eye. *He's the younger of the two men, but evidently not any smarter,* Noah's thinking to himself, then he asked, "You seriously believe that I would let you take me away from my family, don't you?"

"Well, I guess maybe we'll jest try again, but yea, we'll have you. Come on, Cal, let's go."

So the two brothers James and Noah stood watching the two sleazy characters skulk down the hall.

James turned to say, "You know, Noah, that bunch of idiots are the most single-minded and sneaky, unscrupulous skunks we have ever had to deal with, wouldn't you say? But do you have any idea what to do about them."

" Not a clue!" Noah answered as he turned to look at his brother. "Can you even imagine why they believe I would let them take me to care for King?"

"The way those people think is beyond comprehension," James said disgustedly.

"You hit the mark on the head, brother," Noah replied with a chuckle. "Now I believe we best go let our wives and the others know that we are okay for now."

Noah and James walked into the dining room, not knowing what to expect there. But both their wives came rushing to their husbands who caught them in open arms.

Elizabeth said, "Oh, Noah, I was so afraid. And why do I get the feeling you two men are unconcerned?"

Noah hugged his wife and smiled down at her with tenderness. "To be honest, honey, I don't know what to think. Those people, as James said, are single-minded in their determination in taking King."

"Yeah. Now they have their minds set on taking Noah as well, with King!" James said as he caught the frown on Noah's face. But he said, "Anyway, Noah, you know as well as I, we all need to be on the alert. So you can frown at me if you want, but we will do what needs to be done to keep you safe."

Elizabeth hugged Noah then turned to James to say, "Thank you, James," then turned to her husband. She said, "Noah, I know that you would like to shield me. But I want to be aware of everything where your safety is concerned, okay, sweetheart?"

Noah grinned down at Elizabeth, and with a flash of white teeth, he said, "Darlin', you may have any wish come true if you continue to sweet talk me that way," then he gave her a quick kiss.

James said, "Now stop that lovey dovey stuff, you two. This is serious business."

Noah gave his brother a grim look. "Believe me, James, I realize the seriousness of the situation. But how do you deal with people like this Howard bunch? And their determination to steal King? In their minds, they have a right to him. Until we can get them all locked up or somehow convince them we are just as determined not to let King go. Now we need to go check on our children."

"Oh my God! You're right, Noah." Ann turned to James. "Let's go get our boys and hope they're okay."

"Ann, honey," James is trying to calm his wife's ruffled feathers. "Honey, think for a second here. If we thought for one minute they were in danger, we would be with them now. But there's no need for them to be upset, right?"

"I'm sure you're right?" Ann reluctantly agreed. "But let's go get them now."

Noah and Elizabeth agreed. After they had checked to be certain the children are safely asleep, Noah asked James to stay with the women and children, because he wished to go check on the other men at the stable.

So Noah left immediately for the stables. He found the same two men hanging around outside the front door. Noah walked up to the one who did most of the talking at the hotel.

He said, "Sooner or later, you people will have to realize that we are even more determined not to let you have our horse King. Can't you understand me?" he demanded.

The two men looked at him with a blank look. Then the one doing their talking said, "We'll have you and that there horse." That is the only comment the man made. Noah just threw up his hands and walked inside the stable.

Noah walked back to King's stall. He asked, "Is everything okay here?"

Harrison was the first to come to his feet. He said, "No trouble yet, Noah. We've not seen hide nor hair of that Howard bunch so far."

"Well, let me tell you all the same two men that was up there at the hotel, and they were there to abduct me. They are outside here now." He pointed toward the front door. "Believe it or not, those idiots have this insane idea to take me to control King! The real insanity of their plan is they believe, just because they tell me that is what they want, I will let them take me away from my family. How do you deal with such ignorant people, Harrison? Do you have any ideas? 'Cause I'm at a loss here."

"I have to tell you, Noah, I am just as concerned as you. They live up there in those hills, where maybe they don't get enough sunshine," he chuckled. "But seriously, these people make their own rules. I do also believe they know better. But they like to push people to the limit just to get their way. We can see that they're not very good at stealing King. Because of their attitude and by their ignorant way of dealing with other people outside their own clan, or the hill country for that matter, I have the feeling they're waiting for reinforcements."

Noah replied, "I don't like the way they have of doing whatever they believe will get them their objective."

Joel stood to say, "I understand, Noah, and I sympathize with your concern for your family. We all need to be concerned. Maybe it's time to get the law involved again?"

"I agree," Toby offered his opinion in the conversation. "What makes these people dangerous is they're sneaky skunks, but wily as a fox too. I believe, Joel, you and Harrison are the two people to go talk to the sheriff. Make him aware of everything that's been happening with that Howard clan."

"I'm sure you're right," Joel said. "So I'll go with you, Dad."

Harrison said, "We may as well go now and get this over with, that is, if we plan to leave for home tomorrow."

"I'll go too," David told them.

So the three of them rode horses even though Harrison isn't fond of riding. He's never been able to get comfortable in the saddle, so he has always kind of envied his sons a tiny bit for their natural ability to ride a horse.

Chapter  22

When they reached the sheriff's office, the deputy on duty told them, "Sheriff Wade had gone home already, and he didn't want to be disturbed unless it's an emergency."

Joel's aggravated enough to say, "This is an emergency, sir. These hill people have been trying to steal our horse King. The same one"—Joel stressed—"that won the derby today. They have tried twice already, even tried to abduct Noah Bennett who rode King in the derby. They have learned he is the only person who can manage the horse. And believe me, they are a very determined bunch. Besides, there seems to be an endless number of them too. Remember, you have some of them in jail here now. There are more of them hanging around the stable door now. We believe they're waiting for others to come. We wish to make the trip back home to Corbin tomorrow. Now, will you get word to the sheriff?"

The deputy gave Joel a long searching look. Then he finally said, "Sounds like an emergency to me. We'll get more men together, be out there right away."

"If you don't mind, we'll wait to ride with you," Harrison told him, "and please hurry."

They did get busy. The deputy sent word to the sheriff and to other people that they needed help. When they arrived back at the stable, there is more of the clan there. Joel pointed them out to the deputy. When Joel, David, and Harrison, along with the deputy and his men, dismounted, they walked to the stable door where the Howards are standing.

The deputy said, "You men are to come inside with us." He gave them no chance to disagree.

Well, it's not hard to tell the Howard clan are not happy. The one who usually did the talking asked, "Why'd you tells us to come with you?"

The deputy said, "Because we have reason to believe you people are here to steal the horse King, the one that won the derby race today. We intend to prevent that from happening, do you understand?"

"Wed's has every right to that there horse," the Howard man said. "Larry claimed that there horse 'fore he be born."

"And how did you do that?" the deputy asked.

"'Cause Larry wanted him," the man replied.

"You people seem to think simply by just wanting something, that gives you a right to take it."

"Yeah, ain't that the way ever-body is?" he asked.

The deputy had the same look of concern the rest of them felt. He motioned for his men. He said, "Bring this idiotic bunch with us inside the stable."

They could hear voices and knew there were more of them back at King's stall.

Joel motioned for the deputy and his men to stay here, "While Dad, David, and I go around and come in from the backdoor. More than likely, they have someone placed there."

They did find another man at the backdoor. These people never change, and it wasn't hard for them to get the upper hand and take his gun away. So when they marched that one inside, Joel called to the deputy to bring the others back here.

Noah said, "We're certainly pleased to see that you brought the deputy with others to take this ignorant bunch of people to jail." Then he turned to the one that seemed to be their leader. Noah asked, "What is your name, sir?"

"My name be Karl."

Noah's thinking this man looks to be smarter than some of the Howard clan, but maybe not, so he said, "Okay now, Karl, I would like to try and reason with you people one more time. And I believe I have asked this question before, but anyway, I'll ask again. When all of you men end up in jail, who is going to be left to take care of your womenfolk and children? Or do you even care? Is stealing this horse more important than keeping your family safe? Make no mistake about it, if you were to get your hands on King, we would bring an army up in your hills to root out every last one of you. I have an idea you would prefer not to have the law up there, am I right?" The look on their faces is laughable.

Finally, this man Karl said, "Larry weren't thinking 'bout that when he made up his mind to have that there horse."

One of the younger clansmen who could look halfway ordinary if he took a bath occasionally spoke up. "Dam Karl, I don't care no more what Larry says, I ain't gonna leave my Berty, she can't do nothin' for herself without me."

So Karl turned to say, "Well, if in you's people tells us you's will stay down here, wed's will stay up there in our hills."

Noah reached out his hand to the man. He said, "It's a deal." This Karl stood there staring at Noah's hand as if it's a foreign object. Noah said, "If we shake hands, then that's the same as signing a paper—a promise."

Then the man's face seemed to clear as if he understands now. He reached out his dirty hand. Noah didn't hesitate to shake it to seal the deal.

"Now, mind you," Noah said, "that if you promise to leave our horse King and me alone, our families as well, then we will stay away from your mountains. Is that a deal?" The Howard man turned to the others again. He said, "You all knows what it means if they comes fer us up there in the mountains, no horse is worth that, do you' all say it so?"

"I say, yeah," another younger one of the bunch said. "I ain't gonna leave my Maggie to starve neither"—he looked around—"what bouts you all?" They all were shaking their head yes. They wanted to know, "Can we all go home now?"

The deputy said, "If these people are willing to forget that you have been trying to steal their horse and frighten, you know, scare, their womenfolk, then it's okay with me. I'm certain it will be okay with the sheriff too. He may even let your family that's already in jail go as well. But be sure you remember that if we find out that you try again to steal that horse,"—he pointed toward King—"then we'll put you all in jail and throw away the key. Now get out of here, go straight back to your mountains, you hear!"

It's almost comical watching them falling all over each other in their rush to leave while shaking their heads yeah to the deputy as their floppy hats are falling off every where. As they run back to get the hats, they are looking as if they're afraid they'll be told they can't leave after all. Then finally they are all gone.

But Noah and the others, including the deputy and his men, were all too relieved to laugh. Noah wanted nothing more than to be in bed with his wife, so he said to the deputy, "I hope you realize, sir, how much we appreciate your help with those people. We had almost given up on making any headway with them."

"Yes, I certainly understand how you would feel that way, sir. The Howard clan live by their own rules. I'm sure you realize the only thing that did get through to them was hearing we may come up in those hills after them. Like the one man said, that's something they forgot about when they decided to steal your horse, but now I feel certain you have heard the last of them, so we'll be on our way."

Now with a deep sigh of relief, Noah said, "I'm going back to the hotel." Everyone else agreed they were ready too. All the men made their way back to the hotel and straight to Noah's room to tell the women that any and all threats from that Howard clan is over. So now they can relax and go to their own bed. After going to their room, Noah had the best night's sleep he had had for a long while now, with Elizabeth wrapped in his arms. It feels so good just to hold his wife. Unfortunately, there isn't time for more, but when they are back home, there will be plenty of time for the loving and to make plans for their future.

* * * * *

Now in the morning, it's still early, but he is awake and it's time to start the day, so Noah threw back the covers. Now with Elizabeth still sleeping, she snuggled closer to him. He had to smile. She looked just like a little girl, curled up like that. He leaned over, gave her a kiss, and he said, "Darlin', I need to go feed King and get him ready to travel. When I return, we will go eat, okay?" But she only snuggled closer, so Noah turned her over. He bent over to give Elizabeth a kiss sure to wake her, and it did bring her arms up around his neck. She pulled him closer.

He groaned and said, "Oh, honey, I wish that we could stay in bed. But there isn't time, but when I do get the chance, I want to do it right."

"Well that certainly gives me something to look forward to, sir," she told him, still a little sleepy. But she also said, "I'll get dressed and see that Susie is too. I'll have everything packed when you return, honey."

Noah gave his wife another quick kiss, rolled out of bed to get dressed, then he left.

* * * * *

Noah's sure that the other men would already be at the stable ahead of him, and he was right, but they didn't tease him. They are just happy to be getting ready to make the trip home. So they all made themselves busy and did what needed to be done. Then they all walked back to the hotel to take the ladies and children to breakfast. After talking it over with Harrison and the rest of the family, Noah had asked Toby and Tansy to come back to the farm with them. He told Toby, "We can use your help if you're willing," which both Toby and Tansy were happy to accept, because they had grown to like the Steele family.

Chapter  23

The trip to the train station was all done this time without a hitch. King is more comfortable traveling now, and besides, he has Little Jo with him for company, so they let him be, and everyone took a seat inside the train.

Noah turned to Elizabeth to say, "It feels so good, honey, to be able to sit here beside you and Susie, to relax for a change." He lifted Susie up to sit on his lap. He asked, "Did you enjoy yourself, sweetie?"

Susie answered, "Yeah, Daddy, I see you ride King, that fun for you Daddy." She's wrinkling her nose in the cutest way so Noah couldn't help but give her a hug.

He laughed and said, "Yes, I suppose it was fun, honey." He put his arm around Elizabeth to ask her, "Did you enjoy yourself, sweetheart? We really haven't had a chance to talk much since we left home. We have plans to make when we are back at the farm, you know."

"What kind of plans," Elizabeth asked?

"About our future, darlin'. Don't you think it's a good idea?"

"Of course," she's smiling as she said. "I realize that is something we need to discuss. But Noah, you need to know I don't like for things to change, I am content now, but I also wish to please you, husband, so, yes, I agree we need to talk."

Susie is beginning to squirm. Noah asked, "What is it, honey?"

"I go sit with the boys." She pointed to Bobby and Jimmy. So Noah put her down with the usual pat to her little bottom.

He watched her climb on the seat between the boys, with Lily in the other seat, then he turned to his wife with a small smile and a bit of unhappy truth as he said, "Those boys rate higher on her list than I do."

"Oh, I don't believe so, honey. Her daddy still takes first place, you should know that."

He's looking at her mouth. "You know, it's becoming a habit for you to use endearments. I like it," he said in a husky voice. "I sure wish we were alone."

"Well, you're not alone, brother," James teased with a grin. Noah looked around for the first time. He realized where everyone else is sitting: Harrison and Ellen are sitting with Bob and Sara Jones, no surprise there, and Toby and Tansy are in the seat behind them, with Johnny in the seat across from them. William is sitting with Joel and David in the next two seats in back of them. Everyone seemed to be enjoying the ride. Noah turned to look back at James, who is sitting in the seat across from them.

He said, "It feels so good not to be always on the alert."

"Yes, I agree," James replied. "Now we can get back home to a normal life."

"We will need to do some work to catch up, I'm sure," Noah responded. "But we would like to plan a party to celebrate our marriage along with the derby win." He turned to look at Elizabeth who is now sound asleep. She has her head on his shoulder. He smiled down at her. She must be more tired than he realized. Then the thought came to him, she may have another reason to be tired. But surely, it's too soon. The thought of her being with child caused fear to grab at his heart—fear for his wife. Noah knew he would want to die if he lost Elizabeth. He could never imagine life without her now. He pulled her close. If it's true that she is with child, he would start praying every day now for God to keep his wife and child safe. The next thing he knew, James was calling his name, so Noah came awake.

James said, "You must have been tired too. It isn't normal for you to fall asleep, brother."

Noah stretched his arm. Elizabeth had been lying on it, so it has gone to sleep. She was trying to get comfortable again, so he pulled her back against his shoulder. James just smiled at his brother. He is so glad that Noah is finally happy. He had been a little concerned back there when he had seen that woman Kate Nelson talking with Noah after the race. He had known Noah had a thing for her once, but he didn't seem to have a problem walking away from Kate. He walked straight to his wife Elizabeth. James had breathed a sigh of relief then.

"What are you thinking so hard about, James?" Noah asked. "You have been staring at me for the past few seconds."

James looked surprised. "I didn't realize I was doing it, brother. Just relieved, I suppose. We're almost back to Corbin. We won't have much time to talk, so let us know when you have made arrangements for your party, okay?"

"Sure thing," Noah replied.

He realized James must have been the only one not to fall asleep. Both wives, all three of the children, with Lily, were still sleeping. James was right about Corbin being close, because the whistle is starting to blow. Now the train is slowing down to a stop at the Corbin station. Noah had waited to wake Elizabeth. She had been sleeping so peacefully, he almost hated to wake her now, but it's time. He leaned over, kissed her lips, and he didn't rush. When he raised his head, she is smiling up at him and said,

"What a wonderful way to wake up, honey. Are we home yet?" she asked with a grin.

"Well, we are now in Corbin," Noah told her. "We made good time so we can go to the hotel to eat supper. How does that sound? And do you think your parents will go for it?" he asked. "What about you and Ann?" he asked James.

Ann had awaken a while back so James looked at his wife to ask, "Are you in a hurry to get home, honey, or could you eat another meal out?"

"Such a nice way to ask, honey," Ann teased, "but yes, I would like to eat before we leave for home."

Noah turned to ask Harrison and Ellen if they are agreeable to go to the hotel for supper before leaving for home. They said yes.

Sara Jones said, "I think it a good idea. How about you, Bob?" who grinned at Noah and said, "It looks like we'll be staying too."

Of course, it was fine with Joel, David, and William. Toby said, "It's fine with us, Noah. Besides, we're riding with you all." Everyone had to chuckle. "But it sounds good, don't you think, Tansy girl?" She agreed. They had taken a nap too. So they all had a good meal at the hotel dining room. Now, they are ready to head for home.

So the men helped their women in the buggies then untied their horses, mounted, and was headed west to the Steele farm. James and Ann went east on their way home. The Jones family rode along with the Steele party till they came to the turnoff for their farm where they said good evening to all. Now it's just a couple more miles, and they were at the Steele farm. It seemed everyone was in agreement it's good to be back home again.

When Noah helped Elizabeth step down from the buggy, he was extra careful and he wanted to know if she is tired. "Maybe you would like to lie down for a nap, sweetheart?"

"But Noah," Elizabeth chuckled, "I had a long nap on the train, remember? So, no, honey, I'm fine, but thank you anyway."

"If you are sure, then I will go see about helping to get King settled and help with the chores, but I shouldn't be gone long."

Elizabeth is watching her husband leave and thinking that he's acting strange.

Chapter  24

Ellen's happy to be home and now since Noah had ask Toby and Tansy, to come back to the farm. With everyone's agreement for them to come here, and their son Johnny. To work here and help with King. Ellen is showing Tansy around. She showed her to the other bedroom downstairs, where she and Toby will sleep. It's next door to her and Harrison.

Ellen is telling Tansy, "This room is where each of our children slept till we thought them old enough to sleep upstairs. And we'll need to work on a bed for your Johnny, okay? There Is the room on the third floor with a bed, but it's up to him. If he doesn't like it, then we will come up with something else."

The two of them had hit it off like a house on fire. It's the same with Harrison and Toby.

Ellen told Tansy that, "It's going to be so good having you all here. I hope you'll feel the same. Do you think you will like living here, Tansy?" Ellen asked as she is showing her the herb basket.

"I am sure we will," Tansy responded. "Toby has always enjoyed working with Noah. And now he and your Harrison seem to get on so well."

"Good," Ellen said and was pleased to hear Tansy say that she and Toby both know something about the use of herbs for healing too. "Oh, I am so pleased," Ellen told her new friend.

Lily was entertaining Susie, so Elizabeth is watching her mother and Tansy discussing the many uses of herbs. When they realized she is there watching them and smiling, Ellen said, "Oh, Elizabeth dear, did you hear Tansy say she and Toby both know how to use herbs for healing? Isn't that great?"

Elizabeth walked into the room to say, "I think it wonderful that you all have found each other."

"You do realize," Tansy said, "that your husband brought us all together. That man of yours is amazing. But then, I'm sure you already know that, don't you, honey?"

"Yes, I know Noah is one of a kind. I also know he can be a little bit,'—she measured with her thumb and finger—"arrogant, though. But I love that about him, too, because he means well. Was there anything you wish for me to do, Mom, before the men come back to the house?"

"No, dear. Why don't you go sit on the porch a while?" Ellen replied. Then she and Tansy went back to discussing the herbs. So Elizabeth walked out on the porch and sat on the swing, and before long, Noah is there to sit beside her to give her a hug.

"This is great, honey. It's so peaceful here after all the problems with the Howard bunch. And I have a lovely wife to enjoy it with, what more could a man ask for?" Elizabeth snuggled against him. He pulled her close, and this is how the others found them as they came to sit on the porch.

"Looks like you two are enjoying yourselves," Harrison teased as he sat in his favorite chair.

Noah told Toby, "Harrison made all the porch furnishings. The chair he's sitting in is the one he made for himself," Noah said, teasing Harrison back.

"It's mighty nice work, Harrison," Toby told him. "But you know it, don't you? And you should be proud of it."

"I am," Harrison answered. "Mostly because I enjoy working with my hands."

"So do I," Toby answered back.

Harrison said, "Yeah. So, what is it you like to do, Toby?"

"Oh, I like to work with leather, I make whips, and I'm good at it too," Toby said with a chuckle.

"I wouldn't expect anything less of you," Noah said, laughing. "But you will have to show us some of your work soon." Toby agreed he would.

"Now Noah," Harrison spoke to say, "I have been thinking on something. It has to do with breeding thoroughbred horses. I know you mentioned that you and your brother, James, have been doing some breeding on your place already. But how would you like to start a business here with us? It's something I have always wanted to do, and you could build your house here for you and Elizabeth to raise your family. You just pick a spot and it's yours."

Noah is so surprised at first; he didn't really know what to say. But finally, he answered, "You should know, Harrison, a lot will depend on what my wife and your daughter has to say about it."

He is now looking at her, and Elizabeth asked, "Are you really asking me to help decide, Noah?"

"Of course, honey. It will be your home too, you know," and he is smiling as she asked, "Could you be happy living here, Noah?"

"I will be happy anywhere you are, sweetheart."

"It is the same for me too," Elizabeth answered.

Then Noah asked Harrison, "Just where do you think would be a good place to build a house?"

He replied by saying, "Noah, you and Elizabeth just go out and look around the farm and choose a place."

"Well then, let's do it now and everyone can go."

Well, Lily and Susie are playing with dolls, they didn't want to go. So the men hitched up the horses to the buggies, helped the women to be seated. Then with Joel and David riding their mounts, they headed out to look around the farm.

Harrison said, "Toby, if you have it in your mind to stay here, then you and Tansy need to choose a place for your home as well."

Toby turned to Tansy to ask, "What do you say, girl?"

Tansy smiled from ear to ear and said, "Yes, it sounds great."

"Well, Harrison, I guess that's the answer," Toby said, so it was decided.

If Noah didn't already think Harrison a fine man, he would know it now. They looked everywhere. But since Joel and David were riding their mounts, they could get around better, and finally Joel went riding up on this little incline. He called to tell Noah he should bring Elizabeth to look over here at this view and the way the land lays. Noah carefully helped Elizabeth down and took her arm as they walked over to where Joel is standing. David is walking with the couple and leading his horse. When they reached the spot Joel wanted to show them, they couldn't believe their eyes.

"Is that the creek where we met?" Noah asked.

Elizabeth breathed then answered, "Yes, it is the very same creek." Her eyes were shining as she asked, "Wouldn't it be great to build our home here overlooking the creek where we met, Noah?"

Noah's watching his wife and knew he would give her the moon if she asked for it. He said, "Honey, I don't see any reason why not. I think it great too. It is a beautiful place. Thanks, Joel, for pointing it out."

"So this is the perfect place?" Joel asked Elizabeth. "I never thought about how pretty this place is till now."

"Me neither," David is saying. "But now I suppose I see it better through your eyes, how bout that?"

"We can start drawing up plans right away, honey."

"Now, boys, we need to find a place for the breeding barn."

So they walked back to the buggy. Noah is holding on to his wife. He helped her back in the buggy.

He said, "Harrison, that's the spot for our house. So now, we need to find one for the breeding barn. Toby and Tansy need to choose the place for their home too."

So Toby and Tansy chose a place for their house to be between the farm house and where Noah and Elizabeth will build their home. Then the new breeding barn will be built over near where the stable is now.

As they are making their way back to the house, Noah said as he pointed, "Would you look over there in the pasture at King? He's certainly enjoying being home again. Watch him kick up his heels and chase those mares. He is a fine-looking horse, isn't he?" And everyone agreed there is no other horse to compare with King.

"It's a lot in the way he carries himself and his racing ability. And look over there beside the fence." Sure enough, there sits Little Jo watching King enjoying himself. But reluctantly, Noah said with a deep sigh, "It's been great out here looking around the farm, but I suppose we should get back to the house before dark."

Chapter 25

The next morning, Noah is up early, as usual, but his wife didn't even stir. He had to smile even though he still had concerns. Her mother, Ellen, delivered four children with success, and after having done hard work in the fields, no less, so he will keep reminding himself that she will be well cared for.

He left to go for his morning run with King. The weather is getting warmer, the chill is gone, and early morning is great for their run. When he returned, the other men were starting the morning chores. So after cooling King down, he pitched in and helped with feeding the animals. Then they were finished in less time with the extra help. So they were back in the kitchen earlier than usual, but Ellen and Tansy were already starting breakfast, with coffee already made, so out came the cups for all the men with a piping hot cup of coffee set in front of them.

"Man, oh, man," Toby is saying. "I can get used to this. Tansy is a good cook, you know, and she is used to cooking for a crowd of people too."

"Well, let's see what she and Ellen will feed us then," Harrison grinned at the others. He knew no one can make better biscuits then his Ellen.

And then the food is set on the table. The women had made gravy to go with the biscuits. They had fried eggs, bacon, sausages, with some fried potatoes on the side. Since Noah had told them how to fry the potatoes, Ellen will prepare them now and then.

Harrison asked the blessing. He said, "Lord, we thank you for the many blessings we receive each day. I would ask, Lord, that you would look kindly on our new friends Toby and Tansy, with their son. We already feel blessed in knowing them and hope the future will be bright for us all. Now we ask that you bless this food set before us and we are thankful for our good women that prepared it. Amen."

With his first bite of a biscuit, Toby had a wide smile on his face. "Oh, man! This is the best biscuit I ever ate. Tansy girl," Toby said while he is licking butter and molasses off his fingers, "You will have to make a point of watching Miss Ellen make these biscuits."

"There is no way I could do it," Tansy replied. "I don't know anyone else who can make biscuits the way Ellen does. Toby, you just need to watch her yourself to see what I am saying in the first place," Tansy explains. "Ellen doesn't measure anything. She has this large bowl she sifts flour in. She takes her hand to makes a hole in the flour and starts with a pinch of salt, then soda and baking powder. She takes her hand to mix all this in hole with the flour, then she dips her hand into the crock of lard, gets what she wants, and she starts mixing it all with buttermilk. When she has made the dough, she will pinch off what she wants and puts it in her left hand, then takes her right hand and rolls a biscuit. Toby, after tasting one of her biscuits, you can tell she knows what she is doing, but as I said before, I do not know anyone else who could make biscuits as well as Ellen Steele." Everyone else at the table agreed.

Toby is still eating more biscuits with butter and molasses. He asked, "Harrison, I don't suppose you made these mouth-watering molasses?"

Harrison answered with pride, "I sure did. A man I worked for while I was still young taught me how to dip off the foam as they boil, and that is how you get the mild taste. Aren't they great?"

"Oh yeah," Toby agreed.

After Noah had eaten, he stood to say, "I don't understand why Elizabeth isn't down yet. So I believe I'll go upstairs to check on her."

He left the table and made his way to their room. He found his wife being sick over the slop jar. He rushed to get a wet cloth and went to her.

He said, "Oh, sweetheart, I'm sorry you're sick." When she could lift her head, Noah wiped her face, then he picked her up in his arms to carry her back to bed. He covered her up and kissed her forehead. He said, "I'm going back to the kitchen to ask if Miss Ellen can give you something to make you feel better." *She looks so pale*, he's thinking, which only fed into his fears. Noah hurried back downstairs.

He took Ellen aside and told her, "Elizabeth's sick. Can you do something for her?"

Ellen wanted to smile at this tall, handsome, strong man who can take charge of any situation. But when he has seen his wife being ill, it's too much for him. Ellen said, "Noah, you should get another cup of coffee and try to relax. You are aware of why she is sick, right?"

Noah answered, "Yes, I believe so, and I have to tell you, Ellen, it scares me half to death! I don't know if you are aware, my first wife died while in labor. My son died with her." And Noah looked like he's facing death himself.

Ellen said soothingly, "I can see your concern, Noah. I understand it, too, but Elizabeth is young and healthy. She is my daughter, so we will take good care of her. Now leave it to me, of course, Tansy too. We know what she needs."

Noah looked at Ellen for a full second, then his face lost that look of concern. He said, "Okay, I trust you, Ellen, and you, too, Tansy. I will do as you say, but shouldn't I go back with you?"

Ellen said, "No, Noah. I am taking her a cup of tea that will relax her, and she will sleep for a while. We will look after Elizabeth, you have my promise."

While they were talking, Tansy had the water ready for the cup of tea. Ellen made the tea to take up to Elizabeth. She was being sick again as Ellen entered the room, so she hurried to get a wet cloth to wash her daughter's face.

Ellen said, "Now, dear, I know you feel awful for now. But it will get better. You do understand that you are with child. And so how you feel is normal."

Elizabeth asked, "Mom, are you certain there is to be a baby?"

"Yes, dear, I am sure you are with child, and you will be just fine."

But Elizabeth isn't listening. "Oh my," she said with a look of wonder. "I am carrying Noah's child, Mom." Elizabeth's eyes are shining with a look of pure joy, but Ellen was able to get her back to bed. She drank the tea. Ellen sat with her till she fell asleep with a smile on her face. Noah was still downstairs anxiously waiting. He wanted to know how his wife is. Ellen had to smile. She said, "Noah, your wife is fine. Once she became aware of the baby, you should have seen her face. She is so happy that she is carrying your child."

Noah's face cleared, the concern is gone. It went from the look of anxiety to a satisfied look, then he grinned. He told Ellen he would be back later to check on Elizabeth.

Chapter 26

Then he left to find Harrison to ask what his plans are for the day. He found him with Toby in the stable. Toby had a whip in his hand. He's explaining how he made it. They both looked up as Noah came in. Harrison was smiling.

He said, "I couldn't wait for Toby to show me how he makes these whips."

Toby is holding the whip and curled it up in his hand before either of the other two men realized what he was about his arm went up and back then came forward lighten fast with a crack! Toby laughed at the look of amazement on their faces.

Noah finally said, "After all the time we spent traveling together, you never once mentioned your experience with making or using the whip. Toby, you can strike like a rattlesnake with that thing," Noah chuckled. "You will be a good man to have around, in case that Howard bunch decide to try to steal King again."

"Hush your mouth, man!" Toby said, laughing. "Let's hope that never happens."

"Is Elizabeth okay?" Harrison asked.

Noah's grinning from ear to ear as he said, "Ellen tells me she will be fine, and she is happy about the baby."

"It's easy to see you're pleased too, Noah," Toby said.

"Yeah, once I got over being scared half to death," Noah said laughing. "After Ellen explained that things will be fine with Elizabeth, that she has Ellen and your wife, Tansy, to take care of her."

"Well, she couldn't be in better hands either," Harrison replied. "Now we need to get some work done today." Joel and David had just come in from taking the cows to pasture, so Harrison said, "The first cutting of hay is ready. Then we will have a break till the tobacco is ready to be cut."

He said to Noah and Toby, "If you men haven't worked with the harvesting of tobacco, it will be quite an experience like no other, from the beginning till it's ready for market. But for now, it's the hay that needs cutting."

"I am with you, Harrison. But after we get everything ready to go to the field," Noah is saying, "I will go check on Elizabeth again, to set my mind at ease."

When he did go to the house, Elizabeth is in the kitchen talking and laughing with her mother and Tansy. *Ellen is right, she has a glow about her,* he's thinking, and leaned down to give her a kiss.

He said, "I can see you're feeling better, honey."

"Oh, yes, Noah. Do you know about the baby?" Elizabeth asked.

"Yes, I am very much aware of the baby, sweetheart. I am a happy man."

"Me too," his wife told him.

"I can see that you are," he said with a tender smile. "You know, there is an old saying that I think fits how you always seem to be. 'A cheerful wife is the joy of her husband's life.' Now I best go, or the others will go to the field without me, and I am looking forward to helping with cutting hay"—but before he could leave—"here comes my little blond-headed sweetie pie." He called her as she made a jump into his arms. He's laughing as he said, "You know, we have talked about how you're getting to be a handful, little one. Why don't we agree that it's not a good idea now that you are getting to be a big girl, do you agree?"

"Am I a big girl, Daddy? I still you girl, ain't me?"

"Yes, sweetie, but we will discuss your use of words later. But for now, you need to eat. Be good for Mommy and everyone, okay? I need to help your grandpa." He seated her in a chair, gave his wife another tender smile, then left.

"That man sure is crazy about you, girl," Tansy is telling her.

Elizabeth smiled as she said, "I know, Tansy, how lucky I am. I see how other women look at him too. He's a handsome man."

"Oh, he is that, alright, but there's so much more to Noah Bennett than a handsome face," Tansy allowed. "But he's going to be a handful for the next eight months or so, you should know."

Lily came into the kitchen to ask if Elizabeth would like for her to watch Susie after they eat.

"Oh, would you, Lily? That would be good of you."

"You like to play with Lily, don't you, Susie?" Elizabeth asked the little girl.

Susie answered, "Yeah, I like her."

After Lily and Susie had eaten, Lily told Susie to go with her. "Let's get your dolls to play with."

Ellen said, "Well, ladies, I need to go to see how much work the garden needs."

Tansy said, "Okay then, Elizabeth, why don't we get things started for dinner?"

The men were busy cutting the hay, and with everyone working, it was done in less time. Now they will hope for dry weather so the hay will have the time to cure before it's put in the hayloft. The men have a little time to rest before doing evening chores. They set on the front porch to rest a few minutes. The women brought out cool water to drink, and it tasted so good. Noah reached out to pull Elizabeth down beside him on the porch swing. He hugged her close as he whispered, "You okay?"

She gave him a bright smile then she whispered, "I feel fine."

The others are smiling at the couple, but Joel said, "Okay, you two, it hasn't been that long since you talked at dinnertime."

Noah looked over at Joel to say, "I want to be around when you meet the one woman you can't live without."

Joel laughed and said, "You may be an old man by then, Noah."

"We will see, Joel. Believe me, that's something you don't plan," Noah told him with a wide grin.

Soon, it's time for the men to go do chores and for the women to finish cooking supper. After working in the hay field today, all the men decided to go to the creek to wash up. David agreed he would go to get soap and towels from the back porch and warn the women to stay away, but they're not worried. So after a good bath, the men all felt refreshed and ready for supper when it's set on the table. After eating a hearty meal, then they were back on the porch again to rest, waiting for the women to join them and visit until bedtime.

When Harrison told them, he's "ready for bed, but we can start making plans tomorrow for the buildings. I suppose you'll want to start on your house first Noah."

"Harrison, we can hire men to help so we can work on all three buildings at the same time and get them all finished before cold weather sets in." Noah explained how they could go about it. By the time he's finished, everyone is aware Noah knows what he's talking about. They also realized, if they didn't already know it before, he's an amazingly intelligent man. *Just listening to him talk, he makes one believe they can do anything too,* Joel thought to himself.

But now, Harrison said, "I believe it is time to find our beds for the night."

Chapter 27

So they settled into a routine. Noah took King for a run every morning, and Little Jo has grown enough. He tries to run with them. When he gets tried, though, he sits to wait for them to return. After they started the buildings, when the crops demanded their attention, they take care of the crops while the hired men continued to do the building, while Harrison and the others are busy in the fields. So it went till all the crops were harvested. Then they could spend their time on the buildings.

The women have been taking care of their work in the house as well as in the garden. They canned and preserved everything in sight, the men would tease them. It wasn't far from the truth. They pickled beets made from a recipe Ellen told the others that she remembers from childhood when she helped one of the church ladies who took turns caring for her.

Ellen told Tansy, "We need about one-half bush of beets to wash them, then cut off the tops, leaving about an inch to keep the beets from bleeding out and losing their color. Then they washed them again to be certain the beets are good and clean. We'll put them in the large pot of boiling water that's hanging over the outside fire."

So it didn't take long, about twenty minutes or so. And the beets are ready to be removed from the hot water. Ellen uses a sifter to dip out the beets so the water will drain away. While the beets are cooling, the two women carry them back into the house. Then Ellen measured out two quarts of cider vinegar into another pot on her cookstove after adding wood to get the fire hot again. Then she adds ten cups of sugar and six cups water while it's coming to a boil. Now the beets are cool enough to peel. Ellen peels the skin off the beets; it comes off no problem. She and Tansy work together. Tansy will slice the beets into a bowl. When all the beets have been peeled and sliced, then they put them into the pot of boiling mixture.

"Now we bring it to a boil again, for about thirty minutes," Ellen said, "but we do not want them to boil over, now that can be a mess."

They take the beets off the heat and now they use dippers to dip the beets into prepared jars sealed with a ring on the jar, then the lid on tight as they can get it to seal.

Ellen said, "Now that the beets are done and they had made a double batch, let's make bread and butter pickles next."

They gathered enough cucumbers for twenty-four quarts to double the batch. They wash them but don't peel the cucumbers, just slice them, put them into a large pan of saltwater, then peel and chop twelve medium-sized onions, not too fine though, added to the one-fourth cup saltwater.

They carried them to the spring house, set the pan where it will stay cool until they are ready to be canned, which is about three hours.

It is now time to prepare dinner, so they will finish with the pickles later. So Ellen, with Tansy and Elizabeth's help, started the noon meal. After the meal is over and the men are back at work, Elizabeth and Tansy do the dishes while Ellen started the mixture for the pickles:

2/3 bushel cucumbers.

Wash but we don't peel the cucumbers and slice them

Then peel and chop 12 medium sized onions

Add both cucumbers slices and chopped onions in pan of
   salt water.

Add ¼ cup salt to 11/2 gallon water in large pan

Let cool about three hours.

Next step, in another large pan:

2 quarts of cider vinegar.

6 tablespoons of celery seed.

2-2/4 cups mustard seed.

10 cups sugar.

2 teaspoons turmeric

Bring mixture to boil.

Use hands to dip out the cucumbers and onions

Start to fill prepared jars. After all jars are filled, then pour
the hot mixture in each jar and seal with a ring and lid. ~4
dozen jars.

Two quarts of cider vinegar, six tablespoons of celery seed, two and two-fourths cups of mustard seed, ten cups sugar, two teaspoons turmeric. When the mixture starts to boil, Ellen goes for the cucumbers with another large pan. After using the same sifter to dip them out of the saltwater, the sliced cucumbers and chopped onions, then pouring the saltwater outside on the ground. She brings the pan into the kitchen and starts to fill the prepared jars. Ellen puts as many sliced cucumbers with the onions that will fit in a jar. After the jars are filled, with a dipper she pours the hot mixture over the cucumbers and seals the jar with a ring and lid (about twenty-four quarts). Everyone is fond of bread and butter pickles. With the double batch, each jar of pickles with the beets, now they have four dozen jars all together.

For the rest of the garden stuff, Ellen and Tansy go to the garden and take what they need for a garden relish: Twelve medium onions (which will come to about four cups when chopped), one medium head of cabbage (chopped, about four cups), ten green tomatoes (four cups), twelve green peppers, six sweet red peppers. Chop into small pieces, mix it all together in a large pan. Then sprinkle with salt. Let stand overnight.

"Okay," Ellen said, "this will go to the spring house for now. Now, Tansy, I believe we deserve a rest."

"You won't get any argument from me, girl," Tansy said with a chuckle.

So the two women who have become fast friends decided it's their turn to sit on the porch where there happens to be a cool breeze blowing.

The next morning, Tansy told Ellen she would make her recipe for buttermilk pancakes with homemade syrup. Since Noah has a sweet tooth, Elizabeth wants to help so she can learn how to make them.

Tansy handed out a neatly folded paper which contains the recipe she had written for the women to follow.

Buttermilk Pancakes

2 cups flour
1 teaspoon soda
1 teaspoon baking powder
1/2 teaspoon salt
2 tablespoons sugar
2 eggs, lightly beaten
2 cups buttermilk
3 tablespoons melted butter

Sift together dry ingredients. Mix with eggs, buttermilk, and butter into the mixture. Mix till just blended. It should be lumpy. Heat a lightly oiled griddle over medium high heat. Pour approximately 1/4 cup batter for every pancake. Brown on both sides. Serve hot.

Homemade Pancake Syrup

4 cups sugar
2-1/2 cups water
1 tablespoon butter
1 teaspoon vanilla

On a separate pan, let the sugar brown for color and flavor. Add water and bring to a boil. When the mixture starts to thicken, add butter and vanilla. *Serve on top of pancakes.*

The pancakes are turning out great. They also have the sliced bacon fried, with enough eggs. And they can hear the men coming in the backdoor now; they are laughing and teasing as they wash up on the back porch.

As Harrison walked in the kitchen, he said, "We must be having something different for breakfast this morning, but it smells good."

Tansy said, "We have plenty of pancakes, so we sure hope you like them."

The food is set on the table and Harrison asked the blessing. After the first bite of pancake, Harrison said, "Say Ellen, there is no doubt you make the best biscuits, but Tansy can make good pancakes."

Ellen said, grinning, "I agree. The pancakes are great, Tansy."

"I agree too," Noah said. "Tansy, you sure hit the right spot this morning."

"Yeah, I hear you've got a sweet tooth, Noah, so I thought maybe you would be pleased."

So all the men ate hearty, all the bacon and eggs with the pancakes disappeared, and they even decided to have an extra cup of coffee and didn't seem to be in any hurry.

After the morning meal is over, while Tansy and Elizabeth do the kitchen chores, Ellen starts the mixture of one and one-half teaspoons salt, six cups sugar, two teaspoons mustard seed, one and one-half teaspoons celery seed, one and one-half teaspoons turmeric, four cups vinegar, and two cups water. Ellen brings the vegetables back to the kitchen to drain and dumps them into the hot mixture, then brings it back to a boil for about fifteen minutes. She then fills the jars and seals with a ring and lid. She made eight pints. After all the canned stuff has time to seal, usually over night will do.

Ellen is telling Tansy, "Then all the jars are stored in the root cellar along with what is left of the apples and peach crop. After canning and preserving them, hopefully we have enough canned goods to last for the winter."

Tansy asked, "Ellen, have you ever dried apples?"

Ellen said, "No, I haven't dried apples before."

"Well, I know how to do it," Tansy's telling her.

Ellen said, "Okay, lets dry some apples."

Tansy's pleased to help with peeling some of the apples, slicing them and drying them by spreading a cloth on the roof of the smokehouse. They laid the apples out so they will dry.

"Of course, we'll need to bring the apples in before the dew falls. then put them out again next day after the dew is gone. Continue this routine till the apples are good and dry. We can keep them in the root celler as well in a cloth bag." This is something Tansy was able to teach Ellen.

Tansy told her, "This winter, we can cook them, but the apples must soak in hot water. Because they were dried in the open, they need to be rinsed good then cooked with sugar and spices, but it only takes a few of the dried apples, no more than two cups is all you need. You must remember they swell up as they cook. Once you get the sugar and spices in, they make delicious fried apple pies. And of course, I make a stack spiced cake with the dried apples, and maybe I can use some of Harrison's homemade molasses, they will be good in it. Usually I make it for Christmas."

Tansy told Ellen, "And you know I have done a lot of canning while working at the horse farm where Toby and I met. The women working there taught me a lot of what I know. But you, Ellen, know more about canning and preserving then anyone else I know. And I hope we may continue to work together and learn from each other."

"Like I said before," Ellen told Tansy, "the church ladies took turns taking care of me after I lost my family. I learned something from each of them. That has helped me care for my own family. I thank God for those women."

"They gave me a home and so much more. The only thing I didn't take to so much is sewing or quilting. I do what I need to do for my family. But I would much rather be looking for herbs and finding more ways of using them for healing," she said with a chuckle.

Tansy said, "I hear you girl."

"But when I met Harrison," Ellen continued, "he also had lost his family at an early age. When we knew that we wanted to marry, we made a promise to each other. If the good Lord would allow us to have a family, we would try to teach them that through God's way, we grow and prosper. The Lord is there to help those who are willing to help themselves. And I have to say, I believe without bragging, mind you, Harrison and I are proud of our children."

"As you should be," Tansy responded. "You and Harrison did good with those children, Ellen."

Chapter 28

Two men, John Collins and Jim Scott, were hired to cut enough firewood to last the three households. Along with the coal brought into Corbin by train cars from the Laurel County coal fields, there's plenty of coal for the people who can afford it. But actually coal is cheaper than wood, that is, if you buy wood at $2.50 a cord, and ten bushels of coal is only $1.00. The hired men brought in enough to last for the whole winter, with the store of wood. In the past, after the crops were in, Harrison, Joel, and David would hitch a team of horses to the wagon, load a crosscut saw with an ax or two. They would go into the woods and cut enough wood to last for the winter to burn in the fireplaces and for Ellen's cookstove. They spent at least two days cutting down small trees in their woods—that is also how they keep down the undergrowth, it serves more than one purpose. After they cut enough trees, they then saw them in the size for firewood, load them in the wagon, take them back to the house, leave them to be split at another time. They would need to make at least three or more wagonloads. Then each of them will take turns splitting the wood in the right size for the fireplaces or the cookstove. Some needs to be cut smaller for kindling to use for starting the fires, then they are stacked against the smokehouse for easy access. So, hiring other people to do their work is new to the Steele men. But they have had more important things to do this winter. They were also pleased that Noah was right about being finished with all the buildings before cold weather set in.

Soon, the house was finished, and what a sight it is—Elizabeth can hardly believe her eyes—with indoor plumbing and no less two bathrooms!

Noah would take his wife into Corbin or up to London. They would even ride the train all the way up to Lexington to look at furnishings for the new house. Elizabeth already knew that Noah is excellent at choosing what colors and furnishings look best in the house. But to her amazement and delight, Elizabeth found she's good at it also.

"I would like for the house to be homey," she told Noah.

He just smiled and said, "I agree, honey." So between the two of them, they chose loveseats in a soft shade of blue, one to set on either side of the huge fireplace in the front room. There are stuffed chairs, some in a pretty shade of rose and others in a pearl-grey color in different settings around the room, with tables and pretty lamps set on them. As for the bedrooms, they have a large bed with the tall posts with a pretty canopy stretched over them in each room, with a feather mattress. The women had made new quilts, all a different pattern. The quilt for the master bedroom is the wedding-ring pattern. One of the others, a star of the bluegrass, another the flower garden pattern. But each room is set up differently. There's the nine-patch pattern and the log cabin. They are all done in colors to match the room but all done beautifully. Each has two chests with four drawers with a mirror on the wall for the men, and, of course, a dressing table with mirror for the ladies.

But each bedroom with a huge fireplace taking up one whole wall, with the bookshelves at each end of the fireplace, something both Noah and Elizabeth agree on. When they have the time, Noah loves to read on a wide range of topics and is a fast reader. Elizabeth reads books of interest to her, but nothing compared to Noah; he's a wonder.

Susie's room is done the way the little girl wanted it to be. Her bed is a simple one on the wall with a window. The bed suits her size, but of course, a fireplace takes up another wall with the usual box to store wood, with the lid to use as a seat. There is also a bench along another wall for her many dolls and shelves above on the wall to the door for her books. They did a bang-up job, according to Toby.

The furnishing is so much more than Elizabeth had ever hoped to have. The kitchen is every woman's dream, with cabinets on one wall and counters underneath, but also a china hutch her father had made to display her pretty dishes which will only be used on special occasions.

Oh, thank God for Noah, Elizabeth is thinking. He has changed her life in so many ways, but most of all with his continuing love. He has proved that he wants her to have everything he can possibly give her. But she has also tried to tell him that she doesn't need all this luxury. *But I wouldn't complain about the conveniences,* she is thinking with an honest thought. She likes them and really does appreciate it all.

She told Noah with a sweet smile, "It just takes getting used to, is all." And they both agreed there will be more added as each decides what they want or need.

The house is huge with three stories and a wrap-around porch which will be great in warm weather. The rest of the family is in awe of how Noah built the house, with up-to-date labor-saving conveniences they would never even have thought of.

"And the furnishings are just lovely," Ellen remarked, and Tansy agreed.

Since Elizabeth's getting along in her pregnancy now, Noah's becoming even more protective of his wife, so Elizabeth tries not to worry him. But Ellen and Tansy are hopeful that Noah will survive until Elizabeth delivers this baby.

"All the crops are in now, and this has been another good year for the tobacco," Harrison says and his "crop is exellent which is great for us. But even more so for the people who's livelihood depends on their tobacco sale, cash to carry them through the following year."

Harrison told Toby and Noah, "I remember what it was like when Ellen and I would try to make the money stretch a full year. But thank God, Ellen and I managed by trading her butter, cream, and eggs for staples such as sugar, salt, and stuff for baking. We took corn to the mill to trade for flour and cornmeal, with the canned stuff, and beef and pork we butchered. We managed. Of course, there is always wild game to hunt. Some people want to forget the hard times but Ellen and I, we don't regret those times because we believe it only made us stronger in our belief in God's will."

Anyway, Harrison's tobacco has been stripped and graded by the leaf starting at the bottom, which is the higher grade, used for chewing tobacco. The middle leaves are used for cigars. The very top leaves, which is lower grade, most often are used for pipe tobacco. Now it has all been graded, tied in a bunch with the tobacco leaves and ready for market. As Harrison had promised Noah and Toby, it would be quite an experience for the two of them. It also served to help take Noah's mind off the upcoming event for when Elizabeth goes into labor to deliver their child, even though her time isn't near yet, but it doesn't seem to matter. He wants their child more than he can say, but he also has this dread that is a constant thing for him. Their life together couldn't be better, but he just can't bear the thought of losing Elizabeth.

Chapter 29

Now that all the harvesting is done, all the ground has been turned over to make spring plowing easier. The farm is now in good shape for winter, so Noah and Elizabeth decided to have an open house party, since it didn't work out for having one to celebrate their wedding or the derby win back in the summer because of building the two houses as well as the breeding barn. Now, it will also be a Christmas Eve party.

All the neighbors have gotten an invitation. Elizabeth has been busy decorating the house with Susie, who is delighted with it all.

Susie will say, "Oh, Mommy, it pretty."

And of course, Ellen and Tansy are helping now that Elizabeth is getting so heavy with the child. Even though it can only be her seventh month, it's hard for her to get around, but she wants to keep busy. Ellen and Tansy both have concerns that Elizabeth will have an early delivery, but she is so excited about the party she will not slow down. So the ladies just let her go and try to stay close in the daytime. Noah's there to watch over her at night, and he doesn't let her out of his sight.

Elizabeth is well aware of what they're doing, but she doesn't let on 'cause she understands their concern; it's because they care. She has to smile sometimes, though, because they are so obvious about it. Nevertheless, everything is done now. The party is tomorrow night. They had asked Ann to buy Susie a new dress for the party. Noah had wanted to buy a new one for her, too, but Elizabeth wouldn't hear of it.

She said, "I'll just wear one of the dresses that were made for me once I became heavy with our child." She's so looking forward to having their baby born, she even dreams of it. There are also to see James and Ann. They have been busy with their work, getting ready for the coming winter as well. Besides, they do intend to stay over Christmas.

The next morning, Noah returned from his run with King, which he still does every day. He and King both enjoy the time together. After he cools King down with the help of his brothers-in–law, he then helps with the morning chores. But Noah had made the decision not to race any longer. So Noah had told Joel he needed to start training with King, so by this next spring he and King will be ready for the race in Baltimore, Maryland. When Noah came through the backdoor into the kitchen the morning of Christmas Eve, he's surprised to see Elizabeth up with Tansy, helping to get their breakfast made. Elizabeth walked to meet her husband. She tried to give him a hug, but they both had a good laugh 'cause she can't get close enough.

But she said, "Noah, you must think I look a fright, don't you? Now don't fib?"

Noah reached for her shoulders. He bent over and gave her a tender kiss. He said, "Darlin', you're carrying our child. Please do believe me when I say you're still the most beautiful woman I know."

"After that kiss, Noah, how could I not believe you? And you're the most handsome man ever. I love you more every day," Elizabeth told him.

Noah kissed his wife again. He asked, "Why are you up so early anyway, darlin'?"

"Because I have more things to do before the party tonight."

"Well then, what can I do to help?" he asked.

"I'm not sure, but maybe you could see that Lily either comes here to be with Susie or take her over there to Lily."

Noah is surprised. "Hey, honey, I can entertain our daughter, you know." She thought he sounded a little hurt. "You know there's no need for Lily to come here just to be with Susie. Besides, your sister may have other things to do, like get ready for tonight."

Elizabeth turned to look at her husband who's looking back at her with a frown. She walked to him to try again to hug him, without succeeding again, so she lifted her hand to lay it along the side of his cheek. "Oh, honey, I wasn't thinking about you wanting to be with Susie. I just assumed you would be busy. I should have remembered that old saying, 'Don't just assume anything,' which applies here, doesn't it?"

By now he's smiling again and said, "Don't let it concern you, honey. We'll get everything done before the party, you'll see. Just let Susie help along with me."

Elizabeth's smiling too as she said, "Oh, how I wish I could give you a little hug, you big handsome man. You always seem to have a better solution."

He asked, "Are you by chance trying to sweet talk me, Mrs. Bennett?"

Elizabeth looked uncertain as she asked, "Is it working, sir?"

Noah reached out to pull her as close as she would fit. He bent over, gave her a passionate kiss, then just held her for a second or two. He raised his head to ask, "Now, what do you think, sweetheart?"

"When you kiss me like that, Noah Bennett, it causes my head to spin, you know. But you may kiss me anytime you like, sir." Then she asked, "Oh, Noah, do you think many people will come to our party tonight?"

"In my opinion, honey, everyone for miles around will be here, so don't worry."

"Now just let me know what I can do to help for now. When Susie's awake, then the two of us will help together."

He put his finger under her chin with a grin. He said, "Okay."

Tansy spoke up, "Noah, if you're so anxious to help, then would you set up some tables in the livingroom for serving drinks?"

He looked at Elizabeth with a grin. He said, "Looks to me like you have someone in charge here already." He asked with a grin, "How you doing this morning, Tansy?"

"I'm just fine, Noah. Sounds like you're feeling your oats this morning, too, so we may as well take advantage of you," as she returned his grin.

"Alright then, where are these tables you want me to set up?"

"Isn't that just like a man? They're in your house and you don't know where the tables are kept," Tansy teased.

"Sounds like you're in fine fiddle yourself, Tansy," Noah teased right back. Elizabeth's watching the two of them interact with each other. She thought how glad everyone is that Noah brought Tansy and Toby here to live, with their son, Johnny, who seems to like it here too. He never has much to say but tags after David. Though he's a few years younger, David doesn't seem to mind.

Joel and David will be going away soon to start riding the racing circuit with King. She is so happily married to Noah. But things are changing a bit too fast for her liking. Just for a second, she felt a little dizzy. The next thing she knew, Noah's calling her name. Elizabeth opened her eyes and can clearly see the concern on her husband's face.

"Darlin', what happened? I looked your way just in time to catch you before you fell to the floor. Thank God I was standing close enough to do so." He had picked her up to carry her upstairs to their bedroom. Noah told her he wanted to get the doctor too, then said, "But I believe I'll ask Joel to do it instead. I don't wish to leave you for even a second, honey."

"But Noah, I don't know what happened!" Elizabeth told him. "One minute I'm watching you and Tansy tease back and forth, and then I wake up here with you calling my name. But I feel okay now, honest."

Noah turned to Tansy, "Would you mind asking Joel if he will go for the doctor?"

She said, "Of course I'll tell Joel and also let Ellen know what happened as well and be back shortly." She's gone before Noah had a chance to thank her.

By the time, Noah was able to help Elizabeth into something more comfortable—a pretty white gown with a matching robe. Noah had bought this set, as well as others, while they were in Lexington shopping for the house.

Tansy's back with Ellen and Lily who came to take Susie back with her. Noah's relieved she's going to watch Susie after all. Lily offered to get Susie up and dressed.

"Then I will take her over to our house and feed her there, if that's okay?"

Noah reached out to give her a hug. He said, "It's more than okay, Lily. We owe you big time for helping out with Susie. Thank you."

"It's okay, really. She looks at Elizabeth. "But are you okay, sis?" Lily asked hesitantly?"

"I'm fine, Lily," Elizabeth told her. "Noah sent for the doctor, but it's just a precaution. And I wish to thank you, too, for seeing to Susie."

So Lily's able to get Susie ready and away from the house before Joel returned with the doctor who was rushed upstairs to see Elizabeth. Noah was sent downstairs straight away. He's not happy about it one little bit. He didn't understand why he couldn't stay in the room with his wife, but he decided that it's more important that Elizabeth get good care, so he didn't want to get on the wrong side of the doctor—the doctor who's an older distinguished man—but Noah doesn't know anything about the man. He just hopes he knows what he's doing.

Doctor Morris introduced himself to one of the prettiest young women he had seen in a long while. He could tell her husband wasn't happy he wasn't allow to stay. He can understand his objection, but as a doctor he just makes it a rule not to let the husband stay. He's always been of the opinion that the wife will be more forthcoming about her condition if her husband isn't present.

"So now, my dear," he asked Elizabeth, "What seems to be going on with you?"

Elizabeth explained what happened. "I have been feeling fine, so I don't understand why I fainted today."

"Well dear, let me take a look at you." The doctor's telling her as he started his examination, "Now don't be embarrassed, dear, this is something I need to do. But in my opinion, an examination should have been done earlier rather than at this stage."

When he's done, he asked, "Now, dear, have you been tired much of the time?"

She told him, "Well, maybe a little, but mostly I have more energy than I know what to do with. Why doctor?"

"Well then, if you have all that energy, then you are more than likely to be more active, right?"

"Yes, doctor, I suppose so. But for a while, I seemed to have very little energy, so I didn't get a lot accomplished. So now that I do have more energy, I've been trying to catch up."

"Okay. But I believe we need for you to slow down now, dear. And I'm going to tell your husband that also. From what I could tell, he seems very protective of you."

"But doctor, if you tell Noah, then he'll not let me come down for the party tonight."

"You're having a party tonight, are you? Do I have an invitation to your party, Mrs. Bennett? If so, then that will take away your husband's excuse for not letting you be there."

Elizabeth laughed out loud. She said, "I believe I like you, doctor. I'm not afraid of you any longer, but I used to be, you know."

"I don't remember ever having you for a patient before, my dear," he told Elizabeth. "I can't see me forgetting someone as lovely as you."

"Oh, this was when I was a little girl," she told him. "You see, I had this cut on my foot that had gotten infected. I thought you hurt it, but I realized later after it healed, you had helped me instead."

"Well then, what time does the party start? I don't wish to be late," the doctor's telling her with a grin.

Elizabeth laughed again. The doctor's thinking her laugh is music to his ears. "Then we'll see you with your wife at six for the party."

"Sorry dear, it will only be me, I'm afraid. I lost my wife a few years back," he said with a sad smile.

"I'm so sorry for your loss, sir," Elizabeth told him. "But we'll be happy to have you here with us tonight, Doctor."

"You must call me Sam if I am to be your guest."

"Alright, Dr. Sam, it's a deal."

Now he said, "You stay in bed and rest up until time to dress for the party. Then you should be able to go downstairs. So, I will say good day for now."

When the doctor started down the stairs, Noah came up to meet him.

"Tell me, how is my wife, Doc?"

The doctor gave Noah a knowing look. "I knew you would nail me right away. I can tell that girl up there is mighty important to you. Can't say I blame you, though, she's a pretty one alright." But he could tell Noah is losing patience, so he said, "Your wife is okay for now, but she needs to rest more, is all. She was afraid you wouldn't let her come downstairs for the party, so I will be your guest tonight, Mr. Bennett, so your wife will be able to be at your party."

Noah couldn't believe his ears. "You mean to tell me you have been up there all this time talking with my wife about the party?" Noah wanted to know.

"Well, yes, sir," the doctor said, smiling. "Now I must go see to my other patients, but I will see you later at the party." Then he left.

Joel walked out in the entry hall. He looked up at Noah who's still standing on the stairs looking more than upset, but he asked anyway, "Well, what did the doctor say about sis?"

"To keep her from overdoing, pretty much is all he said, and that he will be coming back to the party tonight. Joel, I think that old coot just fell in love with my wife, can you believe it?"

"Well now, Noah, Elizabeth is my sister and all, but I can still appreciate that she is a beautiful woman."

Noah gave him a look that left no doubt he's not happy with the doctor.

Joel hid a grin but asked, "So, Elizabeth's okay then?"

"She needs to rest more. I'll see she gets it," Noah told him.

"Alright. I have things to do, so I'll see you later, unless you need me," Joel told him, then left.

The rest of the family is waiting to hear what the doctor had to say. By now Noah realized how silly it is for him to be upset with the doctor. Elizabeth is, as Joel said, a beautiful woman. He himself fell in love with her almost immediately. But dang it all, that's different. But what's different, he reminded himself, is that Elizabeth fell in love with him too. So his face brightened. He walked down the rest of the steps and walked into the front room to talk with the family. He told them what the doctor had to say then he said, "If everyone is willing to help, we will need to prepare for the party. Then before the party starts, I will bring Elizabeth downstairs to seat her in a chair. She needs to sit there, too, if she wants to stay for the party. So ladies, do you know what the plan is?"

Ellen and Tansy both told him, "Yes, and we'll get started on it right away."

Noah said, "I'll go up to talk with Elizabeth then and ask her if she has anything special that needs to be taken care of."

When Noah walked into their room, his wife's sitting on the side of the bed ready to stand. Noah rushed to her and asked, "What do you think you're doing, missy?"

"Oh, Noah, I hate it when you call me missy, remember that's what you called me so arrogantly the day we met," Elizabeth told him.

"I'm not arrogant, I'll have you know," he said with a kiss. "I can be guilty of taking charge, or impatience, which was the case the day we met. But you fell in love with me in spite of it, didn't you, wife? Just as I fell in love with you, darlin', in spite of my argument against it. If you remember, I had decided never to fall in love or to marry again. But when I met you, my dear wife, that plan went out the window. Now you, young lady, are to stay in bed and not get up unless there is someone else in the room, okay?" He tapped her on the nose lightly with his finger. "Now, is there anything you wish to have done that Tansy or your mother isn't already aware of?"

"I don't believe so, but, oh, Noah I do wish I could help. This will be our first Christmas together, I wanted it to be special," Elizabeth told him.

"But honey," Noah told her, "it will be special. All the work you have already done in decorating the house. The front room looks like a winter wonderland. The children will love it Christmas morning. And it will be special because we will be together. So don't fret about it. Now try to rest." After she promised to stay in bed, he said, "I'll go down to help the others." And so everyone pitched in to help and had all the preparations done for the party in good time to dress and be back downstairs before people start to arrive.

* * * * *

Tansy is there in time to help Elizabeth dress. They decided on a blue dress, of course, it has always been her color.

"Even as heavy with child as you are, Elizabeth darlin', you look glorious," Noah told her.

"I'm so proud of you, sweetheart. I do want you to enjoy your party, but you need to behave and stay seated, okay?"

"I promise, Noah. I also promised Doctor Sam too."

Noah has a frown on his face as he said, "Yeah, he informed me that he will also be a guest tonight." Noah had insisted on carrying his wife downstairs. "Now which chair do you wish to sit in, honey?" After he seated her in a chair where she has a clear view to see everyone as they arrive, she's content, though, since she had no other choice really but to let the others take care of the party. Elizabeth is just happy to be sitting here; it's the best option she has.

Chapter  30

T he party seems to be a great success. It looks as though most everyone they invited are here. But that doesn't mean Noah is having a great time. He's having to watch the doctor, and William Jones as well, hanging around Elizabeth. He hardly left her side all evening while he himself has to play host. And his very own brother seems to be enjoying himself with his own wife. *James doesn't seem to have sympathy or help for me*, Noah's thinking, he is getting a kick out of the doctor and William playing the fool over Elizabeth too. But he also realizes he needs to get a grip here. He looked around the front room. It's crowded as is the dining room. There are children here, So far everyone seems to be enjoying themselves and behaving as well. Lily is smiling even though she is keeping an eye on Susie. *Everyone's having a good time except me.* Joel walked over to visit with his brother-in-law and asked if he could be of help but right away knew by the thunderous look on Noah's face something's not right. Joel turned to look in the direction that Noah's sharing, then had to turn away to hide his grin when he realized what Noah's looking at.

But David caught his grin and came over wanting to know. "Why are you grinning like a fool?"

Joel put a finger to his lips to let David know not to say anything more. He tilted his head in the direction of their sister. Now David had to hide a smile as well.

But Noah knew what they were doing. He turned to say, "I hope you two are enjoying yourselves." That statement had the desired affect to wipe the smile off their faces. Then Noah smiled and said, "I know it's foolish of me. But just look at William Jones. He has hardly taken his eyes off my wife. I understand, Joel, that he's a friend of yours, but right this minute, I just want to go over there, take William by the nap of his coat and the seat of his pants, and walk him to the door then outside."

"Well, I do understand how you feel, Noah. But it wouldn't solve anything, you know."

"I do know it, Joel, but it makes me feel better just thinking about it. Just look at the doctor, he's just as bad."

Elizabeth seemed to sense his feelings. She looked his way and gave him a bright smile that restored his good cheer somewhat. He looked around the room to see Harrison and Toby, with Bob Jones, and their wives enjoying themselves with other neighbors. In fact, everyone but himself seems to be having a good time. So he turned to his two brothers-in-law. He said, "Well, guys, let's see if it's time to feed these good people."

After speaking to Tansy and Ellen, it was time, so the food is being laid out for a buffet supper on the sideboard, and more in the dining room as well, and more refreshments.

Noah walked over to Elizabeth. He asked, "Darlin', what would you like to eat? You tell me what you want, I'll prepare a plate for you and one for me and bring them back to eat with you."

"But Noah," William spoke to say, "I had already planned to prepare Elizabeth a plate." Then Noah turned to his wife and the look on his face spoke volumes.

His wife, bless her heart, used diplomacy. She turned to William and she said, "You should go serve yourself. I wish to talk with my husband now, but thanks anyway for your offer." So William had no other choice but to leave her to her husband's care.

Noah grinned at her. "Very good," he said. "That was very diplomatic of you, sweetheart. I'm impressed and love you for it too. I have reached my limit, you know, with Old Will and the doctor hanging around you."

"I know it, honey," Elizabeth answered. "I realize how you feel, Noah. It has been hard for me to watch those girls, over there in particular, drooling over you, husband. They're the very same girls who, when William introduced me to them at his party, dismissed me then, too, as they have here tonight. It's just a little hard to take, especially with me like this." She lay her hand over their baby. "It has been really hard for me to keep my focus here," she said with a frown.

Noah said, "But Elizabeth, honey, I have no idea what you're talking about. Besides, the only woman I can see here is you, darlin'. Now just tell me, what would you like to eat? So I can fix you a plate then one for myself so I can come back here to eat with my beautiful wife. Now hold tight, honey, till I return."

"Oh, Noah, I would like that so very much. I'll be waiting."

After Noah left, her friend Connie walked over to her and said, "I have been waiting to say hi, Elizabeth. And all I can say is, you being big as a cow with your baby, it hasn't taken away from your beauty, dear friend. In fact, you seem to have this glow about you, but are you okay? I've been concerned since I noticed you sitting here."

"Well, I had a little dizzy spell this morning," Elizabeth is telling Connie. "Noah sent Joel for the doctor who told me I could only be here for the party if I stay seated. Of course, Noah will not let me up. He even carried me downstairs, for goodness' sake!"

Connie asked, "Elizabeth, do you realize how lucky you are? I just hope that I will find someone who will care for me the way Noah cares for you."

"I do know how lucky I am, Connie. I love Noah with all my heart too," Elizabeth told her friend. "To me, he is the most handsome man here, or anywhere for that matter."

"I hate to tell you, honey, but you're not the only one to think him handsome." Connie nodded to the group of young ladies eyeing Noah.

"Yes, I've noticed. With me, as you say, big as a cow, it isn't easy to watch either. But I can't say I blame them." She's looking at her husband now across the room as he's juggling two plates while putting food on them. He's wearing a black suit of evening clothes with a white shirt and a string tie. He looks so good with the light streaks in his dark-blond hair, and his green eyes seem to sparkle tonight.

Connie's saying, "Those young women do try to attract Joel's attention as well. But he doesn't seem to notice any more than your husband does. Maybe they think them too forward. But your husband and brother do have to be the two best-looking men here. Well, there is David, too, even if he is still a little young," she's saying.

"What about William?" Elizabeth asked her friend. She knew Connie had always had a crush on him. *She's looking very pretty tonight too*, Elizabeth's thinking, and couldn't understand why William doesn't notice her. Connie's wearing a beautiful green dress, and it goes so well with her dark-brown hair and her hazel eyes. Connie also has a good sense of humor, too, for which she herself has always kind of envied.

"Oh well, there is William," Connie replied with a grin. "But he always has had eyes only for you, Elizabeth," Connie's telling her as Noah brought back two plates loaded with food.

Connie turned to her friend and said with a wide smile, "Looks like your husband plans to feed you, dear friend, so I'll leave you two to eat your food."

"There's no need for you to rush away, Connie. By the way, Elizabeth tells me she doesn't see nearly enough of you these days, and" Noah asked, "how have you been?"

"I've been okay, Noah. Actually I have thought of coming to visit but didn't want to intrude," Connie's saying.

"Connie!" Elizabeth and Noah both said at the same time. So the three of them had a good laugh.

"But seriously," Noah told her, "don't stand on convention. When you have the time, stop by, please." She agreed that she would then went off to get herself a plate of food.

Noah looked at Elizabeth to say, "Connie's looking pretty, don't you think, honey?"

"Yes, she's looking very pretty, and thank you, Noah, for being so kind to her. She has always had such a huge crush on William, but he has totally ignored her tonight."

"Are you kidding me, Elizabeth?" he asked seriously. "I gave her more credit than to be in love with Old Bill."

Elizabeth started laughing then almost choked on her bite of food she had just put in her mouth. Noah's amusing look turned to concern.

He reached out to pat her on the back and said, "Maybe I should just give up trying to be funny, sweetie. I wanted to spend some time with you, not cause you to choke on your food," he said with a worried look.

"Oh, please, honey, don't say such a thing. It isn't your fault. I inhaled at the wrong time. You were funny, Noah," she said, smiling, "and sweet too. I adore you, husband." But she caught her breath this time.

Noah asked, "What is it now, honey? You look pale."

"A sharp pain," she said, "so maybe you should take me upstairs now, Noah."

That's all he needed to hear. He stood and reached for his wife and was rushing for the stairs with her.

Joel is there to ask, "Is the doctor needed?"

Noah said, "Yes, please, and your mother as well." Noah continued up the stairs to their bedroom. He stood Elizabeth on her feet so he can help her undress, when suddenly her water broke.

Elizabeth sucked in her breath. "Oh, Noah! What's wrong with me!" she cried.

Noah pulled her to him to hug her close. He said, "Honey, that's perfectly normal. Your body is doing what is needed to prepare for our baby to be born. I believe I heard the doctor coming now. So let's get this dress off you."

"Where's Mom?" Elizabeth is asking in a child-like voice, "and Tansy too. Noah, will they be here?"

"Yes, honey, I told Joel to get Ellen and the doctor as well. I'll see that Tansy is here, so don't worry, honey."

Ellen was the first to arrive, and after realizing what happened, she said, "I'll just get a clean gown." She took a plain white gown from a drawer and she's back to help Noah with undressing her daughter, and into a clean gown.

The doctor hurried in the room out of breath but managed to say, "I expected this may happen tonight, one reason I asked to be here at the party. Now, Mr. Steele, you will need to leave. I have a rule about not allowing the husband to stay during labor. They tend to get overly excitable."

Noah tried to stare the doctor down, but it didn't work. "Okay," he said. "First thing, my name is Mr. Bennett! Now I will go. But you better be good to her."

He walked to Elizabeth. He said, "Darlin', I'll be just downstairs if you want me." He kissed her then made himself leave, but before he went out the door, he told Ellen he would send Tansy up to help.

The doctor said, "I don't believe we need anyone else." But Noah had already walked through the door and closed it behind him.

Dr. Morris said, "My, but he likes his own way, doesn't he?"

Ellen replied, "My son-in-law likes being with his wife. He may even have been of help, you know." Just then Tansy came hurrying in the room. She said, "I was out of the room downstairs, so I didn't see Noah bring you up here, sweetie," she told Elizabeth. "But now don't worry, your mom and I are here to help."

"Well then," the doctor asked, "do you suppose I could do an examination on my patient now, ladies?"

He and Tansy took one another's measure then decided to work together to help Elizabeth who gave a sigh of relief. All of these strong-willed people care about her, she's thinking, but, oh, she didn't need all the bother just now.

As another pain started, she called, "Mom…oh, it hurts!"

Ellen reached for her daughter's hand to say calmly and soothingly, "Take short breaths. It will soon go away, dear," and the contraction finally eased and went away, so she told Elizabeth, "Relax, save your strength if you can."

The doctor's watching Ellen soothe the girl, and he admired her. He can see where Elizabeth gets her beauty, too, he's thinking, because she's still a very handsome woman. As a doctor, he can't help but be impressed with the mother's way of reassuring her daughter.

He said as much, but Ellen told him, "It's only common sense, sir, but thank you anyway. Elizabeth is a sensible young woman." So she lay her hand over Elizabeth's as she said "My daughter will be a model patient, you'll see." Ellen squeezed Elizabeth's hand.

"Well," the doctor said, "you should be pleased to hear things are going along as it should, dear." He also lay his hand over his patient's.

Chapter 31

But things are not going well downstairs. Noah's pacing the floor, making noises like any other man being kept from his wife when he feels there is a need for him to be with her. He keeps hitting his right fist into his other hand. Harrison's watching his son-in-law, although he understands how Noah feels. His son-in-law has to come to the realization that his wife is in labor. Her mind is consumed with bringing their child into the world. Her husband has to stay on the sideline for now till the baby is born. Then he's the first person she wants to see and to be with him and their child.

So Harrison walked over to say, "Noah, we're working on something in the barn. We could really use your help, if you don't mind, that is."

On one level, Noah realized what Harrison's doing. He still wants to stay, but Ann said, "Noah, you know I will let you know immediately if there's a need for you to be here."

He looked up the stairs again, then James said, "You know, Noah, Harrison and Toby understand as well as I do. We know how you feel about being shut out of what's going on in that room up there. But you know that Ellen is there with Elizabeth, as well as Tansy. And right now, she needs to concentrate on what the doctor and Ellen is telling her. So your best bet, brother, is to try to stay busy. It's not easy, and I understand, but let's try. We'll all be waiting with you, right guys?"

So Noah let the other men take him to the barn, where David and Johnny are. Toby's working on one of his whips. He's going to show the men how he made it. Even though Noah's watching, because its so interesting to him, still he's watching and listening for Ann at the same time. Toby is telling them how he made the handle round and smoothed it by taking a piece of wood the width, fullness, and length of it. "Then I shaped it by cutting it down till it's round with my knife, then using sand to smooth it." Then he said, "I cut the strips of leather. Also I used small nails to attach them on the handle, then used one strip of leather to wrap it around and over where the nails have been used to attach the leather strips to the handle." He worked it in and out with the other strips of leather as he starts the braid. He keeps working with both hands, overlapping the strips into the braid till it comes to a small end which he leaves about one inch and a half unbraided. He does this as before to work one of the strips in and around and ties it off to keep it all in place. Then Toby took a piece of paper and lay it on the work table. And as Noah and Harrison had seen him do before, he stood back about six or seven feet. With a grip on the whip handle, he coiled the whip up with his right hand. Then almost quicker than the eye can see, he split the paper in two pieces. All the other men were just as amazed as Noah and Harrison were when they had watched Toby do this same trick, Noah thought to himself.

But soon afterwards, Noah could hear Ann calling, and he's out the door running before the others knew what had happened. Noah met Ann then passed her at a run before she could tell him anything. He ran in the house straight up the stairs to his wife.

Standing at the door, he can see Elizabeth laying propped up with pillows, with their baby in her arms. Noah's thinking it's the most beautiful sight he has ever seen. When she looked up to see her husband standing there with this look of pure wonder, she could also see love there. Elizabeth reached out her hand to him. She said, "Come say hello to your son, sweetheart."

Noah felt his chest ready to burst with pride for his wife and the son she has just given him. He's thinking with a deep sigh, *God did listen to my prayer to keep my wife safe while she carried then delivered our child.*

"So thank you, Lord," he breathed as he leaned down and kissed his wife tenderly. He asked, "How are you, darlin'?"

"Oh, Noah," Elizabeth said, "I feel so happy. We have a healthy son. Isn't he beautiful?"

Noah gave her a wide smile as he leaned down, kissed her sweet lips again, and whispered, "Darlin', I think you're wonderful," for her ears alone, then he said, "I'm well pleased to have a healthy son. One can tell he is okay by his wanting attention now. I can tell he's going to be an impatient one too."

Elizabeth laughed then, still with a grin, she asked, "Now he wouldn't be his father's son if he didn't show his impatience now, would he?"

"Now you, young lady, deserve another kiss for that statement."

The doctor's watching this touching scene. He felt pleased they had an easy delivery, but he said, "Now we need to let the women clean up this little man."

"Yes, you do that, doctor," Noah told him with a look that leaves no doubt. "But just know I'm not leaving this room, or my wife and son again tonight, until I spend time with them."

"Well, your wife has to be tired, sir," the doctor told Noah. "When Elizabeth's ready for sleep, Doc, I will see that she gets it. Now doctor, we do appreciate that you helped my wife in delivering our son safely."

Doctor Sam knew Noah wouldn't budge, and he grudgingly admired the man for it. *There's no doubt that he loves his wife and is a very happy man, as he should be because his wife is not only lovely but worthy of her husband's love and admiration.*

The doctor's brought back to himself and where he is by Tansy as she asked, "What do you want us to do about this little guy? He's hungry, and just like his daddy, he has no patience in waiting any longer."

The doctor laughed then he said, "Well, I would say if his mother's willing, then let him nurse.

Elizabeth asked excitedly, "Really? May I let my son nurse now, Doctor?" The doctor gave a nod yes. Tansy took the baby and handed it to his mother. Elizabeth said, "Alright now, honey, we'll need to learn this together. So here you go." She lay the baby in the crook of her left arm and helped him find her breast. She put the nipple in her son's mouth. He latched onto it and started nursing. Elizabeth's thinking the feeling is incredible. It hurts, but yet to actually have their son nursing, she feels it is a blessing. She looked up to see her husband who has this look of wonder on his face again. He sensed her look and switched his gaze to her.

"He seems quick to learn, don't you think, darlin'?" His next words were, "Everything seems to be as it should be."

Ellen looked at Tansy, and they both were aware of how much Noah had worried. He had been afraid for his wife and child, so now it's a time to be thankful. By mutual agreement, they left to go downstairs to let the rest of the family know that it's a boy and that Elizabeth and the baby are just fine.

The doctor agreed it's time for him to leave as well, so he said, "Good night now and let me know if you need me." The happy parents were no longer aware of anything but being together with their child.

Chapter  32

J ames is laughing after being informed the baby is a boy and mother and child are fine. "Noah will be the impossibly proud father, you know."

"And you weren't, James Bennett?" Ann asked him, smiling.

"Well I suppose I was. I'm sure Harrison, as well as Toby, was too. We still are proud fathers, right men?" They both agreed.

"We should give them time to be alone now with their baby. Elizabeth will need sleep, as we all do," Ellen said tiredly. "So Harrison, if you don't mind taking me home, I'm ready."

"Sure thing," he told her.

Tansy and Toby were of the same mind. But James and Ann are staying there for Christmas.

"But James will need to go with you, Harrison, to get the boys," Ann is saying.

"But why not just leave them for what's left of this night? If Joel and David wouldn't mind to just stay here," Ellen asked.

Her sons agreed it's fine by the two of them, so James and Ann also agreed it's a better idea.

"The boys are more than likely asleep," Ann allowed.

So Joel and David told James they would help bring in more wood and buckets of coal to be certain there's enough to keep the fireplaces going for the rest of the night, since Noah had built one in every room. Joel looked around the Bennett's new home and thought about how Noah placed a fireplace in every room. Joel remembered his reaction the very first time the house was finished, plus the other days that followed.

* * * * *

"It's beautiful!" Joel exclaimed as he walked in the huge living room of the newly finished Bennett house.

Of particular interest to Joel was that Noah had built a fireplace in almost every room. There's one in each of the six bedrooms, too, a huge one in the front room, one in the dinner room, with another huge one in the kitchen that has an arm that swings back and forth for a large iron pot to hook on. The iron pot was used to cook beef stew, soup, beans, or mustard greens with a chunk of pork for seasoning. Cooking over the fire that way is great, everyone agreed. But Noah had also bought an excellent wood and coal cookstove with a wood box beside it. There's a wood box beside each of the fireplaces with a lid which can also be used as a bench for sitting. Of course, there are coal buckets as well. They all had joked at the time that Noah thinks of everything. Noah had a crew of men come to build all the fireplaces, with the inside firewalls laid with bricks and the outside wall from rocks that have been picked up off the farm over the years.

Harrison told Noah, "I just knew these rocks would be of use to someone."

There is a chimney at each end of the house. So each of the fire places to be connected through out the house.

There was another crew of wood-finishing carpenters to make all the wood furnishings, except the dining room table that was made with inlaid wood by no other than Harrison. But the side tables and a large one for the entrance hall was made by the woodworking crew. They made beautiful mantels, too, with Harrison's help. Elizabeth and Noah both agreed they would rather have wood shutters for the windows inside the downstairs rooms, too, rather than heavy drapes. So that is something else the men made with Harrison's help.

They all had pitched in to help, after the building was all done, with the help of the hired men. Then they turned their attention to butchering a beef and three hogs so all of the families will have enough meat to last hopefully through winter. Of course, they will be doing some hunting for deer and rabbits. The butchering was done the week before because there was a need for meat to serve at the party. After this night makes the party now yesterday.

The women made sausages by mixing in herbs and spices, then making it into patties to fry. They put the fried meat in jars and covered it with the grease, to seal with the rings and lids, to keep for winter stores. They did the same thing with some of the other meat as well. With the help of the men, they cured the hams by rubbing them with brown sugar and wrapping them in cheesecloth. Then the hams are stored along with the sides of beef and pork after being rubbed down generously with salt and hung from the rafters in the smokehouse. But the hired men also helped with cooking some ribs outdoors, along with beef steaks rubbed with a great-tasting sauce Tansy had made just for the party yesterday. But then there had been fried chicken as well, along with all the other food that had been prepared. It turned out to be a great party till Elizabeth started labor. But then she did fine and gave Noah a healthy boy.

* * * * *

Joel is smiling thinking how happy the couple is now with their son. So after banking all the fires tonight downstairs, he and David did the same in all the bedrooms upstairs, except Noah's— they will leave that to him—so they were off to their beds now.

Elizabeth and the baby both are asleep. The baby still has his mother's nipple in his mouth. When Noah lifted him up, there's a drop of the milk on his lips. Noah almost felt jealous of his son, but he wiped the milk away and made sure the baby is still dry. He wrapped him up good in blankets and lay him beside his mother, covered her up, and gave her a light kiss.

Not wanting to wake her, Noah turned to check the fire to be certain there's enough wood with coal to keep it banked for the rest of the night. Then he found a couple of blankets with a pillow to make a pallet for himself on the floor beside the bed. He hoped to sleep a little while anyway. He was awakened a few hours later to what he thought is a cat mewing. He wondered how in the world a cat could get in the house. *Only if one of the children brought it inside*, he's thinking. So it took him a few seconds more before he fully realized it's his son crying. He was up in an instant to reach for the little bundle of blankets. He uncovered his son. The baby is all red-faced from crying. Noah cuddled him close. He stopped crying for a short minute, then he is crying again because the poor little thing is sopping wet. So Noah looked for and found a diaper to change his son. He had learned what to do by taking care of Susie when she was a baby. When the baby's all dry again, he's still not happy, though, so Noah knew there's no help for it but to wake Elizabeth. So that's what he did.

When she came awake, she smiled, "I like waking up to see my two men looking down at me."

"But I believe one of your men is hungry, darlin', and not in a mood for waiting," Noah told her teasingly.

As he lay their son in her arms, the baby started rooting for her nipple and smacking his little lips as both his parents are laughing. Noah's sitting on the side of the bed now. He leaned over and gave his wife a tender kiss, after which, Elizabeth said, "Honey, why don't you lie here beside me, 'cause our son and I have missed you."

So Noah lay down with his wife and son after the little one ate his fill. Noah made sure he's still dry. Then, because of the baby, he checked the fire again. Husband and wife fell asleep with the baby in his mother's arms. She's lying on her side, wrapped in Noah's arm's.

Chapter 33

They were awakened by Tansy the next morning with breakfast for both of them. "Good morning, you two, and it's a good morning indeed, wouldn't you say?"

Noah said, "Bless you, Tansy. How can we ever thank you enough?"

"Upon my honor, Noah Bennett. You hush your mouth now. I don't want to hear talk like that. I do what I do 'cause I want to, and well, you know it. That was that! Noah, I do have to say, though, I'm impressed with you for taking such good care of your son."

"Thanks, Tansy, but I only did what needed to be done"—he picked his son up—"I'm bonding with him, don't you think?"

"Not to worry, Noah, you're going to be a good father," Tansy told him, and Elizabeth agreed with her. "Now, do you two want coffee with something to eat?" They both wanted coffee.

Noah said, "I'll eat with the others downstairs.

"Then you need to go down now. Ann's serving breakfast as we speak. The children stayed over at the farm house last night."

Noah chuckled, "Poor Susie must think we have farmed her out."

"Oh, I'm sure Lily has explained to her about her baby brother," his wife reminded him.

Her husband said, "Well, that makes me feel better."

Noah said, "But that's something else we need to thank Lily for."

"Maybe we should think of a special gift to give her."

"Did you remember today is Christmas?" he asked her.

"I had forgotten. Maybe because something else of importance happened," Elizabeth is saying with a wide smile.

Noah's laughing as he leaned over to give her a quick kiss. "So true sweetie."

Tansy told Noah, "I would give you a chance to wash, get a change of clothes, then you go eat. I will help Elizabeth freshen up and take care of the little one. You know, you two need to think about a name. We can't keep referring to him as *your son* or *the little one*."

Noah chuckled again. "Leave it to Tansy to state the obvious. Have you thought about names for our baby, sweetie? Do you have a preference, maybe?"

"Not really," Elizabeth said. "Have you thought of names, Noah? What was your father's name, and would you like to name our son after him?" He gave her a thoughtful look then asked, "Darlin', would you have a problem with it?"

"Of course not, maybe we could name him after both our fathers," Elizabeth is saying. "What do you think?"

"I think that's what we should do then. Alexander was my father's name," Noah told her.

"Okay, how does Alexander Steele Bennett sound?" she asked.

"Well, I like the two names," Noah answered, "but should it be switched around?"

"No, honey," she said. "He's your son and your father's name should be his first name. I'm sure it won't be a problem for dad. More than likely we'll call him Alex, don't you think?"

"Yeah, that's what my father was called. I'm fine with it," Noah said with a pleased smile. "I'm just happy to have the decision made, and Merry Christmas to you and our son, as he is the very best gift I could have, and for you to have delivered him safely, I am a happy man."

"Now, I best get a move on before Tansy comes back," he leaned down and gave his wife a kiss.

* * * * *

Noah washed up quickly then dressed and hurried downstairs. James, Joel, and David are still at the table having coffee, more or less waiting for him, Noah's thinking with a smile.

And it was proven to be true when James teased him by saying, "About time you finally came downstairs. We have been waiting to hear how the new mother and baby are doing."

"Great," Noah announced. "Elizabeth is more beautiful then ever and little Alex is a healthy baby boy, brother, and now I know how you felt when Ann delivered your healthy boys."

The look on his brother's face was so touching when he asked, "Noah, you and Elizabeth named the boy after Dad, didn't you?"

"Yes, we did," Noah told him. "Actually it was Elizabeth's idea. And I am so pleased we named him Alexander Steele."

He looked to Joel and David to ask, "Do you two think your father will be okay with having a grandson named for him?"

Joel said, "Seriously, Noah, I'm sure Dad will be pleased as punch to have his first grandson have his name."

David agreed. "Dad will be pleased, no doubt."

Noah asked, "Did any of you remember that today is Christmas?"

"We all know what today is, Noah," James teased. "We would like to celebrate Christ's birthday as well as the birth of yours and Elizabeth's son. So we need to get busy and get things set up before the children get back here. We can exchange gifts upstairs in your bedroom. That way, we will meet little Alex at the same time. What do you say, brother, since it's your home?" James asked with that hallmark crooked grin of his.

"I think it an excellent idea, people, and thank you," Noah told them. "And it means a lot to me. I'm sure Elizabeth will be delighted as well. So, what do we need to do to get things ready?"

"As a matter of fact, the gifts are stored in the other guest room where I was sleeping," Joel told them and agreed to bring them downstairs with David's help, "if he's willing," Joel said teasingly as he turned to his brother.

David said, "Yeah, I'm ready to help," and followed Joel upstairs.

Ann, came in as they returned to say, "You can put those gifts in the living room under the tree if you wouldn't mind." So thats what they did. "The gifts will be there when the children are brought back here. Then we can take them upstairs as we all go up later."

"Speaking of the children, I wish we had something special to give Lily. She's been such a great help with the children, don't you think?"

"I do," Ann told him. "So let me think on it; I will come up with something then I'll let you know." So everyone went to work getting the morning milking and feeding chores done and helped wherever else they were needed in the house.

Chapter 34

So since it had snowed during the night, Joel and David hitched up Noah's buggy to bring the children back. Joel in the buggy and David on his horse were on their way to get the parents with children. When they reached the farm, Harrison is out at the shed getting ready to hitch a horse up to the sleigh.

Joel called to say, "Hey, Dad, I'll do that. And taking the sleigh is a great idea. We're taking gifts to open upstairs with Elizabeth so we can take a peek at little Alexander Steele Bennett." As Joel told his father, he couldn't hide his grin while watching Harrison's face.

"Is that so?" Harrison asked, smiling, "I think it great, we're all looking forward to meeting the little guy. But Joel, while you're getting the horse hitched up to the sleigh, I have something to get from the barn."

Harrison came back with something wrapped in a blanket. He said, "Maybe we need both the sleigh and buggy after all. So if you would take Lily and the children in the sleigh, I believe they will enjoy the ride, don't you?"

Joel's smiling as he said, "I agree, Dad. It will be a treat for them too. I remember how we as kids loved riding in the sleigh, with the snow falling on our faces."

David will stay with his horse though, but he did help load the kids in the sleigh. Then they were off. The children thought it exciting. It's still snowing just enough to make it truly a white Christmas. The children like having the snow falling so they can taste the flakes of wet snow. So it's starting out to be a great day. It will all be a surprise for Elizabeth too. When the sleigh and buggy arrived back there, Noah and James, came out to help get the children in the house.

Noah said, "We should all shed our coats and warm up a bit, so go over by the fire. Then later we can go up to surprise Elizabeth." He smiled as he sat down with his daughter on his lap.

He told her, "Mommy has a big surprise for you, too, sweetie. But were you and the boys good for Lily? And did you all enjoy the sleigh ride? Was it fun?"

Susie, Jimmy, and Bobby all said almost in unison, "It was great fun. We liked the snow falling so we could catch it on our tongue."

"Then did you thank Grandpa Harrison for the sleigh ride?"

"Yeah, we did, Daddy, and we be good," Susie said. She looked at Lily to ask, "Didn't we?"

"Of course you were, honey, and we all had fun playing hide and seek outside, and hide the thimble inside, till naptime."

"Well, we parents are all very grateful for your help, Lily! So thank you," Noah told her.

Lily laughed and said, "You know I wouldn't have been allowed to stay anyway. I'm not far enough from being a child myself. But I didn't help matters by behaving like one for too long."

"You're helping repair that part by admitting it," Noah told her seriously. "You're maturing okay, Lily," he told her with a grin.

"So now, you are all are aware today is Christmas Day, right?"

They all said as one, "Yes."

"Okay, see, Old Saint Nick has brought all these gifts under tree. Soon, Uncle Toby and his family will get back here with what Santa left at their house. Then we will all go upstairs to surprise Elizabeth. How does that sound?" Noah asked. "And it's to be a surprise for her too."

So when Toby and Tansy came with Johnny, who seemed excited as well as the other children, Ann whispered to Noah that she was able to find just what he was looking for as a gift for Lily. She had wrapped it and handed it to him.

So everyone was ready to go up to see the new baby. The men would bring up the gifts after having a good look at little Alex. Noah put the gift under the tree then he picked up his daughter and put her on his shoulders then led the way.

When they came to the bedroom door, Noah knocked.

"Come in," Elizabeth answered.

"Are you ready for company?" he asked.

"Yes."

Noah opened the door. He walked to the bedside with Susie.

She said "Oh, Daddy, Mommy has baby with her, Why she have baby?"

"Because, sweetie, we would like for you to meet your new brother. What do you think?"

Susie's eyes were round as she asked, "He for me?"

Everyone chuckled as Noah said, "He's for all of us. He is mine and Mommy's son. He's your brother, just like Bobby and Jimmy are brothers, do you understand?"

"Yeah. He pretty, Mommy"—she is wiggling—"I hug mommy," she said.

Noah set her down on the side of the bed to let her hug Elizabeth. Then Susie gave her mommy a wet kiss and said, "I love you."

Elizabeth had tears in her eyes when she used her other arm to hug Susie.

Noah said, "Here, let me have Alex, and let the others get a peek at him."

Joel's standing nearby, so he reached for the baby, looked him over, then looked to Elizabeth to say, "You did good, sis." Joel looked so natural with his nephew tucked in the crook of his arm, holding a little hand in his large one, smiling as if he were the father. Noah gave his wife a kiss then said, "Well, I believe I should get some credit."

Joel gave him a wide grin as he said, "You, Noah, there could be no denial of this child as being yours if you wanted to."

"Well, there's no chance of that happening," Noah replied smartly.

Lily had come to get a peek at the baby while Joel's holding him, so he reluctantly handed the little guy to her. Then David's looking over Lily's shoulder to see his new nephew. Then the baby was passed to his Grandpa Harrison. Ellen is thinking her husband has that same look of wonder as when he had his first look at his own children.

He said, "Well, I believe this little guy will grow into his name just fine, don't you all?"

"I think it a good name," James replied when the baby was passed to him. "I'm pleased his parents named him after both sides of the family. And isn't it tradition to name the first son with his mother's maiden name as his middle one, which is to honor the grandfather?" The children were all in awe of the tiny baby. But soon they were ready for the gifts. So the men all went back downstairs to bring the gifts up.

Elizabeth is pleasantly surprised herself. She looked around at her family and thanked them, along with her husband, for making this a special Christmas Day. As the gifts were handed out, everyone's pleased with what they had received.

Ellen had gotten a new bonnet from Tansy. She put it on to show how proud she is. Tansy received a new apron from Ellen. She tied it around her waist with a wide smile as she said, "How did you know, girl, it's just what I wanted?" The children all were pleased with their toys as well. Jimmy and Bobby opened a toy wooden train together from Harrison. Then each got a new snow sled from "Santa." Susie opened a new dollie, and Lily, when she opened the gift marked "From Everyone," she looked surprised to find a beautiful hand mirror, comb, and brush set. She had a look of pure joy on her face.

Noah said, "Lily, we all are so grateful to you for your help with the children. So again, thanks."

She blushed prettily, everyone thought. But she said, "It was no trouble, really."

Harrison had left the room again while he was gone. Noah reached in his pocket and brought out a small box. He handed it to his wife as he said, "I should have given this to you long before now, darlin'."

Elizabeth opened the box to find a beautiful wedding ring. Her eyes were filled with tears when she looked to her husband. She said, "This is such a sweet thing for you to do, Noah. I didn't regret not getting one when we married, you know. But I will treasure this ring always, darling."

The look on Noah's face is priceless! When she called him *darling*, a spark of passionate fire leaped into his eyes. He was looking at his wife. She was the only one to see his face with the look he had given her. It's going to be a long, hard wait for him to show his wife how much that remark means to him, but it will be worth the wait, he's thinking.

But for now, Harrison had returned, so Noah stood as Harrison brought in something wrapped with a blanket to set it down on a low table. He took the blanket away to show a beautifully made cradle.

"For my grandson," he announced. "I started it a while ago, but I wanted it to be a gift, so here it is. Next thing will be a bed when Alex is ready for it," Harrison added.

Elizabeth and Noah thanked him wholeheartedly.

Then Elizabeth asked, "Joel, do you have something for Noah?"

"You bet, sis." Joel reached in his pocket. He brought out a box and handed it to his brother-in-law to say, "From your wife, sir."

Noah took the box and opened it. There lay a watch just like the one his father had carried. He looked at Joel who said, "Elizabeth asked me to get it for you. I was lucky to find this one in London, though I had looked other places."

"Thanks," Noah said in a husky voice. Then he turned to his wife with a look of amazement and then with tenderness. He asked, "How did you know, sweetheart?"

"James told me that you have said that it's the one thing you wished you could have of your father's—his pocket watch. It's the best we could do, honey, but I wanted to get you something special," she told him. "With help from James, Joel found this watch."

"I love it," he told her, and when he opened the lid, there is a place for a picture. His heart swelled with love. "We'll discuss it later," he said with another tender look.

Ellen and Tansy went to work immediately to prepare the cradle for the baby. So when it's ready, Noah reached down, picked up his son, and lay him in the cradle while he was sitting on the low table for easy reach.

"This is great, Harrison. It will allow Elizabeth to go downstairs to eat Christmas dinner with us," Noah said. "We can take Alex downstairs too."

Both Elizabeth and Noah thanked Harrison again. It's easy to see he's proud of his gift. Noah also thanked James for helping with his gift. James told him he was happy to do it. He had bought his wife, Ann, a beautiful pin, and her eyes are still shining when she happens to catch her husband's eye. Tansy had received some new hankies from Elizabeth, for which she is also proud.

Chapter 35

The other three women went back down to the kitchen to finish up their meal. After one last look at the baby, Lily followed them. Soon, the men gathered up all the wrappers from the gifts to take downstairs with them. Before they left, Noah asked Joel if he would want to carry the baby downstairs.

Joel asked with a grin, "Are you sure, Noah, I am to be trusted to carry your son?"

"Don't make me regret it, Joel. He's precious cargo, you know."

Joel agreed. He said, "I best carry little Alex then. So, David, will you bring the cradle?"

"Oh, sure. So I get the hard part here, but yeah, I'll do it," David teased.

Soon Noah had mother and child downstairs with the baby in his cradle. Elizabeth is sitting in a chair at the table with everyone else around her. With the food laid out, there's plenty of everything to eat. Joel and David, along with James, had gone out early this morning to shoot the huge turkey which they dressed out for the ladies to bake. Ellen made a special dressing to go with the rest of the Christmas dinner. There's fresh-baked bread, as usual, potatoes saved from the fall crop just for today, cooked with green beans that had been canned and seasoned with salt pork. There's baked squash with lots of butter and honey, pumpkin pies with whipped cream to go on them; a special cake made with dried apples and some of Harrison's good molasses, it's called a spiced stack cake, made by Tansy with a recipe handed down through her mother's family. Ann had made her special chocolate cake with the recipe that came from her mother, which the children like so well, and, of course, Noah too; coffee and cold water brought in from the spring house to drink and to make tea with, milk for the little ones.

Harrison said a prayer to say, "We thank you, Lord, for all our many blessings this day and the newly born child, as we remember the birth of your Son, Jesus, this day." Then he said grace, "Thank you, Lord, for this food and the loving hands that prepared it." Everyone gave their silent prayers; even the children are thankful for their gifts.

Now it is time to fill the children's plates first, then everyone else can enjoy their meal with good conversation and laughter. But all too soon, after the dishes are washed and everything is put in its place, it's time for the day to end and the others to go to their homes, except for James and Ann—they are happy they won't be leaving today.

"But tomorrow," James made it known, "We need to get back home." Both his boys had long faces, so James told them they best make good use of the time they have left today. So the boys went off to play with Susie and can be heard now laughing and having a good time. Their parents may relax for now.

Elizabeth said, "Noah, I don't feel right not helping with the cleanup chores."

Noah had picked up his wife after the meal is over to seat her beside him on one of two loveseats that have been placed on each side of the huge fireplace. With a fire blazing and the baby's crib on a table nearby, it's very cozy.

Noah said, "Elizabeth, please don't worry about such things. You will be back to doing house chores soon enough, but are you tired now, or can you stay up a while longer?

"I would love to stay as long as our son will allow," Elizabeth teased. "He's sleeping good, don't you think?"

James and Ann had come in to sit in the loveseat across from them. "You should hope he can sleep for at least four hours now, till you get your strength back, anyway. But from what I have seen, Noah is going to be good help with the baby, like his brother," Ann is telling Elizabeth.

Smiling, she said, "It must be a family trait."

"Hardly," James said with a chuckle. "Mom couldn't keep Dad at home long enough. He would rather be out working with horses. But he did love Mom and us, right Noah?"

"I believe so," Noah answered. "When he wasn't working with a horse, Dad would do things with mom and the two us. He was always laughing, happy-go-lucky, so to speak. He would take mom in his arms, dance her around the room, tell her the horse he is working with is going to be a winner, then we'll be rich. But one day, two of the other trainers brought dad home. He had been busted up bad by that very same horse he was so sure was to make his fortune. He only lived a few hours, which was a good thing because he was in terrible pain. But it was the end of our life as we knew it," Noah is saying. "Our mother never recovered. Even though she did remarry, it was mostly for us two boys that she married our stepfather, which was a huge mistake on our mother's part, because he really didn't want us, did he, James?"

"No he didn't. I, too, believe it was a sad fact," James said with a deep sigh. "Mom and dad were such a handsome couple, and it was not hard to tell they were madly in love either. Mom was so pretty. She's where Noah gets his fair good looks. But don't let it go to your head, brother," James teased.

"And dad had the dark, handsome look, such as you do, James. Even though your hair isn't quite as dark as his, but you did get his blue eyes."

About now, they hear the baby making noises. "Sounds to me like we are going to have company here," Noah said, grinning. And he was already on his feet to get his son. *Not hard to tell he's a proud father,* the others were thinking while watching him check the baby's diaper. It's wet.

He said, "We need a dry one, don't we partner?" He's talking to his son as if the baby knows what Noah's saying. Elizabeth is amazed at how well he's doing. *But then Noah is good at whatever he does,* she's thinking. Then Noah picked their son up. He came back to sit down with him. He asked Elizabeth, "Are you ready to go upstairs, sweetheart, or do you want to try and nurse him here?"

Elizabeth asked Ann, "Do you think it okay if I feed him here?"

Ann said, "I don't see anything wrong with it, Elizabeth. Here, let me get you a blanket as a cover. Don't make the little thing wait to eat. More than likely, he is just like his father and uncle who are not good at waiting for what they want," Ann said teasing after she handed the throw to Elizabeth.

"Now, you come here, miss prissy," James said as he took Ann's hand to lead her back to the loveseat. "You could have gone a long time without saying something like that. I will just have to punish you." He bent his head to give his wife a kiss she won't soon forget.

When Ann could get her focus back, she said, "You know it's true, James."

"Yeah, but it gave me a good excuse to kiss you senseless, my dear wife."

"Alright, you two, it should be *me* kissing my wife," Noah groaned.

"Yeah, well I have already been in your shoes, brother. Don't be too hard on yourself. Learn to be inventive, if you know what I mean," James gave his brother a devilish grin. Then he took Ann's hand again. "Come on, honey, we need to get those three little Indians in bed. Then we can help Noah get Elizabeth and their son upstairs."

And so finally Noah has his wife and son back in their bedroom. Alex is sleeping and Elizabeth is already in bed. She looks tired but said, "I'm determined to wait till my husband is in bed beside me, so we can at least cuddle before sleeping."

After undressing, Noah climbs in bed and immediately takes Elizabeth in his arms to kiss her the way he has been dying to do all day. It pleases him when she said, "I had been looking forward to this time as well." And they fell asleep in each other's arms and slept till their son decided he wants attention.

Noah's the one to wake first, and after changing his diaper, he brought the baby to his mother. Noah felt this would be the way of things, for a little while, to come. But he really didn't mind. He enjoys this time with his son. When their son woke them for the second time, it's still early morning, but Noah is in the habit of waking around this time anyway. After Alex has a dry diaper and has been fed, he's back to sleep in his cradle. Noah told Elizabeth he's going to take King for a run now.

"I should be back before Alex needs to eat again. So you go back to sleep and enjoy being pampered for now."

He gave her a quick kiss then she's back to sleeping peacefully.

Chapter 36

W hen Noah reached the stable, Joel's already there getting King out of his stall for Noah to take him on their run.

"Do you believe you can take King out for his run yourself, Joel?"

"I'm willing to try, Noah, if you believe King will allow me to ride him," Joel answered.

"We won't know unless you try, so just remember, don't rush and let him decide if or when to run," Noah's telling Joel. "I believe he will accept you. Besides, you raised him. He'll remember you."

King stood back, just looking at Joel for a few seconds, then he finally started walking toward him. Joel stood still and let King come to him. It was slow but King came then let Joel touch him. Joel rubbed his hand down King's nose all the while asking if he would mind going for a run. Joel managed to get the bridle on, then the saddle. He walked outside with King then mounted.

Noah said, "Just give him his head, he'll do the rest."

So Joel did, and King is running almost before Joel's ready, but he managed to keep his seat. He just let him run for about two miles down the road, then he pulled the reins back to turn King back toward home. This time, Joel's ready for the quick start.

Noah's waiting with his watch when James came out. He wanted to know what's going on.

Noah replied, "I'm waiting for Joel to return from a run with King."

James laughed, "I was under the impression, Noah, that King will only allow you to mount him."

"In the past, that was true," Noah told James. "But did you realize that Joel raised King? He's been around him from day one."

Just then, they can see horse and rider coming at a dead run. When Joel brought King to a stop, Noah clicked his watch. He said, "Just look at this watch! His time is even better, Joel. You must have the touch. How far did you go?"

"Two miles," Joel told him, laughing. He almost ran out from under me here starting out though. He can run, and if you're in the saddle, you best be ready when he is. And it's different sitting in the saddle, right Noah?"

"Yeah," Noah agreed, "just a mite." He grinned as he said, "Now there's no doubt in my mind, Joel, that you and King can win at the race in Maryland."

"Well, I'm getting excited now myself," Joel told them. "I did have some reservations, you know, but thought that I could pull it off. But now, well, I plan to work hard to be ready for the race, to continue to work hard to get King on my side."

"Joel, you have King on your side, or you wouldn't have gotten close enough to put the bridle on him. But you're wise not to take him for granted," Noah told him.

Toby's just now walking up to see Joel leading King into the barn. He wanted to know, "What's going on here, guys?"

Noah said, "Well, Toby, believe it or not, that young man just took King for his morning run and clocked a better time then I did."

Toby laughed and slapped his hand against his leg. He asked, "Now how does that make you feel, Noah?"

"Oh, I have to admit it's a little bruising to my ego," Noah said, laughing, "but I'm pleased as punch for Joel. I told him that now I have no doubt he and King can win at the Maryland track. But he'll need good help with him."

"Well, I wouldn't miss the race," Toby said. "And he can count on me to help too."

"For now, I reserve my right not to commit myself. It all depends on how things are with Elizabeth and Alex," Noah said. "They are my first priority, you know. But if at all possible, I will be there too."

James spoke up to say, "I'll try to be there also. It will be a pleasure to help get things ready for the race. We have some time yet to plan because the Maryland race isn't till third week in May, right?"

"You're right," Noah answered. "Two weeks after the Kentucky Derby. Now I best go back to check on my wife and son. See you guys later," he said with a wide smile as he turned toward the house.

"If there's a happier man than Noah Bennett," James said as he's watching his brother go inside, "I don't know anyone. Well, except maybe me." He grinned.

* * * * *

David was late coming over. It was his turn to take the cows to pasture. Toby and James are still standing in front of the barn. They were still excited about Joel taking King for his morning run.

David asked, "Whats going on here? Did I miss something?"

"Yeah, just the fact that Joel took King for his run and clocked a better time then Noah."

"Are you kidding me?" David asked. He's excited now too.

"Nope," Toby said with a wide smile. "But Noah is okay with it. In fact, he's the one to clock them."

So David went straight in the barn to help Joel with cooling down King. He said, "Hey, I just heard you took King for his morning run," he said with a wide grin.

Joel said, "Yeah, David, isn't it great?"

"You bet,' David answered. So after he and David finished with King, the two brothers came out of the stable. All four men are headed back in the house for breakfast.

As Noah entered the bedroom, he could hear Tansy talking to the baby. Elizabeth is watching with a smile. When she turned her lovely face to him, his heart swelled with love and tenderness. *She's so lovely*, he's thinking. As he walked over to sit on the side of the bed to lean over for a kiss, she surprised him by putting her arms around his neck and pulling him down to her for their kiss.

He said in a whisper, "What's that for, darlin'?"

"I've missed you, husband," she told him, smiling.

"Maybe I should go out then come back in again," he chuckled.

"Don't you dare, sir," Elizabeth teased.

"I second that," Tansy replied as she brought Alex to him. "You stay right here with your wife and son."

"Tansy, I was only teasing," Noah said, laughing. "But so you know, I'm staying right here, 'cause this is where I want to be." But since James and Ann are taking their boys and leaving for home today, Noah left his wife and son asleep to see James and his family off, with a promise from James to see them soon.

Chapter 37

Noah never gets tired of spending time with Elizabeth and Alex. But he and Harrison with Toby are making headway with getting their horse breeding barn in working order. Joel and David, also with Toby, spend time working with King. But they also do help out with the work on the barn. Harrison is well pleased with the barn. It has been a dream of his to start breeding thoroughbred horses. And now, with Noah and his sons and with Toby's help, his dream is coming true. For now, it's hard to believe how quickly the time is passing.

Normally, farmers hire other men to help with the corn shelling, and Harrison is no different. But sometimes, the farmers around the neighborhood like to have a corn-shelling contest at different farms. Today, the corn shelling happens to be at the Steele farm. Each person puts fifty cents in the hat for whoever wins. Harrison and sons can hold their own in the contest, Toby better than others. Noah has finally found something he isn't so good at, but he just takes it in stride with the good-natured teasing. He thinks the contest is fun anyway. They get together in the barn with bales of hay to sit on while they work. They just pitch the cobs aside when they're done. The women like to keep the cobs to use in their cookstove. Seems they are good to get the fire up when it's needed. Some of the men are amazingly fast at shelling the corn off the cob. Noah would almost rather watch than participate, but he gave it his best try. Finally, Mr. Boggs was voted the winner this time, and everyone is pleased for him. Next time it may be their turn to win.

The women meet in the house. There's a quilting frame set up for whoever needs their quilt finished. Then it's the one put in the frame. The women sew and enjoy each other's company. There's also food ready when the men are finished with the corn shelling. Ellen and Tansy take care of the food while the other ladies do the sewing. Ellen made clothes for her family, also made quilts for the same reason but never cared much for quilting bees, and this is another thing she and Tansy agree on. They still enjoyed getting together with the other ladies though.

Because she is a new mother, Elizabeth is excused from sewing, but she enjoys being part of the gathering. When the men came in to eat, they were full of good-natured teasing for the fun of it.

Harrison said, "Ellen dear, we managed to get quite a lot of corn shelled tonight."

Next time they will meet at the Boggs farm. And so it would go for the next few weeks. But Noah and Harrison wanted to spend most of their time with building the breeding business. Alex is now three months old, a healthy happy baby, his parents couldn't be more proud of him. Of course, so is everyone else. Alex never lacks for attention but Noah spends more than his share of time with his son. He enjoys helping with the baby's bath. He and Elizabeth laugh at how their son is kicking and splashing in the water and making noises and then stop to smile at his parents. It is a time that is much appreciated. But afterwards Noah goes back work.

When the weather turns warmer, Harrison takes time away from their work to start preparations for the tobacco bed, so the others decided to help. Noah and Toby are amazed at the process which Harrison uses to prepare the ground before planting the tobacco seeds, then to cover it with a cheesecloth to help the seeds to germinate. Harrison knows how long it will take so when he removes the cloth, there are plenty of these tender green plants. Then the ground for the tobacco patch is prepared, by which time the plants will be ready for planting. Once that is done, the corn fields are next to prepare for planting. Now that's all done, the time for the race in Baltimore, Maryland, is near. So there's lots of preparation in planning for that as well.

The women have been busy, each planting their gardens. Ellen, Elizabeth, and Tansy each have a small garden near their house, but there's a huge one which is planted later for canning and preserving in the fall. The women enjoy working together, and the men are wise enough not to interfere. The weather is so nice, it's almost unseasonably warm spring, so it's much appreciated.

Now the time for the race is here. And the whole family has made the decision to go to Baltimore to watch Joel ride King in the race, with the exception of James and Ann who regrettably can't get away after all. It's something that can't be helped. Noah and Elizabeth have decided it's okay to take Alex. So preparations are underway to make all the arrangements which are being made by Noah of course. Everyone is in agreement that he is so much better at that sort of thing. Joel's feeling good about the race, so are Noah and Toby. They feel confident that Joel is ready to meet the challenge, but one can't leave David out either. He also has an important role to play in getting King prepared. He always helps with cooling him down after a run. And of course, there's Little Jo, he won't let them leave him behind. So everything is pretty much the same preparations as for the Kentucky Derby, where Noah won with King.

They made it to the train station just fine and the trip is uneventful. They all agreed Maryland is a beautiful state, with the old country estates that can be seen from the train, horse farms along the way, and some fine-looking horses, the men are all thinking. Then from the train station, they arrived at the Grand Hotel which Noah tells them is where they want to stay. "We'll have good service there."

"It's definitely grand," Elizabeth said with a smile for her husband.

Noah's carrying their son. He returned her smile. She's thinking, *My husband is still the most handsome man ever,* as he's telling her, "We should be comfortable here, honey. And it will be great since we do have Alex with us."

"I should think so, Noah. You do think of everything, don't you?"

"When it comes to my family, I try, darlin'. We need to ask Susie what she wishes to do, though, she's spending so much time with Lily now. But maybe Lily would rather have some time to herself."

"You can ask, Noah, but I believe Lily enjoys having Susie around as well. I have thought about our childhood and maybe we, as in myself, Joel, and David, didn't try hard enough to include Lily back then."

Noah reminded his wife, "Honey, I remember how spoiled Lily was, so I don't think anyone would blame you and your brothers for not wanting to include her."

Noah continued, "So it's a little hard to believe how much she's changed in the time since I first met her."

After the whole family is registered and they have their room numbers. Which Noah signed for Joel and David. While they took King to the stables to get him settled in a stall. But everyone else is pleased with their accommodations, and Lily is happy to have Susie with her.

Susie asked, "Daddy, it K I stay with Lily, please..." She is looking up at him with that cute trusting face.

Noah's thinking, *With that face, how could I say no if I wanted to?* Instead, he said, "Honey, if that's what both you and Lily wish, then it's fine with me, sweetie."

So Susie clapped her hands, "Goody Daddy," and raised her arms for him to pick her up. When he did, Susie put her arms around Noah's neck and gave him a big hug and a wet kiss before he put her back down. He's laughing as the two girls go off with Harrison and Ellen. Then he turned serious as he said, "Lord, but she's growing too fast for me. I am afraid I don't spend enough time with her since Alex's birth." He turned to look at his wife with that look of self-doubt that she hates to see, especially since it isn't true.

She said, "Come, Noah, let's get Alex settled." Then Elizabeth walks to her husband to put her arms around his neck to give him a tight hug.

She said, "Noah, darling, you're an excellent father. So don't doubt it, please... as Susie would do. I don't like to see that look on your handsome face." Then she kissed him. That's when he took over to kiss her breathless. Finally, he let her come up for air. Elizabeth lay her head against his chest till she regained her balance. She looked up at him to say, "Noah, I do hope this is something that never changes."

"You have no need to worry on my part, honey, I enjoy kissing you too much."

He gave her a look that spoke volumes and he said, "I wish we could just get in that bed there so I could prove to you that I mean what I say, Mrs. Bennett. But for now, I'm afraid we need to prepare to get with the rest of the family and go to the dining room."

Noah is helping Elizabeth get Alex ready, then they go in search of the Steele's room to wait for Toby and his family. Then they will all make their way downstairs to the dining room. After Noah made sure the family is all seated at a large table that will accommodate all of them, he turned to Elizabeth and said, "I'll go check on those brothers of yours, sweetheart, and hopefully bring them back here to eat with us."

While Noah is gone, Harrison is holding little Alex who's perfectly content with his grandfather. Toby told his friend, "You look so natural with Alex."

"Surely, Toby, you haven't forgotten Ellen and I have four children of our own."

Toby started to say something more as this handsome man walked up to their table to stand where Elizabeth is sitting. She's talking with Ellen and Tansy so she wasn't paying attention to the gentleman, so he cleared his throat loudly, "Uh...hum."

Elizabeth turned to look up at him, along with everyone else. Harrison asked "May we help you, sir?"

The man never took his eyes off Elizabeth as he said, "I wish to speak to this young lady here whom I have been admiring since coming into the dining hall and noticed her. Would you care to dine with me, miss? My name is—"

Then a voice behind him said, "It does not matter who you are, mister. This is my wife. And you need to apologize to her immediately!"

The gentlemen turned to face Noah. He started to say, "What the...," then he recognized Noah.

He said, "You old dog you, Noah. What are you talking about? You married? I don't believe it for a minute."

"You best believe it, Casey, because this is my wife. Now apologize!" Noah firmly stated.

"Yes, of course, Noah," the man said as he turned back to Elizabeth. He said, "I hope you will accept my apology, Mrs. Bennett."

Elizabeth responded with, "Yes, I accept your apology, sir," but she looked at Noah with uncertainty. Noah came to her and put his hand on her shoulder. He said, "It's okay, honey, Casey is an old friend." So he introduced his friend to the others as Casey Sears. "We met on the racing circuit too. Casey, do you remember Toby Tyler?"

"Of course. How're you doing, Toby? Are you settled down too?" Casey asked.

"Yes, I am, Casey, and this is my wife, Tansy, and here is my son, Johnny. We are doing fine. We are with Noah and the Steele family now, near Corbin, Kentucky. They have a horse-breeding farm there. We're here because their horse King will be competing in the race tomorrow."

"You don't say! I'm riding a fine horse in the race tomorrow too. So I wish you luck, Noah."

Noah laughingly said, "Oh, I'm not riding King tomorrow. Joel Steele here is. I rode King in the Kentucky Derby. We won and even set a record there. But I am retired now. Joel here is as good, or better, rider, so good luck riding against him and King." So Casey Sears, a good-looking man who knows it (he believes he's the answer to every woman's dream), gave Elizabeth another searching look, but finally admitted he has no hope with this beauty.

He said, "Noah, you always seem to have a way with your women."

Noah turned to say, "Watch what you say, Casey," in a warning voice. "Elizabeth isn't just any woman, she is my wife. This is my daughter and my son here; they are what's most important to me now."

"I best leave then," Casey replied, "while I can still call you friend. Good day." He tipped his hat to all and walked away.

Elizabeth gave a sigh of relief, but Noah's grinning when he said, "There was really no need for concern, honey. Casey is mostly all talk, right Toby?"

"Yeah," Toby answered. "Casey likes to think he has a way with women. Most times he does, I guess. But he had trouble believing he didn't have a chance with Miss Elizabeth." Noah watched Casey leave as he's thinking, *I can't really blame the man for his attraction to Elizabeth. She is a beautiful woman.* Today she's dressed in a simple blue dress, but it's a perfect fit to her slim figure, with sleeves to the elbow and a square neckline, but simplicity seems to suit his wife best with her hair brushed back in a bun. With her kind of beauty, she can wear her hair anyway and it still suits her. But then he could be prejudiced, he thought with a smile.

Then he happened to look Lily's way and drew in his breath. The girl's face may as well be cut from stone. He's pretty sure he can guess at the reason, but best to ignore it. The girl can be pretty if she just lets it happen. He is pleased that no one else seems to have noticed though. He also is pleased they are able to enjoy their meal after all. Alex was on his best behavior, too, and it's a relaxing time.

Elizabeth said, "Noah, I was thinking it's too bad James and Ann couldn't make the trip with us. But I do realize there is the spring planting and Ann's garden to be planted."

"Yes, I agree," Noah said. "But they would appreciate knowing you miss them, darlin'." "Joel, how's King behaving? He's getting to be an old hand at traveling, now, don't you think?"

"Yeah, Noah, he's doing fine. But I'm glad he'll have all the time he needs to rest up for the race tomorrow."

"Oh, don't you worry about King," Toby assured Joel. "He could run the same without rest."

"I think maybe that's true." David put in his two cents' worth. "I don't believe there's another horse that can beat him, 'cause he won't allow it." Everyone had to a good laugh at David's little joke.

Chapter  38

After a restful night, Noah, Joel, Toby, David, and his charge Little Jo, left early with King for the track. Harrison is again left to see to the women and children. As it was for the Kentucky derby, they all slept later, but it's still early when they made their way down for breakfast and had just gotten seated.

When Noah's friend Casey came to their table, he spoke to Harrison first, then concentrated his attention on Elizabeth, asking how she's doing this morning. Elizabeth said, "Fine, thank you, sir."

Casey asked her, "Do you mind if I ask? Where did Noah have an opportunity to meet someone as lovely as you, my dear lady?"

Elizabeth looked Mr. Sears straight in the eyes as she said, "How Noah and I met should not be of importance to you. What's important is we met and both of us fell in love at first sight, and we couldn't be happier, sir."

"Well, you all have a good day now," and again he tipped his hat before leaving.

Tansy said, "Upon my honor, I do hope that man finally gets it through his head that you're Noah's wife and proud of it."

Elizabeth said, "Thanks, Tansy, and I certainly hope he does too."

By the time they need to leave, the women were all dressed and ready to leave for the track. Harrison had been taking care of Alex so Elizabeth could get dressed. They were all wearing the same dresses they wore to the derby race and looked just as good in their hats. Noah had helped to get King prepared, and he's ready to go check on his family. He thought maybe Harrison would be here with them by now. Noah also wanted to watch the race from the stands for a change.

He reminded Joel, "Just remember to keep your cool and let King have his head. He knows what to do."

"Thanks," Joel answered.

"Now I'm going to sit with my family and watch you and King win this race," as he gave Joel a slap on the back.

* * * * *

Elizabeth is pleasantly surprised to see Noah walking toward them and sitting down beside her. He gave her a hug and reached for their son. "I wouldn't miss being here with you and the family, honey."

He can see Susie is sitting with Lily. She said, "Daddy, I stay with Lily, K."

Noah said, "That's fine, honey, just enjoy watching Uncle Joel ride King and let's hope they win." He finished with a wide smile for his daughter, then he said, "I hope it's not a problem for you, Lily. And I hope you enjoy the race too."

It's almost as if Lily forced herself to speak as she said, "It's fine, Noah."

"Okay then, let's relax and enjoy watching Joel and King win this race."

It's time now for the walk over to the stands. Joel felt he's as ready as he can be. Toby and David are with him and it helps to have them there. King acts and looks the champion he is—Midnight King—It's how Joel has always thought of King because of his jet-black color. They walk to the stands then get the call for riders up.

So Joel gets a leg up in the saddle, which is totally unnecessary but part of the routine, and he's now in the saddle. He and King are walking in a circle so the people can get a look at horse and rider together. Then he can hear his name as "the rider of the horse, King, winner of the Kentucky Derby last year." Everyone gave a cheer.

Now the announcer's saying, "It's time to line up for the start of the race." Their number is nine, so they are in the middle of the pack, but Joel thought he knew that wouldn't be a problem for King. When the signal to start is given, Joel knew he had to be ready.

Now King is moving. He refuses to be held back. He's moving up one horse at a time, then he's in the lead. Now he's running away from the pack. He's more than a length, then two now, three lengths ahead. When King comes across the finish line, the crowd is going crazy.

Joel was so relieved and thanked God as he rides King over to the winner's circle. He looks for Toby and David, but he isn't able to see them 'cause people are crowding around them. He's getting concerned for King. The horse doesn't like crowds. But then he can see Noah coming toward them and he's pleased, 'cause he's the one person Joel wanted to see. Noah came to take hold of King's bridle. Joel can almost feel King's relief too. So things went off as planned.

The winning horse and rider is announced. "Joel Steele is the rider of the horse named, simply, King." There is a roar from the crowd and the ladies are there trying to touch Joel.

Noah grinned at Joel and said, "Welcome to the world of being a winner, Joel. But be careful it doesn't go to your head. But I do believe you can handle it. Not everyone can, you know."

Toby and David are there with Little Jo who is handed to Joel to keep him quiet. Now, the rest of the family are there and so happy for Joel. Noah brings Elizabeth and the children to him. Noah can see Casey Sears nearby. His friend gave Noah a look of envy, then a nod, and melted into the crowd. But Noah didn't take the time to think about Casey; there's just too much excitement and happiness, and the announcer is telling them, "King has just set another track record."

Noah caught Joel's eye. The two of them shared the same proud feelings for King. Walking back to the stable to cool King down, Joel got to see and feel what Noah had warned him about. The women were crowding around and Joel is feeling real concerned. When Noah showed up again to take King out of the crowd so Toby and David can start cooling him down, Joel is left to deal with his fans. Noah's watching and he can see Joel is doing just fine. He smiles and nods at the women but keeps them at a distance. And it's easy to see Joel is just too happy to be bothered by anything. Harrison took the women and children back to the hotel so they can get the children freshened, and the women need that, too, but they also need to plan for the supper meal to celebrate Joel and King's winning the race.

But Lily asked Elizabeth if she would have food brought up for her and Susie. "I'll watch Alex too, if you wish?"

Elizabeth said, "But Lily, wouldn't you rather eat in the dining room?"

"No," Lily answered. "I will stay here and read after the little ones are asleep. I have been looking forward to reading this book I brought."

Elizabeth wasn't convinced but didn't know what more to say. She did, however, ask her father to have what food Lily and Susie want brought up to their room. She would talk to Noah when he returns. But when Noah asked Lily, "Are you sure this is what you want?"

"Yes, Noah, as I told Elizabeth, I have this book I want to read. Go ahead to supper now." Noah gave Lily a searching look for a second or so then said, "Okay, Lily. However, you will let us know if Alex wakes, right?"

She said, "Of course, Noah, I will. I know it's important I let you know if Alex wakes up."

"Okay then. Elizabeth, honey, lets go. The others are waiting."

So they finally left. But Lily thought they never would! She just wanted to be alone. Both Susie and Alex are asleep now so she is alone to cry if she wanted to. But she isn't sure now that's what she wants after all. *I've been jealous of Elizabeth for most of my life,* she's thinking, *but then, she isn't a mean person. She wouldn't hurt me, I'm sure. But it's just when that man picked her for his attention today instead of me, it hurt, and Elizabeth didn't even want his attention; she really loves Noah, and he's so crazy about her. What if I never find anyone to care for me in that way?* "I will just die, I know I will," Lily cried with a hiccup and cried till she fell asleep.

However, downstairs, there's a celebration for Joel and King, and everyone in the dining room is willing to celebrate with them, even Casey, but from afar this time. Joel's so happy and proud of King, and that's what he said to everyone.

Noah spoke to say, "I know exactly how you feel, Joel. It's like nothing I have ever felt before, except maybe loving Elizabeth," he said and winked at her.

Oh, how I love him, she's thinking.

But too soon, Noah said, "People, I know we all are proud of Joel and King, and I hate to break up this party. But we may have a baby that wants his mommy. So, if you will excuse us, but we'll see you all in the morning."

"That's okay," Joel said. "I am sure everyone else would like an early night, too, but maybe David, you will stay a while longer."

"Okay, brother, I believe I will stay," David admitted. "I need to unwind myself. Is that how it is for you, Joel? I would like to think so anyway."

"Yeah, David, that's it," Joel told him. "Like Noah said, it's like nothing I have ever experienced or felt before. And King, I am so proud of him! There has never been another horse like him."

"I agree, Joel, all that time you took care of him and he wouldn't let you touch him. I didn't understand why, but you didn't give up on King. But now I know that you sensed then that he is special, didn't you, Joel?"

"I suppose so. All I know is that when Dad wanted to sell King, I just couldn't let him go. Well now, enough of this. I believe I'm ready to retire after all," Joel said with a deep sigh. "How about you, David? The waiters are waiting to clear the table, I see."

So the two brothers, tired but pleased, made their way upstairs to their room. Joel went to bed. He didn't think he could sleep, but he and David both slept better than they had for a long while.

* * * * *

Noah and Elizabeth had found their children fast asleep, including Lily.

Elizabeth said, "I hate to wake her, she's sleeping so peacefully."

"Well," Noah told her, "if you will open the door, sweetie, I'll carry her to your parents' room." As Noah's walking out the door, Harrison is coming for Lily himself, but Noah said, "If I hand her to you, that may wake her. So if you will just go back with me to open the door to your room, I will carry her in and lay her on the bed." It worked, and Lily didn't wake. So Noah said good night to Harrison and Ellen and went back to his wife. He's been looking forward to having her alone all day, but as Noah opened the door, it seems Alex has other plans for her. He stood inside the room and watched her nurse their child. He thought, *I can wait till that little guy has his turn.* Elizabeth looked up to see him standing there. She gave him the sweetest smile.

He went to her to say, "You know, don't you, that I had plans for us tonight. But it seems our children have other ideas. So will you accept an IOU, sweetheart?" Noah asked with a crooked grin.

Elizabeth said, "Noah, darling, whenever we're together, it's special to me."

"Well," he told her, "then we will just make the best of our situation." And they did when Alex was back to sleep. Susie, however, is asleep in their bed also. Noah took pillows and lay them on the floor, reached for her hand and said, "Let's get comfortable, honey." He took the extra blanket and they made their bed on the floor. He hugged her to him and they kissed. "I will still want you to hold that IOU, you know. Now lay your head here on my shoulder; let's go to sleep." And so they did, only to wake up and decide they wouldn't give up their bed after all. Now that they have been awakened by their son, they thought after Alex is dry and has eaten, maybe they can relax on the bed for a while.

* * * * *

It's daylight when they wake again. Noah stood and stretched. He turned to Elizabeth, who's watching him, smiling.

He said, "Honey, if I happen to ever think it a good idea to sleep on the floor again, remind me that I'm past that time now. You're still smiling and I'm serious here, I have you know, Mrs. Bennett." Noah walked back to where she's still lying on the bed. He bent to kiss his wife then started tickling her. She's giggling which woke Susie, then Alex who started crying.

Susie said, "Daddy, Mommy, what you do? I wake up and now Al wake too," since she can't pronounce *Alex*.

"Sweetie," Noah said, "Mommy and Daddy were only playing. We didn't want to wake you and brother," as he leaned over to pick up his son. "I'm surprised this little guy didn't wake us before now, aren't you, Mommy? He has a wet diaper again which could be the reason he's awake now." So Noah changed the diaper then handed Alex to Elizabeth.

He said, "Susie come here." She crawled across the bed to him. Noah was sitting on the bed beside Elizabeth now where she's feeding Alex. Noah took his daughter, seated her on his lap to say, "Susie, I missed you, honey. You were asleep when Daddy and Mommy came back here last night. You're such a good little girl, you know."

"Yeah, Daddy," Susie answered.

Noah chuckled as he hugged her. "That's good, honey."

Chapter  39

On the trip home, Noah is able to stay in the train car with Elizabeth and the children again, and he is so pleased about it. He said, "Elizabeth, honey, I would like for us to spend more time together. We never did get to go horseback riding now, did we? Do you still have those riding skirts?"

"Oh, yes, Noah. Do you really mean it? You want us to go riding together?" she asked excitedly.

"Of course, darlin'. I didn't realize it meant so much to you though. And I'm sorry I haven't had the time, or taken the time, to take you riding. But we'll definitely do it. And soon and as often as we can get away, okay? I don't get a chance to ride my horse Ebony nearly enough anyway."

"Yes, it sounds great. You know Dad frowned on me riding Joel's horse, the General, once. But to give Dad credit, at the time, I was wearing a pair of David's pants that he has outgrown and one of his shirts."

"Elizabeth, you didn't? I can just see your dad who likes to keep things proper." Noah said laughing, and he kept laughing till Toby asked, "Whats so funny, Noah?"

When Noah was able to speak, he said, "Elizabeth was telling me she wore a pair of David's pants and shirt to ride the General once, and Harrison caught her and frowned on it."

"Well, Noah," Harrison told him, "I didn't want Ellen to see her daughter, whom she thought to be so proper, wearing a pair of pants and a shirt."

Ellen said, "But you know, Harrison, I did see Elizabeth riding that horse. She did try to ride in her dress. But of course it wouldn't work. That's something any woman would understand." She put her hand over her husband's and gave him a smile. She said, "But I do appreciate the thought, dear."

Noah grinned at Elizabeth as he said, "Your mother still manages to surprise me. And you, my darlin', are so much like her. I mean that as a high compliment too."

They reached the train station in Corbin without incident, which is a good thing after past experiences with the Howard clan. So the trip to the farm was made in good time, which is a relief to everyone. It was late afternoon so they had time for a short rest before the men need to start their milking and feeding chores and for the women to start supper. Their rest revived them, and soon things were back to normal and life couldn't be better.

* * * * *

In the following days, Elizabeth and Noah found time for their horseback rides and sometimes they would take along a picnic lunch and thoroughly enjoyed their time together, when either Ellen or Tansy was able to take care of Alex, of course. Those were wonderful times. They also went for buggy rides with the children. Those were happy times as well. On one such occasion, they came across a mid-sized female dog along the road. The dog seemed to be in need of food and love, so Noah picked the dog up and set her on the seat beside Susie, who's happy to give the love.

She said, "Daddy, the puppy has curly hair."

When they returned home with the dog, it's taken to the stables and put in one of the stalls. Susie wanted to be the one to feed her new dog, which she calls *Curly* because of its white with brown spots on its curly coat, but of course, the dog is fine with its name. Susie is delighted to have her very own dog and wanted to take it in the house to sleep with her, but finally agreed to leave it on its new bed of straw. The next morning, Little Jo was found with the new dog. It seems Jo no longer feels the need to stay with King. He has finally found where he belongs.

Joel, David, and Toby were thinking about going on the racing circuit with King in a few weeks, but not before the crops are all planted. Elizabeth had noticed that Lily had become more silent than ever. She mentioned it to Noah.

He said, "I believe Lily is jealous of you, honey, through no fault of your own though. But as you said before, it's partly the way she was left to herself and her daydreams so much of the time when she was younger. She didn't have the same chance at maturity as the rest of you did. But it will catch up to her, you'll see, honey," Noah told her.

Elizabeth looked at her husband in awe. She said, "Noah, you are a wonder, as usual. What you have just told me sounds perfectly reasonable, as always. And we can all hope you're right, for Lily's sake."

Chapter 40

The spring has been mild, but there has been a spell where it has rained almost every day, but it's clear that summer is just around the corner. The vegetables, such as green beans, are coming on; lettuce, green onions, and radishes are ready now; plus wild greens, which Ellen has always favored so much, have been coming on; and berries will be ready soon to pick, and pies and preserves with jelly to make. It's a busy time for everyone, but you won't hear one complaint because it's just their way of life, and a good one at that. The hard work just goes along with it.

The crops are all in the ground. Now the horse breeding business is taking off. Harrison has known since meeting Noah and then having him as his son-in-law that Noah is an intelligent man. But with designing the new breeding barn, he has now a new respect and a recognition of just how talented Noah Bennett really is. With the designing of his and Elizabeth's new home, and now that the new breeding barn is finished, it is so much more than he ever dreamed of. But Noah says it's not really a totally new idea.

The barn is huge with fourteen stalls built in the center of the building with a track around the stalls which allows them to exercise the mares they board inside during bad weather. People from miles around are bringing their mares to be bred with King. Joel needed to change his plans for a little while longer 'cause everyone wants King to breed their mares. But the time came when Noah said, "Joel, if you don't leave now, you'll miss an important part of the racing season. We have enough good-blooded stallions, my horse Ebony for one, and others to keep our business going. So you all go and enjoy it. If the time comes when you no longer enjoy the racing, then reconsider if that's how you want to spend your time, okay?"

So that's what they did. Joel and David were getting prepared to leave, and Toby's going with the two young men.

"They need someone with common sense to keep them out of trouble," he said, laughing.

"Yeah right," Noah teased. "I know you still haven't gotten racing outta your blood yet, old man."

"You keep on with that kind of talk, Noah Bennett, I will show you who's the old man here." Toby laughed.

Joel's certainly pleased Toby will be with them. There's no one better, if you do need help. And when the arrangements were made, the three of them left with King, but without Little Jo this time, "'Cause he's in love," they all said teasingly. And it seems Little Jo has found his place finally.

Tansy wasn't happy to see her husband leave, of course, but she knew what Toby had said to be true. Those two young men needed him along to watch their backs. And she will stay here with their son Johnny, and Elizabeth needs her help with the children. Ellen can use her help, too, with gathering herbs, so she's thinking she'll stay busy.

* * * * *

Some days later, Noah and Harrison were busy in their barn one afternoon when they were surprised by the women with snacks and drinks. Elizabeth had carried Alex, and Ellen had a basket of food. Tansy has the drinks. Lily is holding on to Susie. Harrison and Noah were so pleased to see them. Noah wiped his hands clean and took Alex. He gave Elizabeth a kiss and a wink to let her know he's pleased she's here.

When the food and drinks were ready to serve, Elizabeth said, "Noah, I'll take Alex so you can eat."

But he told her he could manage to get what he wanted and hold the baby too. "What's the occasion, ladies?"

Elizabeth said, "We thought we would like a tour of the new barn; but if you are too busy today, then we will wait for a better time."

"We are busy today, but we do appreciate the thought, and we will certainly look forward to giving all you ladies a tour."

Even though Lily is with them, she's withdrawn and has been for too long now. Noah decided he would talk to his wife later about it. He's afraid it is something that shouldn't be let go any longer. He had an idea that may just be what Lily needs to bring her back around to her family. So when he had a chance, he talked to Elizabeth. He told her that he had noticed that Lily's still withdrawn.

"I have been thinking, honey, if Harrison and Ellen is okay with it, I would like to talk to Ann about taking Lily to visit her sister Joan in Louisville. Lily could even start to school there if she wishes. They have a good girls' school there, you know. Maybe they can help Lily gain the maturity she needs. So what do you think, honey?"

Elizabeth is looking at her husband with a smile. She finally said, "You never fail to surprise me, Noah Bennett, and usually pleasantly so. Why don't we go talk with mom and dad now? I think they may like your idea too. Not that they will want to let her go, but they want what's best for Lily."

Noah said, "Okay, let's go now."

So they took Alex and Susie to walk to the farm house to talk with her parents. Of course, Susie wanted to be with Lily, so they went to Lily's room. When the others sat down to talk and Noah explained to them about his idea, Harrison responded thoughtfully by saying, "I have to admit I've also noticed a change in Lily, and I have been concerned. He turned to Ellen. "What about you, dear?"

Ellen was never one to make up her mind quickly, but she said, "Yes, Noah, I believe you have hit the nail on the head. Sounds like just the thing for our Lily. Mind you, not that I am ready to let her go. But I know she needs some time away. And if James and Ann are willing to do this for Lily, we'll be grateful to them. But first, I think we best ask Lily, what she thinks about it, don't you?"

So Lily was asked to come downstairs. She, with Susie, came into the kitchen where her parents are with Elizabeth and, of course, Noah is holding Alex. Lily looks a little uncertain as she sat down, so Noah said, "Don't be concerned, Lily. We just have an idea you may like very much. But just know it's totally up to you what you decide."

So he told her what the deal is. As he's talking, it isn't hard to see she's getting excited. Noah smiled as he asked, "Is it safe to say, Lily, you agree then?"

Lily laughed out loud, something she hasn't done in a long while. She said, "Yes, oh yes, very much so."

"Okay, but we need to make plans. I will get a letter off to Ann. There's a matter of clothes. You'll want some new ones, right?"

Now her eyes sparkled as she asked, "Really, Mom, Dad, may I have new clothes?"

Ellen smiled at her youngest daughter as she said, "Yes dear, I think you should have new clothes to take with you. So I believe that calls for a shopping trip." She looked at the others to say, "Right?"

Noah laughingly said, "I believe you're right, Ellen. So instead of writing to Ann, why don't we just go by their place on our way to Corbin? How does that sound? And we could go tomorrow and get this show on the road."

Lily's happiness shows in her face. When Noah and Elizabeth are ready to leave, Lily came to give both of them a hug, but she whispered thanks to Noah.

"You're welcome, Lily," he told her. "We can take Tansy and Johnny with us and make a day of it. We all can use a day off." So Noah took Susie, and Elizabeth has their son as they walked back home.

Elizabeth said, "I think that went well, don't you, Noah?" He smiled at her and gave a nod with a thoughtful hum in response.

* * * * *

So the next day, Noah and Elizabeth were at the farm shortly after the chores were done as soon after breakfast as it was possible. They stopped by to talk to James and Ann who were in favor of the plan.

Ann said, "I have been wanting to visit Joan anyway. And James promised to take me. So this gives us the excuse we needed, right husband?"

"Now what else can I say but yes," James teased his wife. "But yes, we'll be happy to take Lily and get her settled."

"Okay now," Noah asked. "Are you taking the boys or do we get them?"

James looked to his wife to ask, "What do you say, dear?"

"It may be best if you take them, Noah."

"Good, that's settled. Now do you all wish to go with us or do we come back for the boys?"

"Well," Ann said, "I should stay and pack so when you come back here they'll be ready."

So it turned out that Harrison and Noah followed the ladies around till they made a bargain that the men, including Johnny with the children, will go to the hotel dining room and have coffee. He can hold Alex and feed Susie along with Johnny, who seems pleased with the idea. The women found a dress shop with clothes in sizes to fit Lily and the colors to suit her hair and match her eyes, which are hazel. *Like their mother's*, Elizabeth is thinking, and it's easy to tell Lily is going to be pretty. Her hair is getting a darker brown with red highlights.

The first dress they found is a pretty shade of pink organdy, which is a color that suits Lily. It's with a round neckline, short cape sleeves, a slim waist, and full skirt that comes to just barely above her shoes, which is also the new style. With flushed cheeks, Lily said, "I love it."

Ellen found another dress in the same fabric in a shade of green, with short sleeves and a square neckline, with the slim waistline; full skirted. Then they found three nice white blouses in the see-through fabric with ruffles at the sleeves, three dark skirts in blue, green, and a deep red. Then they bought underclothes and a new pair of shoes with three pairs of gloves, plus two hats, and now Lily is in heaven.

Tansy said, "Lily girl, we won't know you when you get all gussied up, but you'll sure look pretty."

Ellen paid for everything then told the shopkeeper, "If you will get these things boxed up, we will be back with our husbands to collect it all."

So the women set out for the hotel dinning room to meet up with Harrison and Noah. All of them had a bite to eat then loaded back into the buggy. Ellen told Noah which shop to pick up the purchases. After this was done, Noah headed the horse and buggy in the direction to James's and Ann's place to collect the boys.

"And guess who will be happy with this arrangement?" Noah teased.

Sure enough, when Susie realized the boys will be coming with them, she clapped her hands and said, "Goody Daddy." But so is their parents coming as well.

James said, "We decided to just come to your place and leave from there for the trip."

Ann asked Lily, "Are you getting excited yet?"

"Oh, yes, thank you so much for making this trip possible for me."

"Well, dear, we are happy to do it; and in making the trip possible for you, I get to visit my sister. So it's a win-win for both of us," Ann said with a chuckle.

So the trip had been accomplished in good time. When James and Ann returned to the Steele farm and were having a cool drink of tea out on the porch, Ann told Ellen and Harrison, "Lily's so happy. She has been enrolled in a good school where my sister's daughter, Jane, has also enrolled. And the two girls get on great. I really believe this was a great idea. Whoever came up with it should be pleased."

Harrison spoke to say, "Well, you should know it was Noah's idea, and we all are so pleased about it. We knew Lily needed a change, but we didn't know how to go about it. Then Noah came up with the right solution. We're so grateful."

"Well, I should have known," James teased his brother. "But seriously, Noah, you did good."

"How could I not do everything I can to help here? This family—Harrison and Ellen, with their children—from our first meeting, you two were good enough to take me into your family, and when Elizabeth and I told you we had decided to marry, Harrison, you gave us sound advice; you with Ellen gave us your blessings. You have also been so kind to James and Ann with their family; of course, there is Susie. You have taken us all into your family and your hearts." Noah continued by saying, "Since I met and married Elizabeth, we came here to live. It was the first time

I could remember being with people who love so easily. Since our father died, both James and I loved our mother, of course, but after she remarried, it was never the same as being part of a family again. James and I cared about each other, too, then after he and Ann married, they had their sons, who are sitting beside their parents now. James and his family was my whole life for a time, which has changed for the better. And there's Tansy," Noah smiled at her as he said, "You and Toby, with Johnny, have added an important part to this family as well. Thank God for King too. It was because of him you three were brought to us. It's a wonderful thing. Our lives have become richer for it all. I wish the best for Joel in his races with King. May God bless him, along with Toby and David."

Holding his son, Alex, in his left arm, Noah raised his glass of tea with his right hand. And with a wide smile, he gave a toast.

"To my wife, Elizabeth, and daughter, Susie. By the grace of God, I have them, and all of you, as my family. Starting with the hard work, Harrison and his family built a beautiful place here, and it's a good life. I have been so blessed to be a part of it. May we always be as thankful and content as we are today." Noah looked lovingly at his wife who was smiling radiantly under the porch lights. "I am so grateful for my life with Elizabeth."

Lightning Source UK Ltd.
Milton Keynes UK
UKOW07f2120141214

243121UK00014B/175/P